THE
CITY
OF DR
MOREAU

Also by J.S. Barnes and from Titan Books
Dracula's Child

THE
CITY
OF DR
MOREAU

J.S. BARNES

TITAN BOOKS

The City of Dr Moreau
Print edition ISBN: 9781789095821
E-book edition ISBN: 9781789095838

Published by Titan Books
A division of Titan Publishing Group Ltd
144 Southwark Street, London SE1 0UP
www.titanbooks.com

First edition: September 2021
10 9 8 7 6 5 4 3 2 1

A CIP catalogue record for this title is available from the British Library.

Printed and bound in the United States.

For Alistair and Benjamin

"Though I do not expect that the terror of that island will ever altogether leave me, at most times it lies far in the back of my mind, a mere distant cloud, a memory and a faint distrust; but there are times when the little cloud spreads until it obscures the whole sky. Then I look about me at my fellow man. And I go in fear."

Edward Prendick, upon his return from the Island, 1890

16TH NOVEMBER, 1877

LONDON

1

Four gentlemen, all at the very top of their professions, sat in the upper room of a certain public house upon the Strand and waited for the storm to pass. Outside, the sky was dark and thunderous. Rain pelted down, densely, swiftly, and without showing the slightest indication of respite. The street itself, usually so populous and active, was all but empty, save for the occasional scurrying, waterlogged pedestrian, a handful of cabs with their miserable drivers, and a single beggar who moved with excruciating slowness through the deluge, turning his head from time to time to peer at the road behind, as if he believed himself to be pursued.

It was not, in short, an afternoon upon which anyone who was not compelled by circumstance to do so should wish to venture out of doors. Not when, in the room where the gentlemen sat, there was a fire banked high, the remains of a fine luncheon still spread out before them and a seemingly inexhaustible array of ales to be borne up by the taciturn, eternally discreet landlord. Indeed, had the times been happier ones, the occasion could most naturally have led to the breaking out both of cigars and of discursive conversation. The remainder of the day might then have been passed in an agreeable fug of tobacco smoke and tale-telling, in the flow of confidences exchanged and in the consumption of fine drink.

Yet this particular afternoon was not to be concluded in such a manner. Instead, events were to tend in quite other, less predictable, directions, ones which would lead first to violence and then to horror before culminating eventually in despair.

II

"Well, I say we call the whole business off," said Mr Bufford, the oldest and by nature the most cautious of the quartet, a lean, silver-haired man who was amongst the most successful prosecutors of his day. "This blasted rain won't cease and, if I'm not mistaken, the tempest's only going to get worse. These are no conditions in which to be doing our work. There's too great a possibility of his making a run for it and getting clean away. Far better that we wait for a clear day when we stand a chance of seeing our hands in front of our faces."

"Bufford," said the plump, rubicund gentleman who sat to the prosecutor's right, "you know as well as I that we simply do not possess the luxury of time. Every day is darker than its predecessor. I say we cleave to our original scheme and make our move as planned."

"My dear Dr Bright," replied the prosecutor (for his companion was a physician of some considerable renown), "might I be permitted to make the case for inaction at greater length?"

Bright, who, from decades of experience, sensed the onset of a monologue, rolled his eyes theatrically.

The threatened speech never came for both Bufford and Bright were overruled at once by the third gentleman, a gaunt, thoughtful-looking priest by the name of the Reverend Douglas Woodgrove. Generally to be seen in the garb of his vocation, today, like all of the gentlemen, he was dressed in sombre, civilian browns and blacks, as though in search of anonymity.

"I am not so sure," said Woodgrove evenly, "that we can set too much store by the weather. Our opponent is bound in any case to have established numerous escape routes. We shall have to keep our wits about us if we mean to get his attention."

"It may even be the case," opined Dr Bright, "that the conditions might make our quarry too confident and therefore more likely to make a mistake. Don't you think? Remember, gentlemen: he needs to make but a single error, and then, most assuredly, we have him."

Bufford arranged his features into an expression of querulous scepticism. He took a breath and appeared again to be upon the cusp of indignant soliloquy only to be interrupted once more.

This time, it was the fourth man who spoke up, a pale, quiet, cherubic-faced fellow named Vaughan who, while not yet forty, was nonetheless the most inventive and far-seeing scholar of the human mind resident at that time in the metropolis.

"I wonder…" he began and, although his tone was very soft and very low, and although one had to strain to hear it over the clatter and hiss of the rain, the three senior men ceased at once their conversation and turned to face him. "I wonder if he knows that we have set our plans against him. Does he see, do you think, that we mean to track him down?"

The Reverend Woodgrove frowned at this terminology. "Track him down only to ask some robust and necessary questions, surely? Why, you make it sound as though we are some hunting party and he the poor doomed stag."

Vaughan smiled tightly. "Is the comparison so very inapt? Upon this occasion, Reverend, I doubt greatly whether mere conversation shall be sufficient."

As Mr Vaughan had been speaking, the sound of heavy footsteps upon the staircase became increasingly loud. Almost at the final syllable, the door to the little room was wrenched open and a fifth man entered, moustachioed, dressed in damp tweed, dripping from head to toe and exhibiting every sign of extreme anxiety and distress.

"Gentlemen," he said, and his voice was rather high and quavering for the individual was very young (not quite four and twenty) and still distinctly green. "We are discovered!"

If this entrance should strike you as being in any way theatrical in nature the assessment may be a just one; the individual was none other than that promising journalist Mr J. G. Kelman who was in his spare time a keen and talented amateur actor.

The others turned as one to face the newcomer, around whom puddles and rivulets of rainwater were forming upon the floor. Naturally enough, it was Bufford who spoke first. "What do you mean, 'discovered'?"

"Moreau," said the youngest man, "has found me out. Found us out at last."

"Are you sure?" asked Woodgrove.

"He knows I'm not a scientist. He knows I'm not who I pretended to be. He used the word 'spy' to my face."

"That is unfortunate," Bufford said, "yet we ought not to be too hasty."

Dr Bright saw an opportunity to disagree with his learned friend. "On the contrary, speed is essential. If what Mr Kelman says is true – and I have not the slightest reason to doubt him – our enemy will even now be making plans to fly."

The Reverend Woodgrove ignored the men who were seated and asked young Kelman directly: "You're certain he said 'spy'? You're sure he's seen through you?"

"Oh, he had no proof," Kelman said and a tinge of exasperation crept into his voice, "but he knew I've been lying to him all the same."

"Did you make a mistake?" Woodgrove asked, not unkindly.

"No! At least, not that I can think of. I can't imagine what gave me away in the end. It's as though he has some sort of... extra perception."

At this, there came more expressions of concern, more questions as to how it had come to this together with much in the way of disputatious indecision.

Then the one person who had not spoken since the journalist's arrival – clever, watchful Mr Vaughan – spoke up. "We're wasting time, gentlemen." He had to raise his voice only very slightly for the others to fall silent as suddenly and as completely as if a stage curtain had dropped.

"Moreau is nothing if not a practical man. He will even now be preparing his defence. I say that we make our move and that we do so at once. Anyone who wishes to stay here in the warm and the dry may do so without fear of comment or judgement from me."

All glanced towards Bufford who shifted his bulk for a moment in his chair. "I concur," he said, apparently with as much conviction as that which he had employed to argue the opposing view scant minutes before.

Vaughan rose to his feet. "Come along, then. If we hurry we still stand a chance to catch him before he makes some desperate move. We'll take a cab. No, two cabs! You're with me?"

The others all agreed that they were and, following Vaughan, the party of five proceeded through the door and down the steep and rickety staircase that led first to the saloon bar and then to the street outside.

"Reverend Woodgrove!" This was young Kelman to the priest who had somehow found himself at the rear of the procession.

"Yes, my boy? What is it?"

The young man's nerves were plain upon his face. "Why do you think he let me go? Moreau. I mean, he could have made me stay. He could have injured me or worse."

Woodgrove did not at first reply. Then he said: "Perhaps there's hope for him yet. Perhaps some sunken part of him realises the nature of his transgressions. Perhaps the doctor can still be saved."

Kelman found himself unable to respond to what seemed to him to be the most wild and ill-founded optimism for then they were out through the snug warmth of the bar, and into the rain again, into the street where Vaughan was making arrangements with two cab drivers. They all clambered aboard, already sodden, and the vehicles moved away, the horses shivering and whinnying at the misery of it. They were off, away from the heart of the city and towards its wilder, uncivilised edge.

III

Into which of those two speeding cabs ought we now to glimpse?

The first, its horse bent and wretched against the downpour, its driver cursing obstinately at the elements, contained within it Mr Bufford, Dr Bright and the Reverend Woodgrove. In spite of the gravity of their mission, these three gentlemen set at once to the revivification of numerous old arguments and disputes which, being of a circular, repetitive and (at least to the participants) an oddly comforting nature, we can probably leave safely to one side.

It is into the second, then, that we should peer. This followed hastily after the first in a quick, slipshod manner as though both horse and rider were closer than they knew to an absolute loss of control. Inside, buffeted and jolted, sat Kelman, the newspaper man. Opposite him sat Mr Vaughan.

For a long while, as the vehicle careered and swayed through the streets, and as the rain beat its mad tattoo upon the roof, these two disparate personages said nothing to one another at all. The little convoy hugged the road by the river, moving first towards Temple, then to Blackfriars and then to the very rim of the financial district. On and on they went, heading ever eastwards.

No doubt the mind of Mr Kelman was still in some uproar given his adventures that day for he fidgeted constantly in his seat and was forever running one finger around the circumference of his grimy shirt collar, presenting the very picture of nervous discomfort.

Mr Vaughan, on the other hand, sat very quietly and very still. His body did not seem to jump or jitter as did Mr Kelman's at the indignities of the journey. He sat straight-backed and pensive, his eyes half-closed at times in a posture that seemed to hint at the monastic.

It was only once they had passed Tower Hill and edged into Smithfield, that Mr Vaughan finally spoke.

He did not seem in any wise to raise his voice yet somehow every syllable of it was entirely audible to his companion.

"Mr Kelman?" he began, his tone conversational and cordial enough if not especially friendly. "Might I ask you something about the man we're to meet tonight?"

"You may meet him," Kelman said, speaking too quickly and with an odd levity, which he surely cannot have felt. "Then again you may not. He is a slippery fellow, you know. Slippery as an eel. No, more than that – a shifter of shapes. Like quicksilver. Like Mercury."

Mr Vaughan smiled. "A colourful description but I rather think you do him too much credit. He's just a man. An eccentric one certainly. And one possessed of uncommon ambition. But when all's said and done he's just flesh and blood and every bit as fallible as the rest of us."

Mr Kelman looked as if he meant to contradict the fellow who sat opposite him only, at the last minute, to think better of it.

"So my question," went on Mr Vaughan, "has to do with what one might call Moreau's… persuadability. And, since you have spent so much time at his side, since you've been able to witness his working practices at such close quarters, tell me honestly: do you think it possible that we can change his mind? I mean, the five of us? If we sit him down and warn him of the consequences of taking the path upon which he's embarked?"

The younger man looked somewhat aghast. "I don't… That is… even if you say that I overstate the case, Moreau's a uniquely determined man. I've no doubt he's quite set now on the path he's chosen."

"Well, that is a decided pity, for I should so much prefer to avoid any unpleasantness."

Kelman cleared his throat. "Mr Vaughan, honestly. I really don't believe that a scandal is at all to be avoided now. Nor, quite frankly, would my editor wish for it to be. Why, by the time we're finished it will be a very unjust world indeed if the very name of Moreau doesn't become a byword for infamy."

Mr Vaughan smiled a small, tight smile. "Oh, but I did not mean unpleasantness of that kind. For I am quite certain that what is left of his reputation will have to be torn apart."

"Then what did you mean?"

The smile of Mr Vaughan did not dim as he reached into the right hand pocket of his dark jacket and withdrew a slim, polished silver revolver.

The younger man leaned forward to see the thing and gaped. "You really think it might come to that?"

"If everything you've told us and all that I suspect of this man is true then, yes, it may very well do."

"But we're not authorised… I mean, we're amateurs, surely. We're not professional men."

"Hush now." Vaughan slid back the revolver into the place. "All will yet be well. At least, that is, if we only hurry!"

And with this, in an unheralded burst of impatient energy, Vaughan reached up one hand and struck the roof of the cab three times.

"Hurry up!" he shouted. "In the name of England!"

The driver shouted down several curses, the details of which, mercifully, were lost to the storm.

"Can't be much further," said Kelman once the shouting had stopped.

Vaughan, now as still again as he had been before, seemed to have recovered his composure. "Almost there." One hand fluttered to the weapon in his jacket again and touched its outline as if for comfort. This done, he folded his hands in his lap and smiled a flicker of a smile which was finished an instant after it had begun.

Outside, the tempest was growing in pace and ferocity as the cab passed further into the East, past Whitechapel and Shadwell, on and on, as the contents of the heavens were hurled down to earth.

IV

In the wake of the resultant scandal, many descriptions were circulated of the laboratory which was owned and operated by Dr Moreau in the part of the old city known then as Ratcliffe. The popular press were most exercised upon the subject and strikingly vivid in their treatment of it. "Hovel of Horrors" was one such description, "Basement of the Bizarre" another. All of the reporting at the time made it sound like some gothic extrusion, some far-flung medieval castle. In truth, such accounts were grossly exaggerated.

The building was located in a region which was at that time filled with warehouses and places of storage. The nearest pub – The Lion's Maw – was ten minutes walk away and the nearest church – St George in the East – almost fifteen. It had been selected, of course, for precisely these reasons: for its isolation and insignificance.

The area was at its busiest in the morning, around the dawn, and by now seemed almost as deserted as had been the Strand.

The laboratory itself was located beyond an archway, taking up the bulk of a large, rather drab courtyard. It should be stressed that there was nothing in the least bit alarming or minatory about its exterior. It was plain, ordinary and drab and was in many ways as wholly an unremarkable structure as one can imagine – a long, broad building formed of a single storey which any ignorant pedestrian would assume to be a warehouse of some kind, another receptacle there to serve the shipping trade.

No signs or notices of any kind had been placed outside and there were no obvious clues as to what might take place within its walls. Yet there was something somehow rather sly about the place (an odd adjective to use about a building but an apt one nonetheless) as though it had been set up to appear inconspicuous, designed to be overlooked.

There was no sign of life within (no lamps were lit, no windows illuminated) nor was there anything on the road immediately beyond. This, at least, was how the five gentlemen discovered it when, at long last, the pair of hansom cabs clattered into the courtyard and ejected their passengers. All were already complaining about the continued inhospitality of the elements as they stepped down, shivering at the intransigence of the downpour.

"So this is it?" said Mr Bufford in perhaps rather too declamatory a manner.

While Kelman, looking about him nervously, confirmed that this was indeed the laboratory of Moreau, Mr Vaughan dealt deftly with the two cabmen, promising them a good deal of money to stay precisely where they were and to wait in a state of preparedness for departure. There was some talk of substantial bonuses as well as a pledge of future employment.

"It's very quiet," said Dr Bright, peering suspiciously through the rain at the warehouse. "Do you think he might already have flown?"

"No." Kelman was emphatic. "He wouldn't just leave his work. His subjects. His specimens."

"You speak as though he has some sense of morality," said the vicar, not without a note of optimism.

"Oh, I think he does," Kelman said. "In his way."

"Then perhaps it's possible…" Woodgrove began, doubtless about to start a new speech about the capacity of man for ethical growth or the rejoicing in Heaven over the late arrival of a life-long sinner, when Mr Vaughan interrupted.

"Wait," he said. "Did you hear that?"

They all fell silent and strained to hear above the sounds of precipitation. Five brave Englishmen – Bufford, Woodgrove, Kelman, Bright and Vaughan – standing, listening in the storm.

For a moment there was nothing.

And then, undeniably, they all of them heard a new sound, an odd, arresting noise which could be heard quite distinctly even above the fierce hissing of the rain.

It sounded like something between a sob and a cry of pain, an elongated whimper, altogether unlike any which this quintet had ever heard before.

No-one spoke, not even Mr Vaughan, so chilling and incongruous was the sound. It went on, too long, before, miserably, tailing away into silence.

In the quiet that followed, Mr Bufford was seen to step back three paces, seemingly without noticing that he had done so. Dr Bright turned pale, blanching more than ever he had in the course of any surgery. The Reverend Woodgrove made some complicated, involuntary gesture before his breast in a manner which seemed most unprotestant.

Mr Vaughan, meanwhile, simply turned to Kelman and enquired in a tone which betokened no more than curiosity: "What was that?"

Young Kelman was ashen. "I'm not sure I could say."

Then the sound came again, high-pitched and desperate, and also (it seemed) closer than before.

"Good God," said Dr Bright. "What is it? Animal or... human?"

"It's possible," Kelman said rather timidly, "that there's somebody here who needs our help."

Beyond the archway, behind the party of gentlemen, the two horses and the drivers of the two cabs were seen to shuffle and pace.

"Gentlemen," said Bufford, the prosecutor, "before we make too rapid a decision we ought first, in light of this new evidence, discuss the wisdom of any action which we mean now to take. Indeed... given the elements and our isolation here, might it not be judicious of us to retreat to a place of safety?"

Words had always been Mr Bufford's greatest strength and his livelihood; these sentences, grave enough if not especially distinguished, were to be his last.

Later, the survivors could never concur on how the creature had crept up on them without any of them realising its approach. It had great guile, they agreed, and the instincts of a hunter.

Out of the driving rain it sprang, a great black dog, dripping with water and loosing a ferocious growl.

It went for Mr Bufford, latching its vast jaws about him and sinking its teeth into the meat of the man's neck, puncturing with ghastly instinct an artery. Blood was immediate and came in great and vivid quantity.

One of the most renowned and well-respected barristers in

the land tried to scream but could barely do so; the sound was emerging as a grotesque, elongated gurgle.

"My God!" yelled the Reverend Woodgrove.

"Bufford, Bufford! Get it off you!" This was Dr Bright who, in spite of this injunction, was seen to keep his distance.

Kelman turned to Mr Vaughan. "Your gun..." he said but Vaughan did not reply. The alienist seemed glassily fascinated (almost mesmerised) by what was occurring: this sudden, intrusion of horror into the long day.

Poor Mr Bufford flailed desperately with his hands but to no avail.

As the rain beat down, the beast held firm. Its claws found purchase about the prosecutor's shoulders and head. It half-squatted there as it fed.

Bufford gave another wet cry of outrage and agony. He staggered forwards. With a final rip at the flesh of its victim, the dog dropped down and wheeled about with inhuman speed and turned to face the others.

"Shoot it!" Kelman shouted to Vaughan. "Shoot the damn thing!"

Mr Vaughan only watched, unmoving.

"Vaughan!"

Bufford fell onto his knees then pitched forward, his blood pooling in the rainwater, crimson in the gathering dark.

In the drumbeat of the downpour, his last breaths could not be heard but they were feeble, ragged things. A look of absolute disbelief settled about his features and his eyes clouded with terror. His final breath came, his body stopped and that was the end of Mr Bufford – he who had once been at the heart of the most famous criminal cases in London – face down in the filth of a Ratcliffe alley.

For a long moment, that homicidal animal seemed to glare at the four survivors.

So engrossed with the atrocity were Bright, Woodgrove, Kelman and Vaughan that they did not notice as, with sundry curses and protestations of disbelief, the two drivers of the cabs urged on their panicked steeds and drove at pace from the courtyard. Following this departure there was a dread silence. Then they heard something else, a high, terrible, altogether unexpected sound.

It was, quite unmistakably, for all that the juxtaposition was thoroughly grotesque in that deserted, blood-sodden place, the hysterical cry of an angry baby – the sound of an infant who has been woken abruptly or left too long without food. It seemed, impossibly, to emanate from somewhere nearby.

The dog barked loudly, at which the sobbing increased in volume and tenor.

Dr Bright and Reverend Woodgrove looked about them in a state of horrified bewilderment. Mr Vaughan touched Kelman lightly on his left arm and, speaking with an imperturbable calm which struck the young journalist as almost inhuman, said: "See there?"

The murderous beast had turned a little and was now moving to and fro beside the fallen Bufford, as if patrolling its territory or protecting its kill. A shadow in the rain.

Yet there was something to be seen about it which all had missed before in the furious violence of the moment.

"Dear Lord," said Kelman when he realised. "Dear Lord, no!"

At this, the others turned. Now they saw it too.

The beast roared and the sound of the crying intensified as the animal strode towards them, picking its way around the cadaver, on thick and powerful legs.

The Reverend Woodgrove said later that he could not have imagined the sight in the worst, most delirious nightmare. Yet the truth of the thing was undeniable.

There it was, like some detail from a medieval vision of the underworld, an impossible sight – the face of a bawling human baby, not more than a few months old, staring out from the left flank of the creature, transplanted by some hideous feat of surgery.

The mite screamed in outrage as its host ran forwards, towards the horror-struck quartet. The dog seemed about to leap, its tiny, unwilling passenger, peering forth like some grisly remnant of a Siamese twin. The cry of the animal and the wailing of the face combined into a ghastly threnody of despair.

"Shoot it!" Kelman shouted to Mr Vaughan. "In the name of Christ, shoot that accursed thing!"

Vaughan only watched, his eyes wide and unblinking.

"Shoot it, man!"

The hybrid monstrosity leapt into the air, coming to claim its second victim. At last a single shot rang out.

The bullet caught the animal mid-air and it dropped, twisting, to the earth, wounded but still living. It snarled and whimpered in shock and the pitiful wail of the baby could still be heard. Another shot followed. Blood burst from the body of the creature before, at last, it all went very quiet.

The rain started to slacken, the heavens having exhausted themselves at last.

Kelman turned to Mr Vaughan, expecting to see the revolver in his hand yet when he did so he found that the little man had not moved and that his hands were empty.

A new voice was heard. "Thank you so much for coming, gentlemen. I only wish that you might have given me more notice so that I might have had the opportunity to have been a better host."

Vaughan was at Kelman's left-hand side now and Dr Bright and the Reverend Woodgrove upon his right. Four men stood in the street, the bodies of Bufford and the dog-baby creature before them.

Opposing them stood the newcomer, who held outstretched a gun of his own.

He was a man in his middle years, rather sallow-faced and already inclined to fleshiness. He was clean-shaven to an impeccable degree. His hair, which had been fashioned into a style which was some decades out of date, glistened with unguent.

His face was assuredly not a kind one. Yet you might pass him daily without guessing for an instant from his composure the deeds of which he was capable. The only feature about him which was in the least remarkable was his manner of dress: a white suit and tie in a design which might have appealed to some missionary or explorer unusually interested in matters of aesthetics.

"Dr Moreau." It was Vaughan who spoke first. "I think it would behove you now to offer us something in the way of an explanation."

Moreau seemed surprised by his opponent's speech and manner.

"You're Vaughan, aren't you?" he asked, his tone even and pleasant as though they were meeting at some scientific soiree. "I've heard of you."

Mr Vaughan murmured something in response. It was lost due to the words that were shouted simultaneously by Dr Bright, though the Reverend Woodgrove swore later that the alienist had said these two words: "I'm flattered."

It was obscured by the furious exclamation of Bright. "How dare you, sir? How dare you?"

Moreau turned to look at him, with a moderately quizzical expression.

Bright thundered on. "This monstrosity! This obscenity!"

The Reverend Woodgrove fixed the white-clad man with his sternest gaze of disapproval. "What you have done here, sir, is against nature and against God."

Moreau looked at these two speakers with the air of an elephant, troubled momentarily by flies. "I wanted to meet you," he said with a drawl, "you men who thought to set yourselves against me. I am bound to say that, having done so, I rather wish that I had spared myself the effort. Pygmies, all of you."

With the hand that did not grasp the revolver, Moreau reached into his waistcoat and withdrew a gleaming pocket watch. He glanced down at it in the manner of a weary commuter. "As for you, young Master Kelman…"

The journalist had by this time (no doubt quite unconsciously) moved several paces back from the others and stood now half-obscured by the slim form of Mr Vaughan.

"I suppose I ought to cheer your courage," Moreau went on, "in bringing them to me. Yet I cannot abide disloyalty. You've always known how it is here: to do my will is the whole of the law."

Kelman started to speak then, perhaps to protest or else to attempt to bargain. Exactly what he would have said none is in a position now to say, for the gun in Moreau's hand barked once more and the young man crumpled to the ground, narrowly missing Mr Vaughan, his arms splayed out in the dirt.

Moreau looked down at his handiwork as if quietly pleased. He hurried away, back in the direction of the warehouse.

Dr Bright seemed struck dumb by the horror of the afternoon but the Reverend Woodgrove called out in righteous fury, not to the murderous doctor but to Mr Vaughan: "You! You have a gun! Strike him down! Strike down that man!"

Vaughan did now reach for his gun and draw it out but he did so with a sluggish thoughtfulness like a dreamer being woken only gradually in the night.

By the time that the thing looked ready to fire, the swiftly moving figure of Dr Moreau had already vanished.

"Good God," said Dr Bright. Although he had recovered the power of speech, his voice sounded numb and very faraway. Two human bodies lay on the ground before them beside the corpse of something, which once had been an animal.

"Good God," said Bright again, helplessly. "What happened here?"

"We've been beaten," said Vaughan, "and jolly easily too. He barely had to lift a finger."

"What do we do now?"

Vaughan shrugged. Given the context, there was something almost grotesquely callous in the gesture. "You gentlemen should do as you please. There are matters to be arranged, surely, with poor Bufford and with the unfortunate Mr Kelman. But I do believe I'll take a closer look in there." He gestured towards the warehouse.

"Vaughan, no!"

"I thought you would say as much, Woodgrove."

"It's not safe. Who knows what else he has in there? Who can guess at the dangers?"

"Oh I think I can guess," Vaughan said lightly. "But I would very much like it to see for myself. Wouldn't you?"

He did not wait for a reply but merely walked away, passing the bodies without sparing them a glance. Woodgrove and Bright stood still and watched as the fellow stepped first into the shadow of the warehouse and, afterwards, into the building itself.

Then they were left alone, surrounded by the dead.

V

Two hours later and Dr Bright and the Reverend Woodgrove were seated side by side in the office of a police inspector (whose name is not important) trying their utmost to explain themselves. The detective, a lean-faced, beleaguered-looking fellow, was examining the visitors with a look of considerable scepticism. For this we ought not to judge him too harshly; both Woodgrove and Bright looked sodden and dilapidated from their ordeals in Ratcliffe and their subsequent tortuous efforts to reach what they thought of as civilisation.

Neither looked very much at all like the prosperous, well-fed gentlemen who had not long before been sitting, quaffing and debating, in the tavern on the Strand.

"I am still not entirely certain," said the police officer, "exactly what you thought you were doing in confronting this gent in the first place. I mean why not go to the authorities from the start?"

"We thought," said Woodgrove with more patience than many in his position might have mustered, "that we might be able to avoid a scandal. We thought that if we could only talk to the fellow that we could persuade him to desist and seek a quiet retirement."

At this, the policeman gave the priest a look that suggested that he would have been unlikely, in such circumstances, to find grounds for such optimism.

"But we didn't realise," interjected Dr Bright, "how far the man was gone. How deep in his insanity."

Woodgrove nodded in solemn agreement. The policeman examined them studiously, weighing up the matter which had been set before him.

"And you swear to me that this is the truth? That you saw what you say you saw? I shall take a dim view indeed if you're gulling me in some way. I do not approve of pranks played by grown men who ought to know better."

"I assure you, Inspector," said Woodgrove, "everything happened just as we've told you it did. Even now it grieves me to admit that the bodies of two fine people are lying in the filth of a Ratcliffe alley."

"In which case," said the detective, "we need to go back straightaway. I need to see it all for myself."

"Not just us," said Dr Bright in a weak, falling voice. "Not just the three of us. We must have… reinforcements."

The policemen gave him an interrogative look, then nodded briskly, mind made up. "I'll attend to the arrangements. You two wait here."

"How long–" the Reverend Woodgrove began.

The policeman, all business now, cut him off. "Ten minutes. No longer. Then we'll all go together. See if we can't smoke out the truth. And if there's been true devilry done… why then, we'll bring the fellow to justice."

Apparently pleased at this little speech, he nodded again, superfluously, at the survivors then turned and all but strutted from the room. The door clicked shut. Woodgrove and Bright were left in silence save for the hum and chatter of police-work in the room beyond.

The Reverend Woodgrove took a breath, thought how very damp his clothes were and was about to try something in the way of a whispered, desperate prayer for success when he felt a hand tugging at his right shoulder, the force of which all but spun him around.

"Woodgrove…" Bright's face was pale and pained. His eyes were bloodshot and he seemed to be beset by a slight tremor – his hands were visibly shaking – which Woodgrove did not think was attributable entirely to the cold. "I don't think I can do it."

"What's that?"

"I don't think I can go back. Not to find them just lying there. And that… thing too." He looked up at the priest with fearful, pleading eyes.

"I understand."

"You don't think me a coward?"

"Not at all, my dear fellow. We were simply so very unprepared for what we found. We hadn't guessed – we hadn't dared to guess – the dreadful scale of the thing."

"Yes, yes," said the physician eagerly, grasping at this explanation with almost pathetic gratitude.

"Still you don't think…" Woodgrove began, gently, as though addressing a nervy parishioner, "that it might not be better for you to go back? To see it all? To face up to it and see if we can't bring that scoundrel down."

"Oh he'll have fled by now. He'll be long gone. You and I both know it."

"Nevertheless… for the sake of settling your own account in this business…"

Bright shook his head almost truculently, like a child. "No," he said. "No, I'm never going back. I can't bring myself to look on what he did. Surely you of all men should understand that. For it's blasphemy, don't you think? Pure blasphemy. And Moreau himself is the very devil."

VI

And so it was that the Reverend Woodgrove went back to the laboratory without Dr Bright but in the company of the police inspector and two dozen of the metropolis' brawniest and most implacable constables. It made, in the end, for quite the procession. The rain had cleared the streets and, even though it had finally stopped, the roads were still mostly empty.

It was a real spectacle to see three great police wagons go speeding along, out of the Yard and into the East, seemingly heedless of the possible perils of flooding as the sewers and drains, unaccustomed to such a deluge, disgorged their contents into the open. No doubt there were more than a few of those pedestrians who had ventured out once again who watched this small but ominous convoy go by and wondered where it was headed and to whom, thinking themselves lucky that it was not in search of them for which the vehicles had been despatched.

The Reverend Woodgrove sat in the first of the wagons, nestled between the inspector and one of his subordinates, a large, squarely-built man who was in immediate want of both a shave and a bath. As they swayed through the streets, retracing the route into Ratcliffe, Woodgrove tried to distract himself by thinking of various inspiring verses from the book of Proverbs only to find his powers of recollection to be most lacking. He tried instead to find a still point within himself, one in which he might hear the voice of his Creator. Yet there was too much noise and the anxiety that he felt was too great to be able to achieve tranquillity. He tried then to think of nothing at all and simply surrender to the dreadful sensation of the journey yet he found even this impossible to manage.

Instead he kept coming back to a memory – not, in fact, a recent one but something from his childhood (which had been spent in comfortable, if rather bohemian, affluence in Cheshire), to an occasion when he had been left alone with his baby brother (now, sadly, long since gone, killed in some distant territory in defence of the empire). He remembered how he had felt an odd sense of power when he gazed down into the cot and watched that pink face look up at him with uncomprehending eyes. He remembered how he had reached in, meaning to tickle the little fellow or to squeeze a plump and tiny hand, only for the infant to set up at once a terrific wail, his features screwed up in outrage, his cheeks damp with tears, the sound of his furious weeping terrifying to hear. Of course, the young Woodgrove had turned at once and fetched his mother, who chided him for bothering the baby, blaming him unthinkingly for the uproar, but who had also soothed the babe within mere moments as the lad glared mutinously out at his older brother from their mother's arms.

At first, Woodgrove wasn't altogether certain why he should think of this now. Then he realised that when he saw that abominable hybrid, the obscenity which had been enacted upon the body of the dog, it had been his brother's face that he had seen there – or, to be more accurate, that the strange processes of human memory had imposed this upon the scene. Now, he found himself murmuring a prayer at last. His lips moved to form the name of the brother who had left him.

An elbow in his ribs brought him back to the present. "I said, is this the place, Reverend?" The inspector was looking at him with irritation. "Are we almost there?"

Woodgrove looked out at the streets. They had come back sooner than he had expected. This was the place all right: the abandoned alleyway, the courtyard beyond, flanked on one side by what seemed to be a warehouse.

"Yes," he said. "This is it."

"Need to stop here then," the inspector said. "Won't get the trucks through the archway."

He shouted instructions and the convoy was brought to a halt. Woodgrove wondered at the wisdom of so unstealthy an approach. He did not believe it to be his place to protest, however, or to offer any advice (the late Mr Bufford, he reflected, would have been very much more forthright in such a position) and so he simply did as he was told. When the time came, he stepped out of the vehicle and walked behind the inspector at the forefront of that miniature army as they went toward the doors of the laboratory.

The way was sodden. They splashed through puddles. It was gloomy and oppressive. The elderly gas-lamp which stood there still showed no signs of having been lit (Woodgrove wondered later if Moreau had somehow made certain of this) and the only available illumination was the light which emanated from the laboratory itself, spilling out on the courtyard beyond.

"Tread carefully," the inspector said to Woodgrove as they moved gingerly forwards, quite needlessly in the priest's opinion since he had never walked with greater care in all his life. "You can turn back if you like," the policeman added. "We can go on from here. You can wait in the wagon till the worst is over."

"Certainly not," said Woodgrove stoutly. "I have to go on."

The place was as quiet as before, if not quieter now that the rain had ceased. Aside from the light, there was no sign of life from within the warehouse itself. Two shapes, however – long and dark – were immediately apparent on the ground. Woodgrove approached them with mournful determination.

"These are your friends?" the inspector asked as he came to stand beside the priest and as the two of them peered through the mirk at the two dead bodies.

"Mr Bufford was my friend," Woodgrove said. "Kelman I did not know so well. But they were both good men, I can tell you that. They deserved better than to be gored in the street and left like carrion."

"We'll take good care of them," the inspector said. "But didn't you say that there was an animal here? A dog, possibly rabid?"

"Yes," said the priest, without further elaboration.

"I can't see it. You said the beast was shot."

There was no denying it. Even in the dim light of the courtyard it was plain that there were two human bodies before them but nothing animal, nothing like the hell-hound that the five men had encountered hours before.

"Someone's moved it," Woodgrove said, and even to his ears the explanation sounded feeble. "Someone must have moved the body of that creature. Buried it somewhere. Or burned it."

"You think it was Moreau?" The policeman was kind enough to keep any suggestion of scepticism out of his voice but the Reverend Woodgrove knew that he must feel it all the same.

"Possibly... I don't know. I feel certain somehow that he meant to flee. He was, after all, discovered, so I really don't know how he would do... something like this."

At this, unexpectedly, a new voice rang out.

"It wasn't Moreau!"

The voice came from the direction of the laboratory itself and Woodgrove saw now that there was somebody waiting there, in the shadows, leaning, it seemed, against the wall of the building.

The voice was a familiar one.

"Mr Vaughan?"

Woodgrove moved towards him, the inspector hurrying in his wake. As he approached, the priest saw that it was Vaughan all right. The alienist had propped himself up in a leisurely manner and was engaged in eating an apple. Woodgrove heard the moist crunch of it, a sound that seemed to him almost obscene in such a context.

"Hello, Woodgrove." Strange indeed: there seemed to be a note of extreme but suppressed excitement in Vaughan's voice. "You took your time, didn't you?"

"Yes," Woodgrove said, inwardly cross at himself for the apologetic nature of his tone. "It's taken us a good long while… as you see… to bring the authorities here…"

The inspector stepped forward. "You'd be Mr Vaughan, would you, sir? The fifth member of this little club."

"Scarcely a club, Inspector. More a loose consortium of like-minded individuals with a common goal." He took another insouciant bite of his apple. "Or so we thought."

"Way I hear it, sir, is that you were last seen going into this building at a time when the murderer had yet to leave the premises. Now we find you here, leaning and chomping for all the world as if you've witnessed nothing less agreeable than a day at the races."

"Inspector, please." The alienist rearranged his features into an expression of something like solemnity. "You must not mistake my current demeanour for any lack of gravity as to what has taken place here today. My reactions are only, perhaps, a little idiosyncratic."

"Vaughan," Woodgrove said. "What's happened here?"

"Moreau's long gone," said Vaughan. "He must have made his escape minutes after shooting poor Kelman in cold blood. But his laboratory I think you will find most interesting. Most interesting indeed. Some of it, I'm sure, he took with him. But a good deal he would not have had time to pack. And from this alone, I can assure you that our worst fears were not only realised but exceeded." With another defiant crunch, Vaughan gnawed away at a further segment of fruit.

"I think we'd better go inside, don't you?" said the inspector. "Vaughan, you stay right where you are."

"Of course, of course."

The policeman turned to address the phalanx of his men. "You there – stand watch over the bodies, I'll be examining them in a moment. Wilkins – stand in the thoroughfare and make sure no-one wanders in, eager to see what the commotion's about." More orders followed, all acted upon by the constables with commendable alacrity.

As this was taking place, Woodgrove turned back to Vaughan. "What happened," he said very softly but firmly, "to that abominable dog?"

Vaughan gazed at him, unblinking, took a final bite of his apple, tossed the core to the ground and said: "I've really no idea. Why does it trouble you so much?"

"Because that thing killed our friend. And without it we look like fantasists."

"Oh, hardly that. It's been a very long night, Woodgrove, so I'll ignore your rather overheated tone. Besides, you may take it from me that after you've seen what's inside this building, people will not only think us very far indeed from fantasists or dreamers of any sort, they will wonder why we did not act much sooner and with considerably more determination."

Before Vaughan could reply, the inspector was back at his side again.

"We're going in," he said. "Do you want to join us?"

"Yes," said Woodgrove, averting his gaze from Mr Vaughan. "Yes, I do believe I have to see this for myself."

VII

The details of what they found in the laboratory of Dr Moreau were at one time well known. The press got hold of it and ran with the story for weeks after the discovery. The little buff-coloured pamphlet known as "The Moreau Horrors" had perhaps the fullest account (amongst a good deal of omissions for the sake of the morale of the British public).

Certainly, the sights which he saw there followed the Reverend Woodgrove for the rest of his life. He was never to be entirely free of them and he had many a sleepless night that was interrupted by some vision, unwillingly recalled – the twisted face of an experimental subject; the remnants of a failed vivisection; the octopoid things in tanks which spoke of a deep interest in the most monstrous creatures of the sea. The smell of the place came back to him often too, as of something halfway between a chemical lab and a fairground, or the sawdust scent of a circus tent with an abattoir reek. There were even nights in the early weeks following the raid when Woodgrove would wake screaming in his bed.

Later, after Woodgrove and Mr Vaughan had departed, after the police had done their necessary work, after the caravan of journalists and ghoul-seekers and the idle had been and gone, it was decided by some authority or other to have the laboratory first cleared and then demolished. Much that was inside was burned. All that was still living there was euthanised.

For years afterwards there were stories told about that particular patch of ground. Londoners knew to steer clear of it and newcomers soon found reasons to stay away. A generation passed before anything was built atop it. There remained widespread, persistent and very similar accounts of some spectral creature glimpsed in the shadows and of the chilling, wretched wail of a long-dead infant.

Indeed, it is not a place that is visited often even now, when London has changed so completely, out of all recognition.

5TH FEBRUARY, 1880

ALLINGHAM EARL, WILTSHIRE

I

"Of course, one does hear rumours…" Mr Vaughan leaned forwards, smiled confidentially and, for an instant, it seemed to the Reverend Woodgrove that there was something absolutely and undeniably satanic in the face of his old acquaintance.

Almost three years had passed since the events in Ratcliffe and in all of that time the priest had never once had reason to encounter again in person the slim and watchful little alienist. Woodgrove's last memory of him, revisited occasionally in the watches of the night, when the wind howled outside and pawed at the window panes, was of Mr Vaughan leaning against the wall of the mad vivisectionist's laboratory and chewing lustily upon an apple, looking as though he had not just seen two men struck dead before him, and considerably worse besides. Yet here they were again, this pair of gentlemen, now the last two survivors of that dreadful night.

The occasion for their meeting was a solemn one: a funeral.

Proceedings had been short almost to the point of being perfunctory. The vicar of St Raphael's, who had not known the deceased, had given a eulogy so bland and scanty in detail that it might have been appended to the life of almost any dead man. The service had been surprisingly sparsely attended, given the distinguished nature of the life. Though a degree of uncertainty as to the precise nature and cause of his death may have kept away several of those friends and family who, had the tragedy happened just a handful of years before, might have been relied upon to attend.

Now, the vicar and the shrunken congregation had hurried away (for there seemed to be no question whatever of any wake or memorial) and Mr Vaughan and the Reverend Woodgrove had been left alone. They sat together upon a bench in the churchyard, surrounded by the markers of the dead. It was a clear sunny afternoon, and the sight of the English temple was pleasing and soothing in equal measure to Woodgrove, its cool lines of stone a seeming reminder of the impermanence of individual existence.

"Rumours?" Woodgrove asked, for Mr Vaughan's remark had struck him as something of a non sequitur. "Rumours about what? Or about whom?"

"Concerning that particular gentlemen whom we met once. In the east of London." It was a topic on which Mr Vaughan now seemed most eager to converse.

"Oh him," Woodgrove said softly. "I don't think poor Bright ever got over it, did he?"

Vaughan nodded in what was presumably intended as a gesture of sympathy. "Poor Bright."

Both fell silent in awkward memory.

"I didn't even know he was from Wiltshire, did you?" Woodgrove asked.

"No idea. But didn't the vicar mention that he grew up here?"

"He stipulated too it was here that he wanted to be laid to rest."

"Oh so he left some instructions then?"

Woodgrove paused and bit his lip, wary of indiscretion. "As I understand it," he said, "he left a note."

Vaughan said nothing in response, evidently unsurprised by the implication.

"Bright was ever a decent man," Woodgrove said, as if to defend his late friend's reputation. "He was an honourable man who only ever wanted the best for everything. Brave too, in his way. And, of course, a very fine physician."

"Hmm." Mr Vaughan sounded noncommittal. "But he couldn't face the truth of it, could he? At the end. When he was forced to actually look the thing in the eye."

"What do you mean? Face what exactly?"

"Why," said Mr Vaughan, an odd lightness in his tone, "with the arc of the future that is coming."

Woodgrove looked uncertain as to how best to respond to this distinctly peculiar remark. "He's in a better place now," he said, before adding: "and I for one don't care to believe that the Lord will mind exactly how he got there."

"Of course," Vaughan said. Then he grinned, almost blasphemously. "And how very comforting it must be to be able to believe that."

At this retort, Woodgrove felt an uncharacteristic (though in recent years, far from unprecedented) surge of anger. "Really, Vaughan, I can't for the life of me see why you came today. Not if you mean only to sneer."

Vaughan put up both his hands, palms outwards, in a gesture of emollient surrender. "Forgive me," he said, even sounding for a moment as though he might mean it. "I wanted to provoke no offence. I dare say I've grown a little cynical – even a little jaded – since... well, since we saw what we saw."

Woodgrove nodded, that quick flush of anger receding as swiftly as it had arrived. "I dare say we all have."

"As for the reason for my presence here today, I only wanted to pay my respects in person. I can't say that Dr Bright and I were ever close friends but I like to think that there was a certain kinship between us all the same. I like to think that he'd have wanted me to attend."

"Yes. Yes. Of course. That's quite right."

"Come along," Vaughan said, his tone still one of mild contrition. "Shall we walk? It's a pleasant day for it and we've at least an hour before your train to London."

"A fine suggestion," said Woodgrove and the two men rose as one.

They strolled first around the churchyard (careful to go clockwise about the structure and not, though Woodgrove would once have scoffed at such skittish superstition, to walk about it widdershins) and then into the village beyond. It was a calm, picturesque settlement, its houses and solitary inn clustered around a large area of common ground, a pond and a well at the heart of it. They passed no other mourners but only the occasional local who nodded as they went with gruff hospitality. As they walked it seemed to Woodgrove to grow colder. Their breath billowed from their mouths.

"Distinct nip in the air, isn't there?" said Vaughan.

Woodgrove agreed that this was so.

"Brandy?" In some deft magician's movement, Vaughan had produced a silver hip flask which he was holding out now to the Reverend Woodgrove.

"Obliged," the vicar said, taking the proffered vessel and taking two swift swigs, medicinal and welcome. Mr Vaughan did the same and the flask disappeared again.

"You're keeping well, I hope," said the alienist. "Your parish in the city… your responsibilities…?" He spoke as though he had but the vaguest idea of what these might be and Woodgrove reflected that Vaughan had most likely already forgotten such details had he ever known them. He was, after all, the kind of fellow who retained only information that was of direct personal use. Everything else would be jettisoned in order to ensure the maximisation of clarity and efficiency.

"Quite well, thank you," was all that Woodgrove said in response.

"I hear you're thinking of going abroad when you retire. To the Continent?"

"However did you hear of that?"

Vaughan shrugged. "One hears things… mutual friends…"

Woodgrove could not think of a single friend whom he had in common with Mr Vaughan (none, at least, who was still living) but he did not say as much. His time with the alienist was coming to an end and, once they had parted, he told himself that he would go to some considerable trouble to avoid encountering him again. This, he knew, was certainly an unchristian sentiment but there was something about the man which was profoundly unsettling, almost reptilian. He supposed that he had always thought this to a degree, even if, on early acquaintance, he had done his utmost to give the man the most generous benefit of the doubt.

"As it happens," the vicar said, rather stiffly, "I do intend to move. Somewhere quite different. Away from London. Somewhere with fresher, cleaner air. Somewhere I can serve my Creator in a different way."

"I wish you joy of it," Vaughan said. "If anyone has earned a peaceful retirement it's surely you."

Woodgrove murmured his thanks. "And you?" he asked. "You're keeping as busy as ever. Your practice goes from strength to strength?"

"Most certainly," said Vaughan, with no false modesty. "But I find that I have other interests now."

"Oh yes? What kind?"

"I've begun to do a little work for our government. As a kind of consultant. More than that I'm really not supposed to say."

"Indeed? Well, you always were ambitious," said Woodgrove, before adding hastily: "and that's no bad thing, not at least so long as one remembers in whose service it is that you labour."

Vaughan pointed puckishly upwards. "Always," he said with a kind of playful insincerity which, although it rankled with Woodgrove, the priest pretended not to have seen.

They had by now reached the inn at edge of the common. The name of the place is lost but it was of a very familiar type: a stout old building with leaded windowpanes and an air of cheerful dilapidation. A sign outside hung unmoving in the still, wintry air.

"How about a drink?" Vaughan asked.

Woodgrove reached for his pocket watch. "It's been a pleasure to see you again, Vaughan, in spite of the circumstances." (This lie seemed, to the Reverend, to be a white one.) "But I really think I ought to be making my way to the train station. It's an hour's walk and I want to get there in good time and before we lose the light."

"Nonsense," said Vaughan, speaking with an odd, clubbable sort of heartiness which hardly suited him. "Firstly, I don't know why on earth you insist on walking when you can surely afford to be driven not just to the station but to your own blessed front door."

"Vanity, vanity…" murmured Woodgrove.

"Secondly, I am myself being collected from this very common by some associates of mine who will be only too delighted to take you at least as far as you want to go. And thirdly…" His words tailed away and Mr Vaughan seemed suddenly pensive.

"Yes?" Woodgrove felt unaccountably nervous at the pause. "What is the third tranche of your argument?"

Vaughan looked almost blankly at him. "I have the strong sensation that we won't meet again. Not after today. And so I think it behoves us to mark the occasion with a proper drink." Without waiting for a response, Vaughan stamped towards the public house and pushed open the door. It jingled and clanked as he did so. Woodgrove, urged onwards not only by ingrained courtesy but by a considerable amount of curiosity, followed.

At the threshold, he hesitated and, on instinct, glanced over his shoulder. Somebody else was on the common: a bulky, heavyset man who was standing quite still. Another mourner? Woodgrove did not recognise him from the church. A villager out for a stroll? He scarcely seemed the type.

Woodgrove peered closer but the man did not move, standing still in the manner of a scarecrow.

"Reverend!" The voice of Mr Vaughan came from within. "What are you drinking today?"

Woodgrove watched the man on the common an instant longer. At last, the fellow walked away but at an idling, half-hearted pace, as if he meant to reverse his course as soon as Woodgrove was out of sight. Telling himself that he was growing old and foolish, jumping at shadows and that his nerves had never been the same since Ratcliffe, the vicar turned his head away and walked into the tavern where the alienist was waiting.

II

"You said that there were rumours…"

Halfway into his pint of porter and with a little of his guard down at last, the Reverend Woodgrove finally nudged Mr Vaughan back onto that conversational line which he had earlier, when still entirely sober, rejected so emphatically.

"Rumours?" Vaughan seemed delighted by the remark, for all that he feigned ignorance. "Concerning what exactly?"

They were seated at a table in a corner of the inn, away from the fire and the small group of locals who sat before it, nursing their drinks and rehearsing old stories. The landlord, a pale, spindly fellow, glared at them from behind the bar as if suspecting that they might at any moment express an opinion with which he fiercely disagreed.

"Rumours about him," Woodgrove said. "About what had happened to him."

"Oh, you mean poor Bright, I suppose?"

"Vaughan!"

The alienist smiled. "Yes?"

"You know precisely to whom I am referring. I do not think it necessary to speak his name aloud."

"Yes." Vaughan smiled. "I believe I know exactly who you mean. But I mentioned it earlier and you waved the matter away as though it was of no issue at all."

Woodgrove, who saw no need to apologise for anything whatever, said nothing in reply.

"But perhaps your curiosity has got the better of you now, eh?"

"If you know something, Vaughan, let's hear it."

"Nothing more than whispers really… Gossip, I suppose, and a few tall tales."

It seemed to the Reverend Woodgrove that several of the locals had fallen quiet and were sitting in deliberate silence, waiting to hear what the alienist would say next. "Lower your voice, Vaughan. We're guests here, after all."

Mr Vaughan leaned forwards and spoke more softly. "He got clean away, of course. Just as we suspected."

Woodgrove, who had long ago reached the same conclusion, nodded. "Out of the country?"

"So I hear."

"Through your… government connection?"

Mr Vaughan tilted his head in such a way that might be interpreted, depending on the agenda of the observer, to mean variously "yes", "I can't say" or "what do you think?"

The Reverend Woodgrove decided to take the first of these as true. "Do you have any idea whereabouts exactly?"

"We think… an island… a rather remarkable island… in the South Pacific. Or, at least, somewhere in that general vicinity."

"And are you… I mean, can I ask, are these high-ranking friends of yours intending to track him down and bring him to justice? By

God, Vaughan, a reckoning with that blackguard is long overdue."

Mr Vaughan looked at the priest as though he were a very simple soul indeed. "Not exactly," he said, then fell silent as though these two words ought really to be considered the finish of the matter.

"What are you talking about?" Woodgrove asked, his voice filled with real exasperation. "What have you heard? What exactly do you know?"

Vaughan's face lacked any discernible emotion. "The only thing I know is this. There are people in the British Government who know where that man is and something of what he is doing. It's their belief that he might still be of some use to us…"

"Use to who? To what? You can't be serious."

"Woodgrove, you ought to lower your voice. You're aware, I think, that we're attracting attention."

The priest turned around and saw that the locals were indeed observing the men with unembarrassed curiosity, seemingly relishing the spectacle.

"We should drink up," said Vaughan. "The coach will be here soon." He raised his glass to his lips and drank more quickly than was probably wise, for all that he seemed afterwards to be wholly unaffected by the liquor.

Woodgrove, uneasily, did the same, though he left a fair portion of it in the end.

Mr Vaughan stood up, consulted his pocket watch and said: "Well, it's really been most pleasant to see you again, Woodgrove, but I think it's probably time we were leaving."

Woodgrove agreed that this was so and the two men walked, with no small amount of self-consciousness, out of the inn and back into the open air. Dusk awaited them, and something else too: an elegant horse and carriage which seemed quite out of place in this modest rural scene, the kind of vehicle which, while a familiar enough sight in the most well-heeled quarters of London, was rarely seen this far from the metropolis.

"Yours, I presume?" Woodgrove said.

"Good Lord, no," said Mr Vaughan. "Though it does belong to friends of mine."

Woodgrove glanced again at the contraption and thought that he saw in the figure of the hooded coachman a familiar outline which he had seen not long before. The man who had observed them from the common? At the growth of this suspicion, the priest felt a great desire to be shot of the whole thing, to get as far away as he could from the little alienist and his mysterious, hinted-at knowledge, away from the memories of the past and the vile, slithering things that had greeted them in Ratcliffe. As had occurred with increasing frequency of late, he felt the siren call of the continent; not for the first time, he considered how his God would judge him, a man who wishes only to wash his hands of it all, a man who is prepared to look the other way in order to ensure a quiet life.

Vaughan was asking him again whether he would like to be taken to the station.

"No, no, thank you, I do believe I'll walk." Then, without understanding exactly why, Woodgrove added: "It was you who moved the dog, wasn't it? That abominable creature."

Vaughan looked at him thoughtfully. "It was," he said. "You're quite right."

"May I ask why?"

"I didn't want the kind of officials who I assumed you'd be bringing to that place to see the extent of the doctor's work." Vaughan spoke as though this was the simplest, most straightforward of conclusions which any right-thinking fellow might have reached.

"Why ever not?"

"The public isn't ready for the truth. Not yet and not in so unvarnished a state. It could take years for everything to come out. Long, perhaps, even after we've both joined Bufford and Kelman and the rest of the majority."

Behind him, the coach door opened and a man stepped out. He looked over inquisitively.

"Your friends grow impatient," Woodgrove said.

"Then I must away," said Vaughan, though he sounded not in the least anxious or impatient. "It's been a pleasure seeing you again, Reverend. My warmest best wishes for your retirement."

"Thank you. And thank you for coming today. In his own way, I fancy that poor Bright would have appreciated it."

Vaughan nodded, turned away and walked towards the waiting coach. The tall man with the flaxen hair stood back in a deferential gesture as Vaughan approached.

Woodgrove called after him. "Vaughan!"

The alienist stopped but did not turn his head. "Yes?"

"Were you acting for them? For whoever these people are? Even back then?"

Vaughan offered no satisfactory response to this. "Safe journey, Reverend!" he called and then stepped on, into the coach. The other man did the same and closed the door behind him. Immediately the coach rattled away. Woodgrove watched it leave, paused for a moment on the common before, grateful to be rid of the day, he began to walk in the direction of the railway station.

III

Later, on the train home, as the fields of England slipped by and transmuted gradually into the inky sprawl of the city, Woodgrove considered the many oddities of the day.

For some weeks, he had started to sleep a little better at night, and it had been whole months since he had last awoken himself by the sound of his own screams. Somehow he did not believe that he would sleep so heavily or so well tonight.

Yet how was it, he wondered, that it was not the memory of those physical horrors which he had once seen (and which had, he suspected, driven poor Dr Bright to the brink and beyond) but rather the clever, almost playful face of Mr Vaughan which troubled him now more greatly? Why was he fearful tonight not of the past but for what was yet to come? Why, as the journey wound on, even as the welcoming lights of London appeared like rows of lighthouses to welcome home lost mariners, did the Reverend Woodgrove find himself considering the possible limits of Vaughan's ambition, of his ruthlessness, of what appeared to be his troubling proximity to power? And why, as the train finally drew in to the station at Paddington, was Woodgrove discovered by a bewildered ticket inspector, leaning forwards in his seat with his eyes closed and murmuring, with a zeal which he had not truly felt for many years, a desperate prayer for the future?

19TH SEPTEMBER, 1890

LONDON

I

When one lives and works in a large, austere, almost empty house in Kensington, in an atmosphere of sustained gravity and importance, one will naturally long for escape, for a burst of good humour and a taste of friendly companionship. And when the daily life of the house in question has about it not only that air of high seriousness but also certain undercurrents of something like corruption and decay, the desire (no, the necessity) to get away from its confines grows to an all but intolerable degree.

These, at least, were the truths of the life of Mr Jacob Berry, a tall, saturnine fellow who dressed, quite deliberately, rather like an undertaker, and who was at this time amongst the highest paid valets in London.

It was the money, of course, which kept him in his current,

unsettling and sometimes bizarre place of employment. He was of this fact neither especially proud nor particularly ashamed for he still lived by his late father's dictum: "You play the hand you're dealt in life, and you keep as many of your winnings as you can."

Mr Berry's current employer (Berry had had five before him, all very wealthy, three of them titled) seemed to arrange his own affairs along similar lines. Certainly, he had always been honest with his manservant, sometimes to a discomfiting degree. In their first meeting (it was not quite an interview since it was well known that, at this juncture in his career, Mr Berry might have his pick of gentlemen) his future employer had stressed the oddities which would be daily bread in his household and the concomitant need for absolute discretion.

"You will see and hear many strange things during your time with me," he had said when they had met, in a private room in Claridge's, away from the prying eyes of city gossips, "and you may even find yourself routinely intrigued and made curious by them. Yet I would ask you to tell no-one of what you see whilst in my employ and to ask me no questions concerning that which you witness. Do you think, Mr Berry, that you can do these things for me?"

In response, Berry had all but waved the question away as something like an insult to his professional pride. "You need not have asked the question, sir," he said, colouring his words, quite deliberately, with a shade of reproof.

"You will forgive me," his future employer had said with a swiftness and smoothness that suggested a man to whom insincerity came easily. "I did not mean to impugn you. Only, based upon certain recent experiences, I have come to understand that one really cannot be too careful."

"Of course," Mr Berry had replied, every bit as smoothly as he who would be his master. "I shall keep your every secrets, sir. I shall take whatever I witness at your side to the grave if necessary."

"That's very good. That's excellent."

And, for the past three and a half years, Mr Berry had kept all of the promises which he had made that day – at least, until one particular evening.

II

Mr Berry's desire for an occasional escape has already been explained. The more that you come to realise about his place of employ, the more you will surely comprehend this desire, if not, perhaps, to entirely sympathise with him.

Still, it had been an absolute condition of Mr Berry's employment that he should be allowed to absent himself from the house and grounds every Friday afternoon and evening, from two until midnight. These occasions were, as you might imagine, much looked forward to by Berry, and, however they began (with, perhaps, an errand to be run, a walk to be had, an agreeably aimless visit to the library) they almost always ended in the same way, with Mr Berry retiring to one particular institution. The name of the place was "The Outpost" and it was, Mr Berry often thought, perhaps his favourite place in all of London, if not in all the world.

On the afternoon in question, Mr Berry left the house of his employer at the usual hour, took the omnibus to Regent Street and strolled there for a little over two hours, enjoying the anonymity of the browsing crowds who moved, herd-like, from one emporium to the next, and relishing, in stark opposition to his home of quiet and secrets, the rattle and bustle of that populous street, the chatter of pedestrians and the jounce and clatter of the carriages and cabs. He looked in many shops but bought not a single thing.

In a small eatery by Covent Garden, he bought himself an early supper at half past five of cutlets, bread and a small carafe of red wine. Thus fortified, he hailed a cab and, heedless of the expense, instructed that he be taken to Richmond and to the easternmost edge of the park.

He must have dozed during the journey – he believed that he had even begun to dream, of the sun upon his back and of the soft whisper of the sea – because the next thing that Mr Berry knew was the sound of the cab driver bellowing down to him that they had arrived at their destination and could he please, if it's not too much trouble, be given the simple courtesy of his due?

Mr Berry disembarked and passed up his fare. The horse stamped impatiently, pawing the ground as if eager to be away again. The cab had stopped by a stretch of dark iron railing, beyond which the verdant expanse of the park could be glimpsed

"Good evening to you, sir!" called down the driver before moving away.

Berry watched the vehicle go. He turned and, with something of the air of a child at the zoo, he walked to the railings and brought his face close to the bars. It had always fascinated him, this sliver of wilderness so near to the city. He gazed beyond the rails, at the trees and grass beyond. In the distance, something moved and he saw the silhouette of a deer, outlined against the horizon, a shadow in the dying light. Mr Berry even, madly, felt a boyish instinct to clamber over the railings and seek a kind of freedom in the park, to run with the stags and sleep beneath the stars and to face only the consequences of the natural world, and not the many constraints of civilisation.

No doubt plenty of us have felt in our lives such an urge. And no doubt plenty of us have done precisely what Mr Berry did: set aside such thoughts as folly and, with only the hint of melancholic sigh, turn once again to the everyday world.

In the middle of the street which stood opposite this long border of the park was an entrance to an unprepossessing alleyway. It was towards this point that Mr Berry now stepped.

"Spare a farthing, would you, sir?"

There was a figure by the mouth of the alleyway, a sad and wretched fellow, clad in rags, who sat sprawled upon the ground.

Without thinking, Mr Berry reached into his pocket, wrenched free a couple of coins and tossed them down to the beggar.

"Thank you, sir."

Mr Berry nodded but did not slow his pace. He had gone some distance into the alleyway before he heard the tramp call out: "I saw you looking, sir!"

Mr Berry stopped, walked back a few paces and, curious, asked: "What did you say?"

The filthy-faced fellow did not look up from his suppliant's position. His eyes had a glazed quality, Berry noticed now, as though he had taken too much strong drink or ingested some substance that served – forgivably, in the opinion of the valet – to remove him from the cares of so uninsulated a life.

"Only that I saw you, sir, looking into the park."

"Well, what of it?"

"Beautiful, isn't she?"

"On a fine, bright day, most certainly." The vagrant did not respond to this so Mr Berry found himself, more to fill the silence than for any better reason, adding: "A most pleasing little pocket of the wildwood."

The penniless man barked a laugh. "Oh but it's only little now, sir."

"Well yes, in the past, I'm sure, it was very much larger." Growing weary of the conversation, he turned again, only for the stranger to murmur something which rather tugged at his imagination.

"Oh but I didn't mean the past, sir. I meant the future. Seen it, I have, in my dreams. One day all of this will be forest again. All London will be jungle." He giggled at the thought and then begun to hum some cracked old tune.

"Have a good evening," said Mr Berry, over his shoulder, as he walked away. Evidently, the man's reason had been unseated, he thought, as he walked, yet somehow the image of the city as a jungle pawed at his memory and would not be entirely shaken loose, at least until the evening took a stranger turn.

III

At the bottom of the alleyway, which was unpeopled and surprisingly clean, stood a bright green door, upon which was affixed a polished brass plaque that read: "The Outpost."

Mr Berry, having straightened his tie and smoothed down his hair, knocked three times. Almost at once, a shutter was pulled back, and a stretch of metal grille was exposed. A deep voice, long familiar to Berry, intoned: "Who goes there?"

"Jacob Berry."

A grunt. "And what is the law here, Mr Berry?"

The valet gave the well-worn words of entry. "To pay heed, but never to reveal."

A grunt of confirmation at this was all that came. The grille was covered once again and the door was opened. Warm low light spilled out from within, a dash of comfort in this chilly place. A large, squat middle-aged man with a distinctly martial air stood upon the threshold. He beckoned.

"Come on in, Berry, for gawd's sake. You're letting in a right perishing draught."

The valet stepped inside and the door was closed behind him. He stood in a spacious vestibule, wallpapered in a shade of dark damson. The doorman sat down upon a high stool, his hands folded against his sizeable belly.

"Good evening, Mr Gibbens," said the valet.

Another grunt was all that he received from this greeting.

"I fear I'm running a little late tonight."

"You are, sir."

"I dawdled in the city. I seem to be a little sluggish today."

Gibbens shrugged, as though these things were to him matters of sublime unconcern. Mr Berry took off his overcoat and hung it on a row of hooks at the back of the vestibule.

"I'll go through, then, shall I?"

"You do that, Mr Berry."

"Have they started yet?"

"Almost, Mr Berry. Almost."

"Then I'll take my leave of you."

A final grunt. Gibbens settled himself on his stool and fixed his baleful gaze upon the door as if daring somebody to knock upon it and once again interrupt his evening.

Berry walked on, towards a door which led to a corridor

beyond the initial space. With his hand upon the doorknob he turned back and said, softly but with palpable concern: "I was very sorry indeed, Mr Gibbens, to hear about your son."

This time the grunt from the doorman was of a still lower pitch than before. With a kind of gruff sorrow, he said: "These things happen."

"Still…" Mr Berry said. "I am sorry."

Then he opened the door and walked on, down a long corridor, papered in the same dull shade of damson before emerging into a room which was arranged like an informal auditorium. Chairs, placed in small groupings with drinks tables at the side of each, were arranged in a semi-circle around a modest stage, raised only a foot or so from the ground.

The place was busy – around forty or so patrons, all of them men – who sat expectantly, with a drink in hand or beside them, gazing at the stage.

Mr Berry slipped into a chair towards the back of the room. Almost at the instant that he did so, a neat, rather dapper little gentleman walked up on to the stage and motioned for quiet. The gesture was all but unnecessary for the Outpost was not the kind of establishment much given to raucousness or hearty expostulations – not, at least, unless the circumstances were exceptional ones.

"Good evening, my friends," said the dapper man. "Welcome to an evening of what we like to call 'Confessions and Recitations'." Another host in another kind of venue might have paused at this juncture for polite applause. Such things, however, were scarcely in the tradition of the Outpost.

"I trust you're sitting comfortably," said the dapper man again, "and I trust that, as ever, you will, as you listen, bear in mind the code of this place, our solemn pledge for absolute discretion."

Silence, save for the odd creaking of chairs and clinking of glasses.

"The penalties for breaking our only rule in any way at all are, as you will know, of the severest kind. And let it be remembered that we are never slow to act. I am pleased to say that there has not been an incidence of rule-breaking since Mr Terris, four years past. I dare say many of you will recall that most unfortunate accident to which he fell victim. If any have joined the Outpost since that time and are not aware of the details, I have no doubt that an older member shall be able to enlighten you."

This was familiar stuff to many, part of an opening ritual meant to heighten anticipation. Berry's mind wandered a little as the dapper man spoke (drifting back towards that odd proclamation of the mendicant outside) though he was able to recollect well enough what had befallen poor Terris, only a month or so after Berry had joined the Outpost.

He was brought back to his senses by a soft hand at his elbow and a young male voice which asked: "Will it be your usual, sir?"

"Not tonight, I think," said Mr Berry. He did not turn around to face his attendant. "Just a whisky and soda, please."

"Would that be lighter on the soda, sir, than on the whisky?" asked the waiter.

"Most certainly it would."

"Very good, sir." The fellow withdrew and Mr Berry settled himself again in his chair, reflecting as he did so how pleasant a novelty it was for him to be waited upon for a change.

On stage, the dapper man was finishing his introduction. "And now," he said, "that all our preliminaries are dealt with, we can proceed to the business which has brought you here tonight."

There was in the atmosphere of the room, although it was detectable only to the habitué, a certain drawing in of breath at this, a surge of highly suppressed excitement.

"We have five stories for you tonight. Each must be heard only under conditions of absolute secrecy. Each is personally painful to the speaker. And every one of them is the absolute truth."

There was more after this, more introductory chatter, and there was now even a smattering of rather muted applause.

Mr Berry did not observe, however, as the waiter had returned with a whisky and soda.

"Here you are, sir."

The valet reached out and took the tumbler. This time he did turn his head to look at the waiter. He was a young man, very slim and with bright blue eyes.

"Thank you," Mr Berry said, and felt his face flush at the man's proximity. "You're very kind."

"Oh but we like to spoil you here, Mr Berry," said the waiter. He withdrew again, slipping back into the shadows at the back of the room.

The valet, left only with the memory of the man, relished this for a moment and took a long sip of his drink. He swilled the liquid around his mouth, enjoying the subtle burn of it and, for an instant, felt something like contentment.

When he looked up again, the dapper fellow had left the stage to be replaced with the first of the night's tale-tellers, a whiskery fellow dressed rather floridly in the costume of a poet. He was sweating and evidently ill at ease. His accent seemed to hint at the West Country.

"Good evening, fellow members of the Outpost," he began. "I'm very pleased and gratified to be able to speak to you tonight concerning a thing which I've never before been able to tell so much as a soul. And I know, kind and decent gentlemen that you are that I can say anything here and it won't leave these four walls." He gulped noisily and dabbed a hand across his brow. "Now, what I have to say concerns the first time I saw a man die, the grandfather clock in my family's possession and what was told to me by a maidservant who was once employed at Buckingham Palace…"

Mr Berry leaned back, stretched out his legs, took another appreciative sip and listened.

IV

The evening passed pleasantly enough. The man who was dressed as a poet finished his tale (a little over-elaborate, in the end, for all of the scandal it might have caused were it ever to be heard at Highgrove) and was succeeded by another man, a burly fellow in his sixties, a former docker whose tale involved attempted theft, cock fighting and the dreadful moment in his life when he had hesitated too long and brought about the death of a close friend. This was a little more engaging but nonetheless Mr Berry found himself consulting his pocket watch on more than one occasion.

He had now been at the Outpost for more than an hour. He drained his tumbler. He was growing uncharacteristically restless. Something in his evening (though he could not say exactly what) unsettled him.

Feeling suddenly decisive, he was about to rise to his feet, pay his due at the bar and call it a night, when a new speaker was introduced. Mr Berry was on the very cusp of standing when the dapper man announced to the still, thoughtful crowd: "Please, gentlemen, please welcome our third teller of tales on this very special night…"

He glanced down towards his hands, where he probably had some note secreted. "Welcome to… Mr Edward Prendick!"

The force of the name was sufficient to guarantee that Mr Berry did not move but stayed firmly in his seat. The barman appeared by his side again.

"Another drink, Mr Berry?"

The valet did not reply. On stage, the man called Prendick, had shuffled into view. He was a rangy figure with thinning blond hair and a skittish manner.

"Mr Berry?" the barman prompted.

"I know him," the valet said, in a burst of rare candour (though he was talking, at least in part, to himself). "I know that man."

The barman frowned and cleared his throat but receiving no reply, withdrew.

On stage, Prendick bowed his head to acknowledge the attention of the audience.

"Good evening," he said. "My name is Edward Prendick and the story I have to tell tonight is one which I have for two years now been struggling to decide whether or not to share with the world." There was an almost musical lilt to his accent, a touch of Lancashire to his vowels. "I've kept it almost entirely to myself. Though I've set down a written account for my own purposes and I've started to speak about it to another, a professional gentleman who, like you all, is bound by oaths of secrecy."

The audience were patient and polite but there was a palpable sense that Prendick was losing them with this somewhat dry introduction. The sole exception to this was Mr Berry who sat upright in his chair, riveted, unblinking and seemingly absolutely in thrall to this quiet man's words.

"Nonetheless, I find myself beginning to wonder whether I

might not owe it to the world to tell all that I know, to make a clean breast of my experiences and let the public decide what must be done. For even now, I hear strange rumours. I believe I see certain patterns in public life – patterns of the most troubling kind. My friend says that I ought to say nothing at all but... somehow... I wonder..." He said nothing then but only stood and looked at his audience.

It seemed to Mr Berry that Prendick was seeing something quite different to the convocation which sat before him, as though he was imposing upon them some distant, though still vivid, memory. There was a growing sense of restiveness in the crowd. Doubtless there were those who were starting to think that the speaker might not be altogether well, that he might fumble or embroider his story, or that he might simply be a fantasist. There were precedents for such a diagnosis; Outpost practice was generally to kindly, but firmly, remove the lunatic from the stage.

Then Prendick spoke a name which got their attention at last. "How many of you recollect a man named Moreau? Ah. I see that there are many of you who do." As he said the name, Mr Berry saw a flush of disgust flare upon Prendick's cheeks. "He was once quite the cause célèbre wasn't he? A villain of the '70s. The laboratory... the dog in the street... you all of you know the story... But then he disappeared. It was assumed that he had buried himself in some foreign land or had met some accident at sea or had taken his own life. Yet none of these things were true. I know this because I met him for myself in '87." He looked around the room at this, sensing, correctly, that the audience were warming to him.

"I found myself shipwrecked upon the island where he had been hiding out. And I saw for myself what manner of wild science he had there been practising. The hybridisation, gentlemen, of humankind with animals! The maniac desire to forge a new species. The creations of his which lurched upon the land and loomed along the shore." He paused, took a deep breath and plunged on. "But I should begin at the beginning. If I'm to tell you my tale then you should surely hear it all." He took a breath, steeled himself and said: "It began with the sinking of the *Lady Vain* when we were but ten days out from Callao…"

V

Prendick's story was the longest that night, and certainly the strangest that had been heard in the Outpost for many years. By the end of it, his audience was entirely spellbound, relishing every twist, marvelling at the horrors that he described and wondering at the hubris of the madman at its heart who had sought to play god and transform a menagerie into a new kind of being. Although he was not a boastful man, the courage and resourcefulness of Prendick himself was clear. He had been brave and determined indeed to have lived for months upon the island, first sharing it with Moreau and his equally deranged assistant before, after their murder by his own creations, alongside the Beast People, as desperate to survive as they. His eventual escape, on a leaky and improvised boat he had constructed himself from windfall and debris, was thrillingly told.

When it was over, Prendick left the stage swiftly, perspiring and ill at ease, his face already showing signs of uncertainty as to the wisdom of making so full and frank a confession. This was not unusual at the Outpost and there was no tradition there of pausing after the speech for questions or applause.

The room was left in silence after Prendick's departure (Mr Berry saw him slip towards the door) until the dapper man returned to the stage. "Time for a rest," he said. "A chance to refill our glasses. For we have another pair of tales tonight. Though I do not envy having to be heard after Mr Prendick's revelations…"

With relief, the room now stirred itself and rose. Mr Berry also got to his feet but he had no intention of staying. His eyes rested on where Prendick had been just a moment before.

The barman was at his side again, for all that he was surely much needed at his station. "Please," he said. "I have to know. That man, Prendick. You said you recognised him?"

Mr Berry wanted to hurry after the tale-teller but there was something so beseeching in the eyes of the barman that he could not help but tarry. "He's visited my employer," he said, aware that confidentiality at the Outpost was absolute. "Many times. He's been telling, I think, that same story he told to us tonight."

"Your employer?" The barman was ignoring the clamour for refreshment from an increasing number of other patrons. "Why should Prendick have told him so much?"

Berry started now to move away. He had, he knew, to speak to Prendick. He called back briskly over his shoulder. "He's a man called Vaughan," he said. "An alienist. A kind of modern priest, I suppose. That is: a man who hears confessions."

VI

Prendick had left the club, walked up the alleyway and was about to disappear towards the heart of Richmond when Mr Berry finally caught him.

"Wait!" the valet called out. He was still struggling to get on his overcoat, so rapid had been his departure from the Outpost.

Prendick did not turn but hurried on, his movements fretful and distracted.

Berry broke into a light jog in order to reach Prendick's side.

"I've not got anything more," said the blond man, not slowing his pace or acknowledging his pursuer in any way. "I told my story in full in there and I'm not even sure I should have done that. I know… that Mr Vaughan doesn't think I ought to say…" He stopped now, Mr Prendick, and looked at Berry as though seeing him for the first time. "Wait. Don't I know you?"

"I work for Mr Vaughan."

"Of course. I've seen you there. Then what… what are you doing following me like this? I… Is this Vaughan's doing?"

"He doesn't know I'm here."

In the distance, a clocktower tolled the time. Ten. It was dark and cold and the streets were almost empty. The two men gazed at each other, nervous and jumpy.

"Then why…" said Prendick.

"Is it true?" asked Mr Berry. "Everything you said?"

"Every word of it."

"Then…" Mr Berry felt at this point that there was a great deal more which he could have said, based upon several years' worth of observations concerning his employer. He could have told Prendick that the alienist was most certainly not the benign counsellor that he appeared to be. He could have said that his employer's repeated advice to Prendick not to speak about his experiences was surely rooted in something other than unalloyed concern for a patient. He could even have told Prendick of certain of the other guests whose arrival at the house he had witnessed: the government men, the military men, the engineers, the financiers, the pleasure seekers and the artists, an unholy assemblage of individuals whose presence hinted at a scheme of the most elaborate kind. He could have told him that he had for many months now felt that he was, in his professional discretion, materially abetting something of troubling magnitude.

Yet, in the end, Mr Berry's pride won out. He had given his word, after all, to his employer. That, from the first, had been the nature of their arrangement and he could not bring himself now to go against it.

"I suppose," he said at last, "that I wished only to give you my greetings. And to thank you for your story. You have been very brave, I think."

"Oh." Prendick seemed almost disappointed by Berry's words, as though he had divined something of the valet's turmoil. "You're kind. But I've really been nothing of the sort. There's no real courage in survival. Just pure instinct." With this, he nodded and went on, his gait that of an anxious man.

Mr Berry watched him go. He fought for an instant with the impulse to rush after him and tell him of all that he suspected. Yet the moment passed and the mariner walked on until he passed far out of sight of the valet.

VII

When Mr Berry returned home, to that big, ominous house in the city, he was somehow not surprised to see that a light burned in the master's study. Nor was he surprised to hear the soft, potent voice of Vaughan call out to him as he trod by.

"Berry? Is that you? Would you be so kind as to step in here, please?"

The valet did as he was told. He entered the lavish but somehow rather chilly sanctum of his master to find Mr Vaughan sitting in his armchair with a book on his lap and a cigarette between his lips. He had evidently been smoking for some time for the room was filled with it, lending the space a distinctly Hadean air.

He waited at the threshold. "Yes, sir?"

The little man smiled. "So sorry to drag you in here like this. I know it's late and your night off to boot."

"No trouble, Mr Vaughan. What can I do for you?"

Vaughan sucked in the last of his cigarette, then ground it out in the ashtray by his seat. "I understand you were at the Outpost tonight and that you heard speak a mutual friend of ours."

Mr Berry struggled to keep his voice altogether neutral. "Sir, I think I ought to—"

Vaughan cut him short with a gesture. "Please don't trouble to deny it. I know that you were there. And I know what Mr Prendick related. No doubt you recognised him from the sessions in this house. And no doubt, being a brisk, clever and, above all, observant fellow, you have started to think of all that you have witnessed here and have begun to put two and two together. Am I in this correct?"

Berry saw no alternative but to speak the simple truth. "Yes, sir."

"Poor Mr Prendick," said Vaughan, scarcely acknowledging Mr Berry's reply. "He simply cannot hold his tongue."

The valet said nothing. Mr Vaughan seemed to gather himself and return his attention towards his employee.

"It seems I have a choice. I can, if you like, send you away from here tonight. I can give you a generous gift before you leave in exchange for your absolute silence and discretion. I can also send you away with a promise that if you breathe a word of what you know I will ruin you utterly. Would you like that, Mr Berry?"

"No, sir. I'm not sure I would, sir."

"Very good. Then do you want to hear the alternative?"

"Of course, Mr Vaughan."

"That you work for me more closely than ever. That you take on some new, additional duties."

"Sir, I don't know what to say…"

Mr Vaughan smiled and said nothing.

"My duties, sir, in this new arrangement, would they be different at all?"

"Oh much as they are, Berry. Much as they are. Though I suppose there might, from time to time, be something slightly more robust that's required of you."

"Robust, sir?"

Vaughan reached for another cigarette, put it in his mouth, lit it and inhaled. "You'll see in time," he said eventually. "Suffice to say that there'll be nothing which isn't well within your capabilities. So then, what do you say? You know me well enough by now, I think, to know that I'm nothing if not a plain-dealing man."

Mr Berry was far from sure that this was the case.

"Whatever you decide, I shan't hold it against you," the alienist went on. "You have my word. So what will it be?"

In the end, Mr Berry found it very easy to give his answer. And he did not regret it either, at least not at first, not until the complete truth began to emerge.

2ND OCTOBER, 1890

LONDON

I

As we have seen, Mr Vaughan was a creature first and foremost of stillness. There was something distinctly feline not only in his movements, which were ever lithe and precise, but in his ability for motionlessness, a facility for calm waiting that befits any predator, however outwardly domesticated. And so the hour of five o'clock on this particular afternoon found the alienist in a pose which might almost have been designed to typify these tendencies.

He sat in his study, surrounded by his shelves and trinkets (a statuette of a mongoose locked in battle with a serpent; an old trophy from his schooldays awarded for public speaking; a jewelled box of murky colonial origin), with curtains drawn against the encroaching night. The air smelled still of tobacco, though Mr Vaughan was attempting now to curb his habit, having in recent days become convinced of its toxicity. There was the loud metronomic ticking of the clock which would have struck many as a distraction but which Mr Vaughan found to be a source of comfort on the grounds of its absolute predictability. He scarcely noticed the ticking, however, as, leaning forwards very slightly in his chair, he listened to two low voices in the corridor beyond.

The first voice belonged to his manservant, Berry, a fellow whose conduct to date (in spite of one minor infelicity) had never given the alienist the least cause to regret his hiring.

"It's a pleasure to see you again, sir," the servant was saying, in a tone of apparent deference.

"Likewise," said the second voice, which Vaughan knew to belong to the visitor, a certain regular client of his. There was an audible quality of strain in the tones of the guest, a common symptom in Vaughan's experience, in those who had undergone great and sustained trauma. "A very considerable pleasure to encounter you again, Mr..." He coughed to hide his evident awkwardness.

"Berry," said the valet.

"Yes, of course."

The visitor paused. He lowered his voice, becoming muffled and all but inaudible.

Stealthily, Mr Vaughan rose to his feet and stole towards the door. His hearing was sufficiently acute to hear now, at this distance, the words that were being spoken in the corridor beyond.

"Did you tell him?" the visitor was asking. "Did you tell him what I said?"

There was detectable in the fellow's voice a quality of what was, at the least, disquiet, if not of outright fear. At this realisation, a frisson passed through the alienist, a quality of electricity, which brought neither pleasure nor pain but a weaving together of the two.

"Mr Vaughan and I share a most gratifying relationship of master and servant," Berry said, "one which, I am very proud to say, contains a considerable degree of mutual respect. He does not pry into my life whilst I make it a point of principle never to notice those parts of his which do not affect my own duties and responsibilities."

The visitor's voice, sombre and sincere: "Berry, answer me truly, did you tell that man in there anything of what you heard at the Outpost?"

There came a long pause.

"Berry. This is important. He has to hear it only from me. I'll ask you again – did you tell him?"

Some prissy throat clearing, then: "I'm a man of discretion, sir. You must know that. It would not behove me to—"

"Berry!"

Now there came the sound of sudden movement, a noisy thump against the wall, a stifled cry from the manservant and an expostulation from the visitor.

Vaughan waited just for a moment, curious as to how much more of his temper the beleaguered gentleman outside might yet lose.

Hearing nothing further, the alienist opened the door and stepped smartly out into the hallway. There the visitor, Mr Edward Prendick, was holding the manservant by his lapels, having lifted the fellow some inches off the ground.

Vaughan cocked an eyebrow, quietly appreciative of his physical strength.

"Would you care to place my manservant back upon solid ground, Mr Prendick?"

The visitor glared at Vaughan. Unspeaking, he put Berry

down and stepped back. He was breathing heavily, Vaughan noticed, and his pupils had expanded. Fourteen separate other indications suggested a heightened state of distress.

Vaughan smiled soothingly. "If you'd be so kind as to step this way, Mr Prendick, I believe that we have a good deal to discuss."

II

Prendick settled awkwardly into the large and exceedingly comfortable leather chair upon which Mr Vaughan invited all of his clients to sit. That it was several inches shorter and squatter than Vaughan's own was, of course, no accident; the alienist beamed down at his subject with an air of exaggerated magnanimity.

"I feel that I ought to apologise," the visitor began.

Vaughan waved away this predictable speech. "Pray do not speak of it. No-one knows better than I the all but intolerable strain under which you have of late been labouring. Besides, between the two of us, Mr Berry can so often be a thoroughly exasperating individual."

At the finish of this second sentence, Vaughan heard from without a motion at the door: the valet, learning anew the old lesson about the inadvisability of eavesdropping.

Prendick managed a quick, nervous, harried smile. "I suppose you must be curious as to the cause of our dispute?"

"Absolutely not."

"No?"

"The *casus belli* is of no concern to me whatever. A small disagreement between men, that is all, and one which is easily ended. So come now. Let us speak of weightier matters. I wish to know of your troubles lately. Has there been any resurgence of... the old thoughts?"

Prendick hesitated, tilting his head in a posture of contemplation. "Not particularly," he said at last, obviously mendacious in the practised eyes of the specialist. "It's been a period of no particular import, utterly without disruption." Each word compounded the lie.

Vaughan, although he gave no outward reaction of any kind, seethed inwardly.

III

After Prendick had finished speaking in a desultory manner, of the modest trials of the days gone by, avoiding the truth throughout, Mr Vaughan said how pleased he was at this progress.

"I owe it to you," said Prendick. "You've allowed me to conquer my demons, or at least to hold them at bay."

"Then that is my privilege," said Vaughan, apparently with feeling.

"But I think it's time now, sir, to stop." Prendick looked a little flustered at this admission. His breath was coming more quickly than before and his posture suggested that he believed there to be some conflict imminent, that the alienist would attempt to push back against his desire.

According to a stratagem which had served him well for all of his life, Vaughan elected to provide the unexpected and to give the man the very opposite of that which he feared.

"I am so very glad," he said, "to see that you've reached this decision and come to such a conclusion. Glad and – if you'll forgive a moment's sentiment – very proud of you too."

"You are?" Prendick could not keep his surprise from inflecting the timbre of his voice.

"That surprises you, I think."

"Yes, yes. I suppose it does. I suppose I had thought…" He said no more, colouring slightly.

Vaughan spread wide his hands, palms outwards – his politician's gesture. "Please. Let us have no secrets here. Let us say only what is on our minds and let us be frank, clear and candid."

"Well then," Prendick said. "In that case… I suppose I thought that you had taken something of an interest in me, and in my story."

"I have. Most certainly. You are my client, after all."

"I mean a more than professional interest. An… anthropological one, if you like. A scientific one."

"That may be true. Yours is, after all, amongst the most remarkable accounts of our age. I could hardly fail to be greatly intrigued by what you have told me. But this is merely my curiosity speaking. Mr Prendick, I am not an investigator. I am a healer. And it brings me nothing but joy to see today that you are healed. Not by my words or actions – I ought upon that point to be emphatic – but by your own. I have given you the tools to ensure your own survival; to see you wield them now with such aplomb is the cause of all my pride."

Vaughan who, although he often permitted others to think of him as inscrutable, had always rather enjoyed speechifying, stopped himself here, concerned that he had gone too far. The man upon the chair beside him, however, seemed both satisfied and relieved.

"Thank you," he murmured, "for everything. Do you know I have even started to believe… That is, I have begun to consider the possibility…"

"Yes?" Vaughan prompted after a long moment of hesitation from Prendick. He was, after all, almost certain of how that sentence was to be completed.

"I have started to wonder whether I ought not to tell my story to others apart from you."

Vaughan feigned surprise. "But have you not spoken often in the past of your fears of public ridicule were you to present the facts of the matter? That you'd be branded a liar or a madman or worse? That there would be dire consequences?"

Prendick exhaled very slowly in an attempt, Vaughan suspected, to regulate his temper. "Yes, Mr Vaughan, I have said that. But I feel more confident now. So much more myself. Thanks, in large part, to you."

"Have you told anyone else of this plan?"

"Not yet," Prendick said, too quickly – with such speed, in fact, that the lie would have been obvious even had Mr Vaughan not known of it already. "No, no. I thought I had first to say it to you."

"Then I thank you," Vaughan said smoothly, "for your good graces and for your most excellent manners." The smile slipped comfortably onto his lips, although, of course, it was false in every respect.

"And I've written it down too," Prendick said.

Vaughan's smile grew still more taut. "Indeed? You have not spoken of such a thing before today."

"I thought I would do it for myself, you see. As a way of taking the story out of me, if you can understand. A kind of exorcism."

"Oh, I understand that very well. And I hope that the no doubt painful process of composition has aided your recovery."

"You're not cross?"

"My dear fellow, why ever would I find myself in such a

temper? I may be a little dismayed that you could not confide in me about this additional labour of yours. But in essence the idea is a capital one."

"But it's one you so often counselled me against."

"Perhaps in that, my friend, I was rather too hasty. The taking of overly precipitate action is not traditionally a flaw of mine but, in this particular instance, I may have acted with too much speed."

Prendick nodded with an odd sort of contentment (such as he might once have exhibited in the years before he found himself upon the island) as though he considered the matter settled, his complicated ledger with Mr Vaughan now altogether balanced and even.

"Well then," Vaughan went on, "seeing as our professional relationship seems about to come to an end, I wonder if there's one more thing that I might ask of you in this, our final session. A kind of favour if you will."

"If it's within my power to grant it," Prendick said, with the confidence of someone who still had not wholly gauged the capacity of the man with whom he was alone, "then I shall do so."

"Thank you, Mr Prendick. So what I wish to ask of you is this: will you let me mesmerise you?"

IV

Somewhat to Mr Vaughan's surprise (and most certainly to his delight), Edward Prendick proved to be entirely susceptible to mesmerism.

The patient sunk easily into a different state as Vaughan crouched over him, swinging a highly polished gold watch and crooning instructions in a soft, low, persuasive voice. The mariner spoke, under the influence, almost eagerly of all manner of secret things. There was much that he had buried, though none of it very deeply. He was a man, Mr Vaughan considered, whose pain was ever close to the surface.

The alienist began by asking three questions to which he already knew the answers. These were of escalating difficulty, so as to test the honesty of the subject while in a hypnotic state.

"What are you called?"

The answer came swiftly, its delivery perhaps a little more leaden than was usual, though nothing which would have raised any alarm in a layman. "Edward Prendick."

"What was the name of the ship which rescued you from almost certain death after the sinking of the *Lady Vain*?"

A momentary grappling with pronunciation, then: "The *Ipecacuanha*."

"Have you ever been in love?"

No hesitation. "I have not."

Mr Vaughan paused. Some might say that he was relishing his moment of power. I would argue that it was more likely a case of his enjoying the anticipation, a piece of pleasure which was for him peculiarly acute. His tongue darted out, very briefly, to dampen the corners of his mouth, like a hungry man spying the arrival of dinner.

"Now, Mr Prendick… I want you to search your mind for me. I want you to ransack your memory. I want you to turn over even the heaviest, dullest stones from your past and see what lurks underneath."

"Naturally," Prendick said, and his tone was almost agreeable. "Anything I can do to help. I like to make myself useful, you know, if I can."

The alienist ignored these pleasantries. "You've told me of the island. Many times. I know now that you have told strangers of it also. Even that you have set down on paper an account of your adventures there. But Mr Prendick, is there anything you have not told me? Anything at all which does not feature in any of these testimonies?"

Nothing was said. The clock ticked on.

"Mr Prendick?" There was an oddly singsong cadence to Vaughan's voice, like a father cajoling a child into good behaviour or a citizen coaxing a cat down from a tree. "Please hold nothing back from me."

A thin moan now escaped Mr Prendick. He seemed to struggle in his chair, as though he were sleeping and in the grip of a nightmare.

"There's something there, I think. Yes? Something hidden."

"Please, no…" Prendick's face was drained and white.

"I cannot force you to say anything which you are determined not to say," said the mesmerist softly. "I can only ask you to speak as fully, freely and frankly as you can. Besides, to let go of one final secret may set you free. It might provide that exorcism."

Silence then, and although nothing was said, a battle of wills between the two men all but crackled in that quiet room, until, at length, Prendick murmured, hesitatingly: "There was something."

"I knew it."

"Something so fantastic that I dare not speak a word of it. Something so strange I almost felt I dreamed it."

"What was it?"

"Something… in the water…"

"Yes?"

"A shadow. Tendrils. A deep, strange voice."

"You mean… Moreau?"

Prendick groaned. "No. One of his creations. But one which had evolved beyond his origins. Into something new."

"You mean…" Once again, Vaughan's tongue emerged to lick the corners of his mouth. "Are you saying that there were experiments which Moreau conducted of which we know nothing at all?"

"I… think so. Not even his assistant, Montgomery, knew of them…"

"Tell me." Vaughan's voice rose higher than before. In a slip of self-control that was most unlike him, he all but shouted: "Tell me now!"

It was too much. Prendick groaned again. He thrashed to and fro.

"Wait…" Vaughan said, as calmly as he could. "Wait and tell me more."

Yet things had gone too far. The spell was broken. Like a man bursting out from beneath the ocean waves, Prendick's eyes were flung open, he struggled, flailingly, to sit upright and took a noisy gulp of air. He looked around him wildly. "Did it work? Did you hear what you needed to hear?"

Vaughan looked at him, calculating the plausibility of the man's response. Wasn't this too neat, he wondered. Too close to formula? Weren't these precisely the sorts of reaction which one might expect to see at the performance of any music hall mesmerist?

Prendick grinned back, seemingly guileless enough. Vaughan watched him, unspeaking, wondering whether he might not have underestimated the man.

The client yawned, stretched and clambered up from the chair. "Well, if there's nothing else, I do believe I ought to be going. I thought I might take a walk this afternoon. I may even treat myself to a little light supper. Creedles, perhaps. It's said to be very good. Do you know it?"

Mr Vaughan, who took very little interest in the vagaries of fashionable dining, said simply that he had heard of it but that he had not eaten there himself, a convenient lie in order to speed the conversation to its conclusion.

"Thank you again," said Prendick, both men on their feet and shaking hands.

"It's been my honour." This was true enough, thought Mr Vaughan, though perhaps not quite in the way that the patient might have assumed.

At last, smiling nervously, as though he couldn't quite believe that he was to be released so easily, Prendick backed away. As he approached the exit, the door opened and Mr Berry appeared, showing at last that breed of punctual discretion for which he had once been well known.

"My servant will show you out, Mr Prendick."

"Thank you, Mr Vaughan."

"This way, sir," said his valet, leading the client away.

Vaughan returned to his chair and to his posture of absolute stillness, listening to the diminuendo of footsteps, the opening and closing of the front door and then the soft, creeping return of Mr Berry.

He stood upon the threshold, looking questioningly at his master.

Vaughan sighed. "Yes? What is it, Berry?"

"Don't you want me to go after him?" Goodness, but the fellow was eager.

"Why ever would I want you to do such a thing?"

"To see where he goes. Who he speaks to. Surely you'll want him to keep his account a secret?"

Vaughan sighed and stretched, languorously, in his chair. "It would seem that Mr Prendick has decided to tell his story to the world. I'm not sure that he'll be listened to. Besides, I don't think he's as cured as he believes himself to be. I somehow think that he'll be dead within the year."

At this remark, Berry seemed exercised. He opened his mouth before, thinking better of it, saying nothing at all.

"Say what you want, Mr Berry."

"Sir, have you done something?"

"Excuse me?"

"Something to Mr Prendick? Have you… I don't know… placed some suggestion in his mind? Some instruction to suicide delivered in the mesmeric state?"

"Dear me, but you do have an imagination. I should never have believed you so fanciful, Mr Berry. Such a thing's quite beyond me."

"I'm sorry. That must have been most… exasperating of me."

"Come now, Mr Berry. Don't be truculent."

Berry said nothing and only waited.

Vaughan sighed. "Yes, Mr Berry?"

"So how do you know? That Prendick will be dead and gone within the year?"

Vaughan sniffed. "Instinct. Nothing more. But, as I believe you know, my instincts have rarely led me down the wrong path before."

"I see that, sir, yes. But Mr Prendick being on the loose… in the wild, so to speak, and happy to tell his story to anyone he meets…"

"Yes?"

"Well, won't that damage your plans, sir?"

A long silence. The ticking of the clock. Mr Vaughan weighing up his options, considering the possibility, all but non-existent in his life to date (except perhaps, long ago, with a certain girl, named Louisa) for trust.

"And what do you know of my plans, Mr Berry?"

The valet winced. "I don't know a great deal, sir. But there's plenty I suspect."

"Bold of you to say so."

"Yes, sir."

"And do you want to know, Mr Berry? Do you want, at long last, to know everything? Do you want to know what we're planning? How all of this connects?"

No hesitation. "Yes, sir."

Vaughan felt the urge for a cigarette and had to push away the thought. "I should warn you: Mr Prendick's island constitutes only the beginning…"

"Yes, sir. I want to know, sir. I want to know everything."

Vaughan grinned, his mind made up. A drink, perhaps, rather than tobacco. "Then be so good, would you, as to fetch me a brandy and soda? And one also for yourself."

"Yes, sir. Thank you, sir."

"Then you may draw up a chair. And you may sit with me awhile." Mr Vaughan found that he was, against all expectation, enjoying himself now, that he relished the possibility of finally making a clean breast of it, of laying out every element to another human being. "And then, Mr Berry, I shall do what you have asked of me and I will tell you everything."

25TH DECEMBER, 1890

SUSSEX, ENGLAND

1

Three times in her life Mrs Eliza Finn had cause to consider that she had made some more than usually severe error of judgement in the upbringing of a boy whom she had raised as her own, he who now walked about the world as Jacob Berry.

The first was when he was ten years old and had been returned from school along with a letter which suggested that it would be best for all concerned if he did not return (a situation which was eventually resolved only by the liberal application of both diplomacy and money). The second occurred five years later, not long after the death of her husband, Mr Thaddeus Berry, and her introduction of the boy to the man (Mr Walter Finn) whom she intended to take the place of the recently deceased around the matrimonial table. On this occasion, the juvenile had disappeared for two days and a night, returning home in a state of extreme sullenness, refusing to admit where he had been, looking as though he had engaged in fisticuffs and bearing upon his sleeves and collars a sequence of troubling discolorations. The third time was this very morning, in the small village church where Eliza had long worshipped, when, at a tender recitation of the nativity of the Christ-child, he had barked out a laugh so sardonic and so blasphemous that his adopted mother would, had it been uttered by any other than he, have considered him to be unequivocally of the Devil's party.

"Jacob!" She spoke sharply but under her breath, so as not to draw attention to the pair of them from the other worshippers (of whom there were many, this service being still, in spite of the godlessness of the age, the most well-attended of the year). "You cannot make such noises."

"Forgive me," murmured her son, though in truth he looked very far indeed from penitence. "It's just the sight of all this… mummery. Hypocrites everywhere."

"Hush!" She glared and Jacob fell silent.

She was about to suggest that he was not too old to be put across her knee but something in his eyes – some new, unfamiliar intensity – made her hold her tongue. *You've changed*, she thought later as she knelt beside him as they prayed together at the end of the service and gave thanks for the miracle of which the day was a commemoration.

But what has changed you? And to what end?

II

After they had returned home from church, the remainder of the Christmas morning was passed in silence or else in vague, elusive chit-chat. Mrs Finn had a good deal of work to do in the kitchen in order to prepare the luncheon while her adopted son, though he offered his assistance, spent much of the time stalking through the sparse little rooms of the cottage or standing outside in that small patch of garden which Eliza had, in the long years of her second widowhood, worked at and nurtured until, in defiance of the unpromising clay of the ground, it had become a respectable, well-tended plot. Even today, overcast and chill, it looked orderly and patient, the neat rows of flowerbeds waiting for the rebirth of spring.

Not that Jacob saw any of this. Mrs Finn caught sight of him through the window, pacing with apparent nervousness up and down and then stopping, as though caught by a sudden thought.

He seemed to be muttering to himself. Once, when she was checking the progress of the roasting goose, she thought she heard her son laugh again, a high wild noise which didn't sound much like him at all.

As they sat down to their food (which, although prepared by Mrs Finn herself had all been bought and paid for by Jacob), Eliza was surprised to find him on theatrically cheerful form, smiling, complimentary and attentive.

"I'm so sorry about this morning," he said once their plates were laden high, just after he had taken his seat and, at his own instigation, said grace with a careful, earnest eloquence.

"It's not for me to forgive," said Mrs Finn, sniffing, although of course she had already done so. "It's for the Lord to give you absolution."

"Well, He does have a reputation for mercy," said Jacob, slicing happily into the hot gooseflesh and adding to his forkful a hunk of roast potato.

Mrs Finn gave him a hard, old-fashioned look. Yet Jacob grinned back, just as he so often had as a little boy, and her heart was melted just as easily.

"Let's not quarrel," he said. "Not today on all days. And not when I've come so very far to see you."

"And don't think I don't appreciate it," Eliza said, somehow contriving to make a compliment sound accusatory. "Don't think I don't. You coming all this way to see your old mum and being so kind and generous to her."

"Oh… well…" Berry spread wide his hands, in an indication of magnanimity. This, thought Mrs Finn, was not a gesture which she could recall her son ever having made before. "It really is my pleasure."

The mood between them leavened now. A thaw was well under way. Mrs Finn even found herself able to remark, a fork halfway towards her mouth, the gravy dripping back onto her plate, "And so very good of your employer to give you these days of leave."

Jacob seemed almost to flinch at the mention of the man who was, in a sense, the founder of the feast. "Yes, yes," he said but he would not meet his mother's gaze. "Mr Vaughan was very insistent that I take some time… away." He paused and, his lips twisted in indignation, withdrew a piece of gristle from his mouth and placed it daintily before him. "He was very insistent about the significance of the season."

"He sounds a most Christian gentleman."

At this, Jacob all but snarled. "He's not that but at least he's no hypocrite. He's never hidden what he is or claimed to be a better man."

Mrs Finn wondered. It was as though, for an instant, someone else entirely was sitting at the table, a person she had suspected before but only ever glimpsed. A shadow version of her son. All she could say was: "Jacob?"

But the storm had passed again and, with palpable effort, her boy was smiling once more and carving at his food. "Please. You should ignore me. I'm very tired, that's all. The stress of my work. The responsibilities…" He seemed to have to force himself to look his mother in the eye. "Let us talk of other things. Let's speak not of London matters. Tell me of village things. And, perhaps, after lunch we should take a walk together? As we used to do?"

"Of course," said Mrs Finn, bending once again over her luncheon. "I'd like that very much." But she watched him now with an emotion which she had not felt with such intensity since he had been a boy; she watched him, fearful for his very safety.

III

Later, just as he had promised, the two of them went for a walk, through the English village and out onto the Downs beyond. They had left their departure too late and had lingered too long over luncheon with the result that the light was already beginning to dim by the time that they set foot outside. Nonetheless, it was pleasant enough at first, at least before the day soured irretrievably.

In the village itself, the couple passed several acquaintances and they were able to nod politely and call out "Merry Christmas!" together with various seasonal platitudes. In such moments, it felt to Mrs Finn almost as though nothing was awry, that the dark clouds above them did not exist.

When they passed out of the village and onto the Downs

(usually so picturesque but today somehow glowering), Mrs Finn's son seemed once again to retreat into himself, turning grim-faced and monosyllabic. He had not been like this for years; often, in fact, to her circle of friends, Mrs Finn had spoken of his natural charm and easy way with people. Why, only last month she had remarked to the postmistress that her boy had "such a quality of happiness. Folks is drawn to him. They put their trust in him and they tell him their secrets."

This description did not seem in that darkening afternoon to hold water at all, as this morose man stalked ahead of her, at one with the lengthening shadows.

Two incidents unsettled them further. The first was when a pheasant, startled by their approach, emerged, squawking, from a bush. Its wings whirred in alarm. Both of them were surprised but Mr Berry, although the creature surely meant him no harm, flung up his hands in front of his face. There was a cringing quality to him which Mrs Finn had never seen before.

Later, as they turned about to come home again, the light now almost entirely gone, Berry let out a cry of revulsion. He had stepped inadvertently in what looked to be a decaying rabbit, torn apart by dogs, and left to moulder on the ground. It was hardly a pretty sight – scraps of fur, a smear of dark blood, a handful of small organs, liberated by the evisceration and abandoned by the corpse – but the countryside provided such scenes, and worse, daily. Yet he squealed, like a child awaking from a nightmare.

Gently, carefully, Mrs Finn touched her son's arm. "There," she said. "There's nothing to fret about. Only a coney, torn asunder."

"Did it suffer?" Berry asked, his voice a high wavering thing.

"No," said Mrs Finn. "Leastways not for long. It wouldn't have known all that much about it."

Berry breathed out noisily. "That's good."

"Let's get ourselves home," said Mrs Finn. "Get in front of the fire with a nice hot toddy. You've not been yourself, you know. Not at all."

"I know," said Mr Berry, "I do know that," and walked ahead of her again. She knew better than to press him. He was moving too fast in any case for her to catch him. She trailed behind at a distance and, in her mind, she asked for help and intervention.

IV

Back home, in the light and the warm, her son rallied. He was talkative enough as they sat by the fireside and almost too grateful for the toddy that she made him. He seemed to want to speak not of recent events but of the distant past. He talked of his boyhood but in a queer, idealised fashion which surprised her. It was as though he had smoothed away all the elements of his youth which had been less than ideal, as though he had edited his own history to make of it a kind of child's fable. She let him speak and did not correct his misrememberings.

It was only on his second glass that a few shards of real truth emerged, and these seemed to fall from his lips almost without his realising.

"They're building something," he said suddenly, hard on the heels of an odd reminiscence about his schooldays.

"Who is?" Mrs Finn asked. Drowsing under the influence of firelight and drink, she wondered whether she had missed some necessary context. "Who's building what?"

Her son stared into the flames. "Doesn't matter," he said.

"Shouldn't tell you anyway. More than my life's worth. Perhaps even yours."

"Oh, but you're being dramatic, surely. What could be so bad about a building?"

Her son did not turn to face her but kept his eyes trained upon that which was burning. "It's not one building," he said softly. "But many. A city. A city underground." He reached his right hand up to his forehead and wiped away the considerable amount of perspiration which had accumulated there. "And then... what they mean to do with it. How they're going to people it. They're going to just take them. Just scoop them up and steal them away and put them in this new place." He sighed. "The scale of it, ma... Why, the sheer bloody audacity of it."

He drifted into silence then and Mrs Finn felt a surge of fresh concern. He had not called her "ma" for many a long year.

"Who is doing all this?" she asked.

"Powerful people. Wealthy people."

"But why? Why are they doing these things?"

Her son laughed then, a single bark. "Do you know," he said, "I think that's the worst of it."

"Why?" asked Mrs Finn. "The worst of what?"

Her son sighed again. "I've said too much. Ask me nothing further. Please, let's forget we ever had this conversation."

"But why? I'm not sure I can."

Her son rose to his feet. "I'll leave in the morning," he said. "And then, please, think no more about any of it. Just say to yourself that I was drinking. That I have a wild imagination."

"Oh my darling," she said, and her voice was very quiet and kind, filled up with all the complicated love that she had for this man. "I think that's what worries me the most. For you have no imagination at all. You never had."

He smiled, bent down and kissed her on the forehead. "Thanks for everything, ma."

Then he turned and left the room and went to bed.

Mrs Finn found that she could not retire just yet, her mind whirling with vague terrors. So she sat up awhile in front of the fire and she prayed again softly, under her breath.

Eventually, weary from the stresses of the day and comfortable in her chair (the same one in which she would die, quietly and without a fuss, fourteen months from now), Mrs Finn descended into an unhappy sleep. In this state, she dreamed unusually vivid dreams of a distant place, one full of sun and hot sand where the screams of the dispossessed could be heard upon the breeze.

20TH AUGUST, 1891

THE ISLAND

I

In the moment that he awoke, the ape-man, M'Gari, knew that he had slept for too long. In the heat of a tropical afternoon had he dozed in sight of the sea, beneath the spreading and accommodating branches of an ancient palm. Having wandered to the easternmost part of the island, he had meant to succumb just briefly to that drowsiness which had been his sole companion since his luncheon of rabbit and vine leaves. Instead, lulled by the comfort of a full belly and by the distant whisper of the ocean, he had slipped into a slumber of more than three hours duration.

During that time, he had dreamed only of pleasant things, of sunshine and food and of the life that was to come with his mate, Skirandar. Now, his eyes flicked open as, dazed and startled, he noted the position of the descending sun. With an odd, ungainly set of movements, he pulled himself upright. His breathing was ragged. His furred feet squirmed against the hot sand. He struggled for a moment to regain all of his senses, together with his equilibrium.

There were two things, he realised, which had awoken him: firstly, an unfamiliar scent in the air and, secondly, a voice, a strange and alien voice, which was most assuredly not his own, echoing inside his head.

"M'Gari," said the voice now. "M'Gari, son of Anse, you must listen carefully to me." It was high-pitched and sibilant, a most curious voice indeed, sometimes keening and sometimes almost querulous but always possessed of a profound and all but irresistible persuasiveness.

"Who are you?" said M'Gari. The words felt strange in his mouth for the language of English, as opposed to the eloquent tongue of his own people, was saved only for ceremonial occasions. "What do you want?"

A human male might have wasted valuable time in querying whether or not the voice had any objective reality or whether it was some symptom of incipient madness. He would have fretted and paced. He might even have considered consulting an expert.

The Beast People of this island, however, still possessed all of those instincts which humanity had long since come to overlook and so M'Gari wondered only at the identity of this intruder in his consciousness as a man might wish to know who a stranger was in his home and what was meant by his presence there.

"I am a friend," said the voice. "One who fears that you have slept too long to stop what is about to happen. You have already smelt it, I think? That strange scent upon the air?"

The ape-man sniffed again. The combination of the aroma was clearer now: perspiration he knew and a half-familiar sort of liquor but the other constituents were new to him. A civilised person, had they shared the ape-man's olfactory ability, might have recognised them as tar and gunpowder.

"Yes," he said. "I smelled it."

"And do you understand…" the voice began, now with a touch of impatience, "what it must portend?"

M'Gari reached for a concept that was almost out of reach – something from the time before of which he had heard his father and his grandfather speak. "Incomers…" he breathed. At the word, he felt a spark of pure and hectic panic.

"They have come at last as I always knew they would."

"Who are they? And what do they want?"

There was a momentary pause, followed by an admission. "I do not know. Not for certain. Yet it is my belief that their arrival means only… danger."

The tendrils of a new scent came now to M'Gari – the first intimation of smoke upon a breeze which had begun to stir.

"There is a burning," said the ape-man. "From the village. Skirandar is there. I must hurl these incomers out."

"Yes. I think that you must," said the voice, speaking in a tone of great sadness. "Do what you can, M'Gari, son of Anse. Save whoever and whatever you are able. Although I fear…" The voice ceased for a moment and there was a burst in the head of M'Gari of something much like rushing water, although somehow a harsher, harder sound. Then the voice came back.

"I fear that you may already be too late."

At this, M'Gari was able to make a series of connections, between the scent of strangeness, the smell of smoke and the stark pessimism of the voice in his head. For an awful elongated second he imagined what all of these might mean. There came a parade of images to his mind's eye – great, unfamiliar vessels on the shore; a mass of new arrivals who walked solely upon two legs and were not as the people of the island were; the little settlement which had been his home for all of his life, ravaged and in flames.

Surely it was his imagination (surely he was too far away for the sound to have carried?) but it sounded to him almost as though he could hear distant, fear-stricken screams. They sounded like they belonged to one individual in particular – though this must be only his imagination.

"Do what you can," said the voice in his head, though M'Gari scarcely heard it now and certainly paid it no heed. "But, above all else, make sure that they remember you."

M'Gari turned away from the direction of the ocean and back towards the centre of the island.

Without further thought, operating purely on instinct, his system flooded with adrenaline, the blood pounding hard and loud in his ears, the ape-man threw himself into the dense patch of jungle beyond. He ran faster than any human and soon swung from branch to branch to speed his progress further.

In a handful of instants he was lost to that lush, green forest, a blur of simian motion. Had any observers been present on the beach a short while after M'Gari's departure and had they chanced to be looking out to sea they might have glimpsed an odd, even disquieting sight – a shadow in the water, a great, dark, gleaming head which appeared momentarily above the surface before disappearing and leaving it as unruffled as before.

II

The ape-man ran on through the forest, ran and clambered and soared. He knew the terrain as intimately and to as high a degree as any other living being. He knew every tree in the jungle, every vine and creeper and he knew of all those many creatures who dwelt in it.

With every step he took he grew more and more afraid. As he ran on other, more palpable signs of the disaster became distressingly plain. First, there were disturbances in the jungle. Small animals running in the opposite direction to M'Gari, fleeing whatever disruption had arrived. Birds, exotically plumed, who had in their time borne witness to many strange sights, squawked overhead in frantic alarm.

Then smoke grew visible: thick, dark, choking smoke. Then the cries of his fellows, which he had hitherto half-persuaded himself that he had only imagined, grew audible and impossible to dismiss as anything other than real – although M'Gari could not help but realise, the closer he came to the village, the more distant the sounds became as if those who were making them were being moved further away at speed, towards the other side of the island and to the sea.

Fear and foreboding were to the ape-man novel emotions, at least in such quantity, yet he pushed them aside and forced himself onwards, out of the jungle, towards the settlement and to the disaster that was waiting there.

Only once as he ran did he call a name in desperation. "Skirandar!"

When M'Gari emerged from the line of trees which separated pure wildness on the island from that little pocket of progress which the Beast People had maintained, he understood the totality of the invasion.

The village was in flames and was already burning down almost to nothing. It had never been a grand conurbation but it represented the hard work of several islanders as well as their hopes and dreams for the future and now, it was so much ash and blackened wood. The huts that had been their dwelling-places, the great hall of convocation, the place of mysterious worship where a complex array of deities had been honoured – all had been razed.

Of the people of this village – M'Gari's friends and rivals, neighbours and competitors – there was no sign at all. M'Gari called out in horrified rage, the name of she who was dearest to him: "Skirandar!"

No reply came at first save for the crackle of the flames. M'Gari was about to leave this place of devastation and run in search of his missing people when he heard a sound amid the flaming ruins – a wet, choked cry of entreaty. He loped swiftly to the source of it.

In the scorched debris of what had been a fledgling schoolhouse, M'Gari came across a familiar figure, the goat-man Aristophani who had until mere hours ago enjoyed a reputation as the wisest creature in the village, a teacher to young and old alike – and the nearest thing to a rationalist of which the beast People could boast.

Now he lay in a pool of his own dark and spreading blood. At first, M'Gari did not see the wound which had caused this debilitation nor could he understand how so seemingly inconspicuous an injury could have brought the goat-man this close to death. He sniffed the air and leaned closer. He saw then what had been done to the creature right enough – a patch of matted fur and beyond it a small, ugly penetration of skin and flesh, just below Aristophani's ribcage. The goat-man panted hard and fast, each breath sounding shallower than the last.

M'Gari, like all of his people, was no stranger to death and did not fear it, believing in a vague, rather nebulous afterlife in which existence would not be so very different to island routine.

Yet the manner of a person's death was of great importance to the Beast People and what had been done to the goat-man – cut down by some impossible machine and left to spend his last moments suffering alone in the ruins of his home – was an affront to that creed.

M'Gari reached out a paw and touched the side of the goat-man's face in a gesture intended to comfort. Yet Aristophani weakly pushed his arm aside. He tried to speak but only a moist desperate gurgle emerged from his thin lips. A long line of spittle fell upon the fur which grew upon his chin in a formation which looked almost like a beard. Unable to form words, the goat-man instead pointed south, towards the sea.

The ape-man nodded to show that he understood – this was where the people had been taken. His instinct was to run in pursuit of them to see if his worst fear was accurate and that Skirandar was amongst them. Yet he could not leave the goat-man dying like this, unseen and unmourned in the dirt like an animal of the time before.

Aristophani seemed to know the trajectory of M'Gari's thoughts. Through what must have been a terrific effort of will he shook his head twice from side to side.

To M'Gari the message was unambiguous. Go after them. Confront the strangers. Save our people if you can.

"I am sorry," M'Gari said thickly, each word heavy in his mouth. Then he sprang once again onto his hind legs and ran on towards the ocean. He did not look back.

III

This was the final stretch of M'Gari's long run and by now even he was growing weary. His movements were growing less focused and controlled. He struggled at times to regulate his taking of breaths, gulping in air too greedily, as he had once lapped up spring water as an infant. Something pulsed and uncoiled itself in his head, some advancing ache.

As he ran on through undergrowth which now grew thinner and more sparse he smelled again the rich, sweet tang of the ocean and, woven into it, those unfamiliar scents of gunpowder and perspiration.

For a while there was nothing to hear save for his own ragged breaths and the pounding of his paws upon the baked earth. There was little sign in this patch of the island of any life but then he heard again first a single scream of shrill fury and then, very close to him now, a collective moan as of a herd beset by misery and confusion.

M'Gari ignored the roaring ache in his muscles and flung himself on. It was not until he reached the shore that he found them.

A great vessel, bigger than any he had seen before – for there could be seen when the day was clear and the sun was high, glimpses of distant ships, and none of them had ever seemed even half so big as this – had weighed anchor in the deep beyond the shore.

Moving towards it were a miniature fleet of smaller boats onto which had been driven, so far as M'Gari could tell, every other inhabitant of the island.

There they all were, the hybrids and created beings. All were watched over by human beings – a race M'Gari had never seen before. Every one of the strangers carried weapons – rifles, muskets and pistols.

These too were alien to M'Gari, although from the way in which they were held and pointed, he could guess at their purpose.

And from all of those boats there rose a low wail of sorrow and anguish, a mingling of horror and absolute disbelief at what had been done to them.

For an instant, M'Gari only watched in utter incredulity, his mind struggling to absorb the bleak disaster of the scene before him. Then he glimpsed her, far out to sea, in the most distant of the smaller boats; the speckled plumage of her fur, the terrible keening of her scream.

He wasted no energy in calling her name but instead, and without hesitation, he flung himself down to the ocean's edge and pushed himself into the water.

That generation of Beast People of which M'Gari was a part had learned to swim in infancy, some collective folk wisdom having advised the tribe of its necessity and so, although exhausted, M'Gari found the going simple enough at first. The water was warm and the sea familiar as the ape-man, with powerful strokes, pushed out towards the line of boats, each containing its terrified living cargo. He did not falter. Only once the initial surge of frantic rage had left him did it occur to him to wonder what his strategy might be – him, a single individual who had already been run ragged against a small army of strangers who had succeeded in first subduing and then capturing a population.

He hesitated in his strokes; his mouth filled momentarily with water. He craned his head upwards to see if he might see the outline of Skirandar. But he had lost the boat in which his mate was held amid the confusion of the fleet. He pressed on, lungs aching, and approached that dread Armada only for the men from the outside to notice him at last.

One of them, in the nearest boat, turned from his threatening and cajoling of the dozen Beast People in his care, apparently startled by the sight and sound of an ape-man swimming ever nearer with grim implacability.

M'Gari caught a glimpse of his lean, drawn face, his close-cropped grey hair and a scar like a sickle moon which was etched beneath his right eye.

As he came nearer to the boat, the eyes of M'Gari met those of the stranger. On both sides there was only incomprehension and fear.

To M'Gari it seemed almost as though the alien hesitated long enough for him to fall back if he wished, to let the water cover him and return to the solitary safety of the island.

But then one of the other humans on the boat spotted M'Gari too and there was a brief exchange between the strangers.

The man with the sickle moon scar brought up the long stick in his hand and levelled it towards M'Gari.

At first, the ape-man's instincts did not fail him. He gulped in air and plunged his head beneath the waves. The bullet (though M'Gari did not know that this was the name of the projectile) passed harmlessly into the water beside him.

Even then, M'Gari might have survived had he given up or played dead. Instead, he rose again above the surface of the sea and, with all his might, bellowed the name of his beloved.

"Skirandar!"

From one of the boats ahead he was sure he heard an answering cry.

"M'Gari!"

This time the bullet clipped the side of his head. Blood sprung up on his right temple. In agony and shock he fell back into the sea, the awful clog and burn of saltwater in his mouth and nose. The face of his mate passed once – searingly, beseechingly – across his consciousness. For a third time, he burst again from the sea. The man with the scar showed no mercy, save, perhaps, for the surety of his aim and the absolute finality of the shot.

A single bullet passed into M'Gari's forehead, puncturing skin and cranial bone and moving into that remarkable, singular and entirely unique tissue which lay beyond.

M'Gari had no time even to call for his lover or to offer a prayer to the deities of the island for the good stewardship of his soul. He sank for a final time into the ocean and his body began to sink.

The boats moved on and the human occupants prepared to move their cargo onboard the bigger ship before their return to what men called civilisation.

The murderer with the sickle scar looked dolefully into the water to see that it remained unbroken before, satisfied, he looked up at the vessel which would bear them away from this place and the grand bronze plaque which bore its name: HMS *Scorpion*.

Meanwhile, into the inky depths did M'Gari sink, down, down into the uncaring waters. Until, at last, though he did not know it, strange but oddly tender tentacles reached out to his body and ran with almost paternal care and sorrow around his handsome features.

M'Gari would have recognised the voice which spoke then, possessed of quiet power and fury.

"Sleep well, M'Gari, son of Anse, Skirandar's mate. Your death shall not be forgotten. It shall not be unavenged. And mark me well: in good time, it shall serve to change the face of the whole world."

3RD-4TH OCTOBER, 1892

STAFFORD RISE, NORFOLK

I

Coral Mayfield had been seven years old when she had truly understood for the first time that the boarding house which her mother ran had acquired an evil reputation. For Mrs Elizabeth Mayfield (the "Mrs", it being widely understood, was strictly an honorary title) had long operated a simple policy when considering those paying guests whom she would permit to rent any of the eight rooms in her establishment: namely that there was no-one at all whom she would ever turn away.

In consequence, the house, which was situated at the edge of the little town of Stafford Rise, had become something of a way-station for all manner of last chancers, no hopers and undesirables. It attracted a clientele who craved anonymity and discretion: runaways, escapees and those who had dallied for too long upon the wrong side of the law. It offered sanctuary to those without capital and to those of bad repute. It hosted lapsed swindlers and the bankrupt; men and women who were not married (at least, not married to each other); those who were slaves to the bottle and they who craved the syringe. It was, in short, widely considered to be no place to raise a child and Coral was made well aware of this opinion by the whispered jibes and hissed insinuations of her fellows.

The dawning of this realisation had taken place four years before this segment of our story begins. Coral was now eleven and much growing up had been done in the meantime. She considered herself to be in all essential matters a young woman, a view that was supported strongly by her mother who had come increasingly to lean upon her daughter as both co-manageress and general fixer of that which had been broken.

It was in this capacity of responsibility that Coral sat upon the steps outside the House late in the afternoon just as the light was dwindling and turning to dusk. The building itself was a long, pale structure made of local stone with something of the schoolhouse about it, although, so far as anyone knew, it had never served any such purpose.

It had a darkened, shuttered look at all times, no matter the hour or the season, as though it were turning its face away from the world. These steps, then, were about the property's best feature, especially since they were flanked on either side by iron railings, freshly painted (by Coral herself) a shiny shade of black which, even in the twilight seemed to gleam.

The girl sat in the middle of the third step, her manner casually proprietorial. She was keeping watch, looking out for customers since she knew that, when it came to a place like theirs, folk could often be shy or nervous and in need of coaxing to persuade them to cross the threshold. She had been waiting for more than an hour, however, and had seen no-one save for a seller of chestnuts (who had ignored her, stepping rather haughtily past the establishment) and a flower girl (who had cast in her direction a single look of doleful camaraderie).

Coral yawned and was even considering going indoors for, although she was wrapped from head to foot and wore a thick scarf, the evening was a brisk one, growing steadily colder and the chill of the air was starting to bite at the exposed skin of her face. She rose, with a weariness like one very much more senior in years, to her feet. She glanced back once towards the street and it was then that she saw him, stepping forwards from the gathering shadow and peering up at the House, his posture suggestive of hopeful uncertainty.

He was a short man, much laden down with bags and cases. He was pushing something before him – a trolley, Coral guessed, or perhaps some unusual kind of bathchair. His face was still hidden by the gloom and she could not see his expression, though she fancied that she could guess it all the same – a certain furtiveness, mingled with relief that he had made it this far and that he was so close to what would constitute at least a temporary kind of safety.

Just as her mother had taught her, Coral beamed at the stranger and beckoned him forward. With dainty steps she walked to the foot of the stairs and waited there, her arms a little outstretched in a universal gesture of welcome.

"May I help you, sir?" she asked. "Would you be looking for bed and board?"

The stranger did not at first reply. Coral assumed that he was still staring behind her, examining the House itself, only to realise that it was she who was the object of his gaze. She could not say precisely why but, unlike the looks which she had begun of late to notice from men of all ages, this seemed to her to be benign, devoid of any sort of appetite.

"Sir?" she asked again. "Was it a bed for the night you were wanting?"

Still he said nothing.

"We have space," Coral added, indicating the man's copious luggage. "We have plenty of space for all of your... possessions."

"So this is it." The man's voice was deep and old and cracked, as though its owner had suffered much.

"This is what, sir?" Coral asked, who, although far from afraid or even disconcerted, was starting to wonder about the fellow's sanity.

"The famous Mayfield House."

"If you say so," Coral said, more pertly than she had intended.

"I have never been to Stafford Rise before. Not even once."

"Truly?" asked Coral, who could not remember ever having been anywhere else. Then, echoing a phrase which she had heard her mother employing: "We're not a place folk mean to come to. We're a place folk pass through."

"I am not so sure that's true," said the man. "You have my word that I meant to come here, after all."

He shuffled forwards, into the light. His baggage clanked and jingled as he moved.

Coral noticed two things about the stranger now that she could see him better. The first was that the object he pushed before him was no trolley or bathchair but rather, of all things, a great black perambulator, covered over entirely with muslin and cloth. Coral speculated swiftly as to its contents – bottles, she thought, most likely, or else old newspapers or some baffling trove of filthy bric-a-brac and soiled trophies.

The second observation which struck her with even greater force than the incongruity of the man's belongings was the strong yet indefinable sense that she had seen him before. His face was lined and browned by the sun, though the summer had been largely grey and cheerless. His hair, white and oily, was thinning and patchy. Beneath his right eye was an old scar, shaped a little like a sickle moon.

For a moment, and more uncharacteristically, Coral forgot herself. "What do you want?" she asked and there was now in her voice something very like fear. "Who are you and where have you come from?"

"Please," said the stranger. "I am a friend. As to my name. It's Grayson."

"Grayson," the girl repeated doubtfully, for from long experience she knew an alias when she heard one.

The man smiled, a tired, sorrowful thing which sat most uneasily upon his face. "Is your mother inside?"

Coral did not answer his question but asked one of her own. "Do I know you, sir?"

The man seemed surprised. He winced, took a breath and appeared to be about to reply when, unexpectedly, something in the perambulator stirred.

Coral heard it quite distinctly – something moving, shifting from side to side or turning over.

"What have you got in there?" Coral asked.

From beneath the muslins, there came another noise of motion.

"Mister, have you got an animal in there?"

And then she heard it, a new sound – a high, thin, reedy cry of an infant.

Coral had come to consider herself beyond shock or surprise when it came to the residents, their eccentricities and secrets. Yet this was quite without precedent.

Before she could say anything further and before Mr Grayson could offer some explanation, the door to the House was opened and the voice of her mother could be heard.

"Now what's going on here?"

Both Coral and Mr Grayson turned to see her – a slight, fine-featured woman who stood silhouetted with folded arms against the gaslight which shone forth from the House.

"Coral, who's this?"

Grayson moved further forwards. Once again, his luggage clanked and jingled. The wheels of the perambulator hissed and squeaked. Another whine could be heard from whatever lurked inside it. Grayson attempted an even broader smile than before, to still less convincing effect.

"Hello, Mrs Mayfield."

Coral's mother shot him a look of what seemed to be pure venom. To Coral, she said: "Come here, my darling. Straightaway. Quick as you can."

Coral, who had good cause to fear this particular timbre in her mother's voice, did as she was bade and hurried to her side. As she tripped up the steps, she heard another squealing exhalation from whatever the occupant of the perambulator might be. She reached her mother.

"Inside now."

Coral stepped into the House – and into its oddly welcoming

scents of turpentine and polish. She stopped, agog, just beyond the threshold.

"What do you want?" her mother asked Grayson.

"Please, I mean no harm. I bring no trouble with me."

"But what do you want?" her mother asked again, her voice simmering with inexplicable anger.

Grayson seemed to be trying to appeal to her. He grinned nervously, his hands tight around the bar of the perambulator.

"Mrs Mayfield," he said, "I only want a bed for the night. Or maybe a few. Certainly – I give you my word – for no more than a week."

Again, there came a sound like something tiny crying.

In response to all of this strangeness, Coral heard her mother use a word she had never used before to a possible tenant.

"No," she said, and closed the door sharply against the stranger.

Coral herself and (she suspected) her mother were both so shocked by this refusal that several moments passed in startled silence before either of them moved or spoke. Coral heard her mother's breathing – too rapid and irregular – and considered that the reaction had been closer to slamming the door against some wild beast or feral dog than a plump and luggage-laden stranger in the final quarter of his life. Coral opened her mouth, prepared to ask a torrent of questions.

Who was the man? Why had he been turned away? Why did she think that she had seen him before? What was in that bizarre perambulator?

Her mother seemed to respond, however, before any of these could be asked.

"Not now," she said. "Later. But first we've supper to attend to."

With this, she turned towards the door and pulled a chain

in place, something which was not done traditionally until midnight, before she pivoted and began to stride back down the hallway in the direction of the kitchen.

"Coral!" she called back. "Hurry up! We're late as it is!"

The girl paused before obeying. She stepped closer to the door, experiencing as she did so the odd but absolute certainty that the stranger, stood still just inches from the other side, looking unflinchingly at the house, laden down with his cargo, the occupant of that unlikely vehicle still shifting and sighing.

Then her mother, out of sight, called her name again and Coral hurried after her to help.

11

There were at that time five residents in the house and four of them were sitting expectantly in the dining room around a homely, battered trestle table when Coral came in to serve. She pushed a trolley before her, fully stocked with mutton, vegetables and potato. The squeak of the wheels put her in mind of the stranger's perambulator, a thought which she tried, unsuccessfully, to swallow and ignore.

As she entered the room the four residents turned to face her – three men and one woman. It was the last of these, Mrs Wootton, a flushed-faced toper whose age might be anything between thirty and sixty, who spoke first.

"Good evening, dear," she said and managed a sickly sort of smile. "Supper smells 'licious."

Coral agreed that it did though, privately, she was not so sure that she agreed with the assessment. Mrs Wootton had been a regular visitor to the House for some years, coming to stay with increasing frequency whenever her family grew tired of her drinking and foul temper, both of which Coral's mother, for the sake of their income, was happy to pretend did not exist.

"You spoil us here," Wootton said as Coral approached the table and prepared to serve up. "You really do."

To this, Coral only bowed her head as if in gratitude, knowing from experience how slippery and uncertain Wootton's temper could be at this stage in the day, how she could oscillate between simpering good humour and embittered viciousness.

The other visitors were nothing like so well-known to Coral – three taciturn fellows, all of them visibly bruised by the world. They had only been here a handful of nights between them. Had any stayed before? Coral could not be certain. So continuous was the traffic in and out of the house that even a girl as perspicacious and clear-sighted as she could not keep track of all of their temporary residents.

One of the men had been smoking a cheap, pungent cigarette which, now that his food was approaching, he stubbed out noisily and messily on the tabletop. He grinned at Coral, baring yellow teeth.

"Thank you, little lady." His voice was tinged by an accent which Coral did not recognise. "You look after us all so well. And you serve us our dinner so very prettily."

He gazed at her very frankly then, a look too close to examination for Coral's comfort. The man touched his stubbled chin and stroked it. "Tell me, girl," he said. "Have you ever been kissed?"

One of the other nondescript men snorted at this. The third man looked away as if suddenly beguiled by the fading papered walls of the room.

Mrs Wootton grimaced. "Plenty of time," she muttered, her tone curdling. "Plenty of time for that."

The yellow-toothed man grinned again. He seemed in a state, faintly paradoxical, of lazy excitement. "But why should she wait?"

With scarcely any warning, Wootton snapped. Her eyes bulged. Sweat stood out on her forehead. "Go to hellfire! Sup on the Devil's teat!"

"What…" said the man. "What exactly did you just say to me?"

The atmosphere now badly soured, Coral hurried to load the dishes on the table.

"Mind your own business," said the first man, perhaps to the group at large.

"Filth," Mrs Wootton hissed. "Filth."

And then, mercifully, Coral's mother came amongst them all, bustling into the room, bright but firm. "Good evening, everyone!"

The four at the table murmured their responses, suddenly dutiful and subdued. Not for the first time, Coral considered how fine a schoolmistress her mother might have made in a different life, had things gone easier for her.

"Eat up, won't you? This is fine mutton. I won't see it wasted."

The party set to noisily, the flare of conflict forgotten.

Coral's mother touched her once on her left shoulder. "Would you take up a tray to Miss Hollow? She's in her room as usual."

Coral, grateful to be free of the yellow-toothed man's gaze, said that she would.

"And after that," said her mother, "we eat."

"Then you'll tell me?" Coral asked.

Her mother only gave a tight, reluctant nod. "Upstairs now," she said. "Don't let Miss Hollow's food get cold."

III

Miss Hollow resided on the third storey of the building, the floor which was generally the least occupied since Coral's mother kept it for the use of longer-term residents, regulars and (or so Coral suspected) those for whom she had acquired a sneaking fondness.

At this time, the floor was empty save for Miss Hollow herself. Mrs Wootton and the three sallow-faced men all occupied rooms on the first floor. Of course, an establishment which was even the slightly bit interested in the cultivation of respectability would have set down strict rules on the separation of the sexes – men on one floor, women on another with immediate eviction being the penalty for any crossing of the lines. Mrs Mayfield had no such qualms or even interest, however, in what took place in the hours of darkness when the house was all abed.

Not that Coral herself was considering any of this when she walked steadily up the staircase to the top floor and, supper tray held out before her, advanced down the long and silent corridor to the last bedroom in which Miss Hollow had lived now for the greater part of a year.

The wooden floor was old and ill-cared for. It creaked as she walked. The walls had a decade past been painted a deep shade of amber which had over time grown only darker and more muddy. Hung haphazardly upon them were a series of framed photographs, all portraits of individuals and family groups.

Coral knew none of the people who had posed for them; her mother had purchased a job lot from a tinker who had passed through the town two Christmases back.

As she walked, these blank, sepia figures – frock-coated and high-collared – seemed to her to watch her progress with unhealthy curiosity. Once a floorboard creaked so loudly that it made Coral jump. It sounded, she thought, a little – maybe even more than a little – like the cry of some wild animal.

Coral hurried on. She set down the tray and knocked twice.

From within came a thin, high "halloa?"

Taking this to be an invitation, Coral opened the door, picked up the tray and, stepping inside, nudged the door shut again, her every motion nimble and controlled. The room was gloomy and malodorous.

Miss Hollow was, as she always was, in bed. A single ancient lamp flickered on an adjacent cabinet.

She was very thin, the skin pulled tight against her bones, her grey hair receding greatly and leaving a smooth, protuberant scalp in its wake. She had few teeth; her smile was gummy. There are children less worldly than Coral who would have found this resident monstrous, an object of terror. Coral knew better.

"Good evening, Miss Hollow."

"Good evening, dear."

The voice was softer than one might expect – gentle and uncomplaining. Coral was pleased. The lady sounded lucid tonight.

"Is this my tea?"

Her accent was educated, much more so than many who passed through their doors, and Coral had often wondered what had led her to such a place as this. Mrs Mayfield, naturally, always discouraged such unnecessary speculation.

"Yes, Miss Hollow," said Coral, moving to a chair on the far side of the bed. "Sit up now if you're hungry."

The old woman raised herself laboriously against the headboard until she was sitting at least halfway up.

Once this was done, Coral balanced the tray on the old lady's lap. "Here it is. Just the way you like it."

All of the food had been cut up by Coral's mother into small segments.

"It smells so good, dear."

Coral did not reply to this optimistic expression but busied herself in heaping high a spoon with a chunk of some mutton and sauce, and held it, just as her mother had taught, to the resident's wrinkled lips.

Miss Hollow opened wide, biddable and willing, and swallowed down the food.

"There," Coral said. "Doesn't that taste nice?"

The old woman nodded then let her jaw hang open, hungry for more.

The process was long and messy and Coral let her mind wander during the laborious course of it, thinking, not for the first time, of what her life might be like in years to come, once she was old enough to make her own judgements, imagining escape.

Towards the end of the supper, Coral heard a cry from the street outside. It sounded male, not angry but anguished. Without being able to say exactly why, she felt that she knew who it was who had made the sound.

For a moment, Miss Hollow ceased her ineffectual chewing. She cocked her head to one side and seemed to listen intently. No further noise came.

She fixed Coral in her watery gaze and said (though Coral had an idea that it was not truly her to whom she was speaking): "It's the circus." She sounded bright-eyed and hopeful, as she might have done, perhaps, decades ago when she had been no older than was Coral herself. "The circus has come to town."

IV

The rest of the evening passed by swiftly, lost in a haze of chores and duties, many of which seemed to take longer than usual and to be still more onerous. It was not until everyone was fed and had retired to bed that Coral was alone again with her mother.

Even their own supper had – most unusually – been consumed at different times and in different rooms. Although, come to think of it, Coral was not convinced that her mother had actually eaten anything that night at all.

It was late and dark and – for now, at least – the house was quiet and settled.

"Come on," said Mrs Mayfield, bustling into the kitchen, where Coral was engaged in stowing away the last of the cleaned utensils, and acting as though nothing so very remarkable had taken place that day at all. "Up to bed now. Tomorrow is another day and bound to be a busy one."

To anyone but Coral, this performance – of poised and unflappable efficiency – would have been entirely convincing. Yet it had been a while since the mother had been able to fool the daughter about pretty much anything.

"But you have to tell me," Coral said, turning from the basin. "You promised."

Mrs Mayfield sighed, yawned and rubbed her jaw with her left hand – a pantomime of tiredness. "It's late, Coral. It's too late now."

"Who was that man?"

Her mother had been expecting the question and her face gave nothing away.

"Nobody," she said carefully, "who has the slightest thing to do with us."

"But mother…"

At this, the line of Mrs Mayfield's mouth set into a picture of stern disapproval suggestive of imminent anger – an expression which she had not had cause to adopt for many months.

"It's time for bed, Coral."

The use of her Christian name made it clear that no discussion would be tolerated.

"You need to get your sleep."

Coral knew that a time was coming when a direct contradiction of her mother's authority would be unavoidable but she knew also that the time was not tonight.

"Yes, mother," she said, bowed her head in temporary supplication, walked from the kitchen and made her preparations for bed. A quarter of an hour went by before her mother came into her tiny bedroom to wish her good night.

Coral was already under the blankets and, in spite of the dramas and curiosities of the day, already close to slumber.

"Sleep well, my darling," her mother said, speaking softly from the threshold. "And thank you."

Coral did not reply, allowing her mother to believe that she was even drowsier than she seemed. She listened as the woman waited by the door, then closed it and walked away. Coral listened for as long as she could for any other sound, for evidence of her mother's secrets.

Yet nothing could be heard and for as long as she could keep her eyes open and the silence remained altogether undisturbed.

She woke once at which time she believed herself at first still to be asleep and in the grip of a dream. She could hear movement outside her room as of several bodies and a long pealing cry which sounded to her even then neither entirely nor wholly animal.

As she struggled into wakefulness, the noise ceased. The sound of movement likewise stopped.

Coral lay still for a while and listened.

A short while later, that keening cry began anew.

Coral rose to her feet and padded the few steps over to her door. She tried the handle but found that it had been locked from the outside, a thing that had not happened since she was eight years old.

Then, from without, above that uncanny shriek, she heard the calm, determined voice of her mother.

"It's only a dream, my darling. Go back to bed. Go back to bed now and all will be well."

As she finished her sentence, the commotion ended and silence resumed.

Coral did not speak or stir.

Her mother's voice came again. "Please, Coral. Please."

The emphasis was unusual, frank and almost pleading. Again, Coral said nothing but only listened and waited.

"Good girl," her mother said hopefully.

Still Coral waited but nothing further could be heard. In the end, she did as she had done many times before. She chose to be patient and returned to bed.

At first, in the morning she was almost able to persuade herself that her mother had been right and that all the inexplicable and suggestive incidents of the previous day had been the products of exhaustion and imagination. At least, that is, until she saw the creature in the hallway.

V

When Coral rose, nothing was said. Her mother had always had a talent for maintaining the appearance of things. Breakfast was hurried before the guests trickled down to eat.

Normally, Coral would have been pressed into service to attend to the residents, bringing them tea and the essentials of the morning – devilled eggs, kidney, kipper if it was a Sunday – but today her mother kept her occupied with other duties, far from the dining room. That this might have been done in order to make sure that she did not overhear the conversation of their guests, and any questions they might ask, occurred to the girl more than once that morning.

Eventually, Coral's mother came to find her in the laundry room.

"Miss Hollow is awake," she said, "and hungry too."

This was by no means unusual. The woman kept increasingly irregular hours, sleeping more and eating less – a kind of mercy in Coral's view.

"Would you take her up her breakfast?"

Deep beneath the words, Coral could sense an echo of that almost-pleading which she had detected in her voice during the night.

"Yes, mother," Coral said. "But mother…" She paused, unsure as to how best to continue.

"Please, Coral," Mrs Mayfield broke in quickly. "She's really quite restless today."

Coral hesitated.

"*Coral.*"

"Of course," she said and was gone.

VI

It was a dreary day outside and only thin grey sunlight illuminated the long hallway on the second floor which led to Miss Hollow's room.

Coral proceeded along it with a tray of food held out before her just as she had done so many times before. Yet something this morning felt different – not just in the house or between her and her mother but something specific to this storey.

Halfway along the corridor, Coral hesitated and then stopped. It was not that she had heard anything unusual or even that she felt that she was in some sense being watched, only that she felt a strange certainty of change; something fundamental had been altered within mere feet of where she now stood. She called out.

"Hello?"

The only response was silence. With a gathering sense of unease, Coral walked on.

Miss Hollow was sleeping once more when Coral tapped on her door and stepped into the old woman's room.

"Good morning, Miss Hollow!"

The thin, birdlike figure in the bed managed only a single puny groan at the girl's approach.

It then took Coral quite some time to wake up the resident (she seemed more sluggish than ever, her movements more heavy and dull) and to arrange her properly in bed in order to receive her breakfast. It was only when Miss Hollow had finished two slices of lukewarm toast and sucked messily on half a poached egg that anything like the light of recognition flickered in the lady's eyes.

"Thanking you..." she murmured. Although she looked at Coral when she said it her gaze seemed hazy and ill-focused.

"Miss Hollow?" Coral asked as she spooned in the last of the slippery yolk. "Did you hear anything last night? Anything out of the ordinary?"

The old woman gave a vacant grin. "Only the circus, dear," she said. "Only the sounds of the circus. Only the sound of them pitching their tent. Only the roar of the tigers and the cries of the ringmaster giving his orders."

Her gaze shifted altogether now, away from Coral entirely to a point some way beyond as though Miss Hollow was addressing another, unseen presence.

It was then that Coral heard the sound. It came from the corridor, a scratching noise, irregular but growing louder. She paused and put down her plate and spoon.

Miss Hollow evinced no sign of having heard anything but only beamed happily into mid-air. The scratching came again accompanied this time by something else – a high-pitched gurgling. Coral stood up.

"Sorry, Miss Hollow," she said and all but ran to the door.

Out in the hallway, clinging to the worn and peeling skirting board was a thing at once bizarre but also wonderful, at least to a girl like Coral.

It was a baby but not like any infant which Coral had seen before. Naked aside from a set of bandages which had been inexpertly tied about its waist, it was covered all over in dark brown fur. Its ears were sharp and pointed.

It was surely still very young yet it moved like a human of at least a year, managing to push itself along in a half-stumble, half-roll. It ceased its motion at the sight of Coral and began instead to make a piteous wailing sound and stretched out its furred arms as though beckoning for help.

Without the slightest hesitation, Coral stepped towards the little creature, stooped and picked it up in her arms. It clung to her at once, one tiny hand gripping a fistful of Coral's dress for purchase and comfort.

"There," she said, with a naturalness that surprised her. "There, there."

She looked down at the little creature and it (no, "he" – she felt certain now that he was a boy) looked back at her.

His face was round and plump-cheeked and the hair upon it was finer than elsewhere on his body. His sobs had stopped almost at the instant when he had been scooped from the ground and he wore now a grin of giddy bliss as though he had always known Coral, for the whole of his short life.

Where had he come from? Coral saw that one of the other doors, was open just a crack and it was through this that the little fellow must have crawled.

Swiftly, Coral looked back in on Miss Hollow who was lying idle, her breakfast tray untouched beside her, staring blankly ahead.

As Coral entered the room again, the old woman turned her head very slowly to face her. She showed no surprise at the furry being that Coral was cradling.

"See?" said Miss Hollow mysteriously. "Didn't I tell you so?"

A look of something close to self-satisfaction flitted across her features. Bewildered but persuaded at least of the old lady's safety, Coral hurried back down the corridor towards the half-open door. The baby wriggled closer to her as she walked, trying to find the point of maximum comfort against her slim, bony body.

Although Coral Mayfield would experience in her eventful life a great many other instances of horror and shock, she was never again quite so swiftly and entirely frightened as she was by what she discovered in the room with the half-open door.

Laid out on the bed, untidily arranged, lay the body of the stranger who had come last night and begged for sanctuary here. She had known – or, at least, she had suspected so strongly that the thing was all but a certainty – that this oddly familiar man had, after all, been allowed across their threshold, that her mother had recanted and made a different choice. That the precious and remarkable cargo which Coral held now in her arms had only hours before squirmed in that perambulator was also to her logical mind quite plain.

Yet by inviting in the man with the sickle moon scar, Mrs Mayfield had also asked in death.

The body of the seafaring man was not the first corpse which Coral had seen but he was the first to have died with such violence. He was still dressed in a filthy white shirt and noisily checkered trousers, though he had removed his jacket and pulled off his shoes. His considerable stomach strained at the fabric and at his belt.

The shirt itself was soaked in blood, plentiful, dark and ugly stains which had spread across almost all of the garment and into the sheets beneath him. There was surely a cleaner, neater way to end a life, Coral would think later; it was as though the man had been killed in the way that would create the most horribly striking effect, as if murder were just theatre by another name. The little furry creature in her arms craned his head around to examine the scene with a frank, and somehow rather unnerving, curiosity.

Coral was brave, and perhaps, wary enough not to scream at the sight of the cadaver but she did gasp audibly, a big, noisy gulping in of air.

She stepped closer, simultaneously fascinated and appalled. She considered dimly how upset her mother would be that such a thing had happened here, upon her premises, and that such a horrid incident may, at long last, be the final blow to the town's grudging tolerance of the House.

She was still thinking these thoughts, the baby peering out over her arms, when, silently and without warning, the body on the bed moved.

Now Coral screamed – a high, petrified wail of terror.

"Coral…" The man's voice was a ragged croak. He can't have been dead, Coral thought, trying to ensure her own sanity. Surely he can't really have been dead?

At this, a clear, logical voice in her head seemed to add: but he very nearly is.

"Coral, listen." A gout of blood trickled down the right hand side of the man's mouth.

Coral found her words: "I have to help you."

"No…" The dying man wheezed. "You have to keep him safe… the little fellow…"

Instinctively, Coral clasped the furred baby closer to her. "From what?" she breathed.

"From the people… in the city… the city of… Dr Moreau…"

These were his last words. For once he had said them, his eyes flickered once in a final surge of energy. Then his breath stopped and he lay entirely still, dead now beyond all doubt.

The baby gurgled once in Coral's arms before he too went silent.

A moment later, Coral heard a soft, snuffling rhythmic noise which it took her a few seconds to identify as the baby creature's snore. With the hirsute infant in her arms, the girl backed away from the dead body. With a final, horrified glance at the bloodied figure on the bed. Coral turned, out of the room, back into the corridor and towards the staircase.

She had gone down just three steps when two things occurred to her. The first was that the baby in her arms was wriggling and cried out (just once but very noisily). The second was that she understood that she could hardly walk through this house with such a being, whatever he may be, held out before her as though he was nothing remarkable at all, no worthier of comment than a teapot. Even in such an institution as this, so good at keeping secrets and at looking the other way, the infant would cause a commotion. She would need to find a way to disguise the fact of him.

Coral hurried back upstairs, her own breath starting to come in short bursts now, the shock of his discovery giving way to a tidal wave of panic.

This time she moved swiftly along the hallway back in the direction of Miss Hollow's room. She did not stop or even slow her pace as she passed by the chamber of the dead man, but she could not resist glancing carefully inside.

A different kind of child might have imagined all sorts of additional horrors – that the man would be alive again or up on his feet and shambling towards her, or even that the room would be clear and empty, the body gone entirely and the whole thing a cruel trick played upon her by her own imagination. Coral Mayfield, however, was, even then, clear-eyed and practical. She believed the evidence of her own senses and so, as she saw again the sprawled cadaver of the stranger, she merely bore grim witness.

Miss Hollow looked up as Coral came into her room.

"Is it time for breakfast, dear?" she asked as though the tray, cutlery and food which had been set before were all but invisible.

"Could you bear with us, Miss Hollow? Just for a little while?" Coral's tone was astonishingly measured under the circumstances.

The old woman nodded vaguely. Coral went to the wardrobe

which had been set against the furthest wall. Deftly, holding the baby in one arm, she opened the drawer at the foot of it and pulled out a thick white sheet. With an inadvertent flourish, she flicked it open before wrapping it crudely around the infant. There was enough of the fabric left over to make a kind of hood for the baby which she could, when the moment came, use to mask his features.

Miss Hollow had watched all of this without comment but with evident delight. "A conjuror..." she breathed. "I always did enjoy a good magic trick."

Coral smiled kindly and paced from the room, the shrouded infant clutched tightly in her arms. Downstairs she went, first one flight then two, then onto the ground floor and towards the kitchen where she hoped to find her mother alone.

She was in this hope to be disappointed.

As she moved briskly down the hall towards the dining room, she heard raised voices, laughter and questions – the sound of her mother holding court with the residents.

At this noise, the baby shifted against her and let out a thin moan. "Hush," said Coral. "Hush now, please. It's for your own safety."

The baby, responding, perhaps, to her tone, fell silent again, though he kept turning his head quite rapidly from side to side. Coral stopped short, stroked his back through the sheet and waited for him to settle himself. This he did at last. Sensing that time was short, Coral covered his head with the sheet, making a little tent of it so that he would still have air to breathe, and walked into the room. There was her mother standing by the trestle table, smiling professionally and encouragingly at Mrs Wootton and the man with the yellow teeth.

Of the other two gentlemen there was no sign. Coral supposed that they had already left for the day, perhaps even for good. Their absence did not strike her as significant at the time; transience was the natural order of things here.

"Mother!" Coral stood on the threshold. At the sound of her voice, the infant stirred. "Mother!"

Mrs Mayfield did not look over from her conversation or show any sign that she had even heard her daughter. Then, using a mode of address which had long been forbidden, Coral, louder than before, called out: "Mummy!"

It was Mrs Wootton who looked over first, attracted no doubt by the note of rising panic in the young girl's voice.

Over the resident's face there stole a look of crafty curiosity. The furred baby wriggled and Coral had to tighten her grip.

"What have you got there, dear?" Wootton asked, seeming more alert than she had for as long as Coral had known her. Then, to Mrs Mayfield, she said: "Elizabeth? Whatever has that daughter of yours discovered now?"

The creature stirred again and gave an elongated yelp of bewilderment.

"It's alive! Lizzie, whatever she's found, it's alive."

Mrs Mayfield saw her daughter now right enough. Her face was very pale. She did not trouble herself even to respond to her paying guest but strode over to Coral.

"Outside," she hissed, her gaze seeming to take in the situation with considerably less surprise than Coral might have expected. "Get into the hallway."

Coral did as she was told and stepped back across the threshold.

Before Mrs Mayfield followed suit and closed the door against the watching residents, Coral saw both of them staring flagrantly at her.

"Is it a puppy?" the man with the yellow teeth was asking.

"Has our little lady found herself a puppy?"

Then the door was shut and her mother was speaking, urgently and low. "Show me."

Coral peeled back the sheet to reveal the little face of the baby.

He looked up uncertainly, nose twitching.

"I think he's all right," Coral said.

"Where did you find him?"

"Upstairs... He was crawling, I suppose, out in the open."

"And... what about... where is the man you met last night? Mr Grayson."

She said this in such a way that Coral was made quite certain that the name had not been the man's real one.

"Mother," she began. "He's..." She tried to get the next word out but tears came instead and for a few moments Coral Mayfield was choked by wracking sobs.

"I'm sorry," her mother said. "Truly I am."

Coral breathed in, wiped her eyes with her one free hand and did her best to regain her equilibrium. "He's..." She tried again. "Someone killed him."

Coral would not have thought it possible but at these words her mother grew still more deathly pale.

"I think... they must have stabbed him."

The memory of the body rose up again and Coral had to work hard indeed to push back down the tears.

As if in sympathy, the baby began to cry – big whoops and wails, its face screwed up and turning puce.

"Give him to me," Mrs Mayfield said, and, grateful to be free of the burden, Coral passed him over. The older woman took him very naturally into her arms and began to rock him back and forth. His sobs lessened but did not stop entirely. For a second,

Coral saw her mother as she must have been more than a decade ago, as a new parent, hopeful in spite of it all.

"What do we do?" Coral asked.

"This one needs feeding," her mother replied, almost absently as she kept on rocking the infant. "And I must make certain… about Mr Grayson. As for you, I need you to do something for me. Can you do that? Can you be grown up?"

Coral nodded.

"I want you to go to the police station and I want you to bring at least one of the policemen back here. Tell them there's been a death. In fact, tell them what you saw. Tell them the truth. They'll come. But don't tell them about this." Coral's mother indicated the infant in her arms, whose sobs had now diminished into gurgles.

"Why not?"

Her mother seemed surprised at the question. "Because they'll take him away," she said. "So can you do that? Can you bring the police back here? I'll have this one out of sight by then. Tucked up. Safe and warm. And quiet."

"Yes, ma."

"Quickly then. Hurry now."

Before she went, Coral reached out her left hand and touched the little creature once on his fuzzy head. "Bye bye," she said and then, without looking back, hurried away, down the hall towards the front door and then out into the street beyond.

VII

The police station was a dark building, not twenty years built though it looked considerably older. It was the largest structure on a side street just off the town square.

Coral had been there before but never, until now, on her own. She ran most of the way, attracting some attention though not enough for anyone to try to stop her or ask where she was headed. Besides, she found that running helped, that it distracted her from her own thoughts.

She slowed down as the police station came into view, wisely given that the combination of speed and growing fatigue meant that taking a tumble was becoming more or less inevitable, and walked the last few yards to the door.

As she did so, she caught sight of two men who, lounging against the wall opposite her destination, appeared to be watching her more closely than seemed polite. They were dressed in rough, ragged clothes and seemed at first glance to be labourers of some kind still looking for work for the day. Yet there was something oddly familiar about them. Unable, for now, to place them, Coral walked on.

The door was wedged open and she stepped into the station. Inside it was cool and dim, more like a shop than a place of justice and incarceration. It was empty except for one young man in uniform, rather fat and rosy-cheeked, who sat behind a long desk, fussily engaged with turning over the leaves of some large book or register.

In the distance someone was singing – a woman's voice, high and sweet. As Coral entered, the young constable looked up. It was not a hot day but the man was perspiring as though it were the peak of summer. He passed the back of one hand across his forehead.

"Little miss," he said. There was a faint burr to his voice which spoke of a country childhood. "Are you lost?"

"No," said Coral. "We need your help. My mother sent me."

The policeman gave her a condescending smile. "Oh yes? And who's your mother?"

In the ordinary way of things, Coral would have known better than to blurt out the name in the town, even (or, perhaps, especially) to an officer of the law. Events, however, had unsettled her and, before she could stop the words, she heard herself blurt out: "Mrs Elizabeth Mayfield."

A look of self-satisfaction spread itself across the man's doughy features. "You're the Mayfield girl." It was neither a statement nor a question but something close to an accusation.

"Yes," Coral said in a small voice. "I am."

"And what exactly is it that has happened at your mother's establishment this morning?"

"There was a body," Coral said quickly. "A man. A stranger, though I believe I'd seen him before, perhaps when I was very young. And he was dead today in his bed. I found him there and I think, I think he'd been stabbed over and over." She stopped herself just in time, in spite of her mother's injunction, from mentioning the strange little creature in the hallway.

"Well, that certainly sounds very dramatic…" said the policeman. "Goodness me, but you must have been so frightened."

He was testing her, Coral realised.

"And what did that mother of yours want us to do about this, ah, dead body?"

"You're to come back with me," Coral said. "Back to the house with me now."

The constable looked at her thoughtfully. "You do seem afraid," he said. "Yes. You really do."

"Come back," Coral said. "Come back and I can show you."

"Well…" He still sounded doubtful but the man was weakening.

"Please?" Coral said, pressing home her small advantage. "I promise this isn't a joke and I didn't make it up and there truly is a dead person in one of our residents' rooms."

There was a long pause.

"I can't go myself," the policeman said firmly. "As I have my duties here, you see. But perhaps... I can call for one of the others... if you promise, that is, that all of this is real."

"Oh, yes it is. All of it. All of it."

"Very well then." The policeman rose to his feet in the ponderous, self-important manner of a very much older person. He walked over to the door behind the desk and opened it. He was seemingly about to call for aid when the interruption came.

"I think we might be able to help, officer."

The voice came from the doorway.

Two figures stood there, blocking out the light.

Coral recognised them as the men who had been watching her from the street. They seemed a great deal smarter now, more upright and formal. Their postures (their very demeanours) seemed to have changed.

"We know this girl and her mother too."

Seeing them as they were then allowed Coral to make a further connection. She *had* seen them before at the supper the previous night. They were the other two guests, the quiet, nondescript ones who had said little and whose every action had seemed designed to be forgettable.

"And who exactly are you two?" the policeman asked, letting the door fall shut behind him.

"We're visitors," said the first of the men, "to this charming little town."

"Just passing through," added the other. "We've been staying at this girl's mother's guesthouse. Though I fear we have already had to make alternative arrangements. It really isn't of the most salubrious sort."

"Anyone round here could have told you that," said the policeman.

The first of the visitors smiled. "The benefits of local knowledge," he said and his voice now was soothing and soft.

"Nonetheless," the policeman went on, "if you were both staying at the Mayfield place, perhaps you'd be well placed to cast light on the girl's story."

"Oh, we would be, officer, yes. Why, I think we'd be ideally placed, don't you?"

The young policeman nodded a little uncertainly. "Go on."

"Clearly, officer, you know the kind of place this boarding house is – better than we did, at any rate, when we secured rooms there. There's a good deal of drunkenness and bad behaviour of every stripe."

"Sundry misbehaviour," said the second, less talkative man.

"Sundry misbehaviour, yes, and I, we, are very much afraid that this is what the girl must have witnessed."

"Not," added the second man dolefully, "that some can be exactly a stranger to such sights."

"That's certainly true," said the policeman, fixing Coral in a gaze of theatrical pity. "But what did she see?"

"One of the other guests," said the first man. "I fear he got himself dead drunk again last night. At Mrs Mayfield's insistence, the two of us lifted him up to his bed and deposited him there. He was quite insensible. Doubtless this is what the girl discovered."

"No!" Coral shouted. "No, he was dead, not just drunk and yes I do know the difference."

"She said," began the policeman, speaking now in a vaguely apologetic tone of voice, "that this gentleman had been stabbed."

"Oh," said the first man. "Goodness me."

He started to laugh uproariously. His companion only smiled.

"You must forgive me," said the first man once he had recovered his composure. "It's just that the idea... the very idea of it!" He began to laugh once again.

"Can't you see?" Coral cried out. "He's playacting. He's putting this on."

The policeman put a finger to his lips to hush her. "Sir?" he said.

"Oh I am sorry, I really am. But you must understand – when we took the toper in question to his bedroom we saw that his clothes were in such a sorry condition. Torn and ripped all over. An imaginative child might very well believe..." He let his sentence tail delicately off.

"There was blood. There was blood!" Coral shouted.

"Sauces," said the first man. "Relishes and condiments of every kind. Stippled and dotted all over his garments. I believe him to be a glutton as well as a lover of the bottle."

The policeman thought for a moment. It seemed to Coral that the signs of doubt flickered upon his features.

"She's a lively girl," said the second man, "but, perhaps, and wholly forgivably, rather too fanciful for her age."

Coral said nothing to this, though her hands were now screwed up into fists. For the second time that day she felt the onset of tears. Fiercely, she shook her head.

The first man spoke again. "Why don't you let us escort her home? Even a mother like hers might have started to worry by now."

The policeman sighed heavily. "Well, I'm sorry," he said. "And I dare say you gentlemen are right in what you say but

I really think this ought to be looked into. A tale like this, however wild and fantastical it may sound to the layman, must all the same be investigated."

As he had done a few minutes earlier before the arrival of the men, the constable turned around and opened the door behind him.

He called out into the recesses of the building: "Harry!"

He spoke no more. For at the first sign of his action, the second man reached into a pocket of his ragged coat and drew out something gleaming and metal.

There was a very loud retort and the air was filled with smoke and the smell of burning. The constable fell, speechless, to the ground. There was a hole in his head, Coral saw, and there was blood.

The first man moved very fast towards her. "Where's the baby?" he said and his voice sounded different. "Where's the baby?"

Coral did not hesitate. She screamed as loudly as she could and she ran full pelt towards the legs of the stranger. He reached out to grab her but at the last moment, Coral swerved around him, dodged past and all but flung herself out of the station and back into the street.

Then she was running again, running as fast as she could, running, she knew now for a fact, for her life.

VIII

She ran towards home unthinkingly and unhesitatingly. Behind her she could hear one of the people who had been dressed (disguised, she realised) in the clothes of labouring men, giving chase. It was, she thought, the second of them, the one who had spoken a good deal less but who had, when it had come to it, shown not the slightest qualm about killing in cold blood. The whereabouts of the other man, the talker, did not for now concern her.

She ran on, faster than ever she had before, still hearing the rapid footfalls of the killer behind her. He must surely know where she was going. Would he dare, Coral wondered as she pelted through the streets of Stafford Rise, to try any further acts of violence in her mother's boarding house in front of witnesses?

Yes, she decided – from all that she had seen of him, she doubted that he would even hesitate. She had to warn her mother and she felt certain that the little furred baby was somehow in danger. Yet she did not think it wise to lead a murderer right to their very door and, Coral realised, she must know this town very much better than the ghoul who now pursued her.

Her decision came easily enough.

They were two streets away from home and the murderer at her heels was gaining on her when Coral veered suddenly to the left, diving down a side alley, at the end of which she doubled back upon herself and started to pelt towards the centre of the town again.

She heard her pursuer swerve after her but she could hear that she was increasing the distance between them.

And so she went on, dodging and weaving her way through the backstreets of the town, circling, looping and taking nonsensical detours. What, you may very well be asking, of those sundry townspeople and citizens who surely witnessed this pursuit in their midst? There were those, of course, who saw and noticed. But many looked away, some at first sight, others upon recognising the quarry, the Mayfield girl. Those one or two who did appear to at least consider the possibility of intervention – one a newspaper seller, the other a disconsolate-looking lounger – went so far as to step forward into the path of the runners, only to step back again at the last moment, once they spied the set expression of implacable fury on the gentleman's face.

At length, her limbs aching and her breath burning in her lungs, Coral heard the man behind her start to slacken his pace. Not long afterwards, she ran along a yew-lined pathway which went through the secondary graveyard of Stafford Rise.

Coral had never understood the reasons why the town had to have two separate grounds for burying the dead – the first beside the church in the middle of the place, the second here, almost in the outskirts – and had always assumed it to be history's business. She was grateful for its existence now, however, as she left a path and went to the largest and most ornate headstones that she could find. Here she hid behind the stone ("In Loving Memory of Susannah Abel, wife of Robert," read the epitaph and then: "Death is Sure") and waited.

Coral stayed quiet and unmoving for as long as she could but no-one at all passed by the graveyard in the long minutes which followed. Certainly, there was no sign at all of her shadow. Had she truly lost him, she wondered, had she shaken him off in the depths of the town? Or, rather, had he allowed her to run on, absenting himself from the scene in order to take up some other strategy?

Fearing the worst, Coral got shakily to her feet. She looked around and saw that she was alone. Keeping a careful eye at all times on her surroundings, she made swiftly for home.

IX

Along the way, she stopped at a shop which sold tobacco, strong drink and an oddly comprehensive range of household implements. Here she asked for two items, to be put on her mother's account.

When she made her request, the proprietor, a spry, elderly fellow with half-moon glasses, who had known her vaguely since infancy, seemed at first surprised and then concerned.

"Are these for Mrs Mayfield?" he asked.

"They're for one of our residents," said Coral, and the lie came easily to her.

"Very well," said the proprietor. "If you're quite certain."

"Oh most definitely I am," said Coral as she took the two items and pocketed them. After that, she ran all the way home.

X

As she approached the boarding house she saw at once that it was quieter than she had ever known it to be in her life before. The front door was standing open and there seemed to be only silence inside. On the threshold she hesitated.

She touched both of the items from the shop which she had in the pockets of her apron, just once, lightly and as if for luck, and went inside.

As she walked down the corridor and towards the dining room (for the last time as things would turn out) she heard a mingling of two low voices, almost whispers. She recognised both of them: the talkative man from the police station and her mother. Then there was something else, the thin grizzling sound of a baby settling into an exhausted nap.

Coral strained to hear the conversation but could make out nothing at all.

When she entered the room the scene appeared to her as a parody of family.

Her mother was settled beside the first man, appearing curiously relaxed in his company. In her arms was the little furred baby. On the trestle table before them was a revolver, abandoned there almost casually.

Mrs Mayfield smiled at the sight of her daughter. "Darling! There you are. We were getting so worried. This is Mr Berry. He's told me what happened."

The infant in her arms turned his face towards Coral who believed that she saw in his features a slow wave of recognition.

In response, she felt within her a surge of protectiveness and anger. She ignored her mother and addressed the man ("Berry"), who had, she noted, taken off his jacket and sat now in her mother's house with his shirtsleeves rolled up. He could scarcely have made himself more at home.

"Where's your chum?" Coral asked.

The man managed a flat, unconvincing smile in response. "He had other duties to perform."

"Reckon he's still wandering about the town."

Mrs Mayfield looked hurt. "Coral, we were worried for you. As you've been gone so long. I know today's been a little surprising for you. And a little upsetting too."

"What's happening?" Coral asked. "Mother, what's happening?"

The older woman sighed. "I think there's been a misunderstanding. That's all. This... creature is the property of Mr Berry's employer. They've just come to take him home again."

"Ma, they killed the man upstairs. They killed a policeman right in front of me."

The talkative man, Mr Berry, smiled without humour. He reached out his right hand and touched the hilt of the revolver. "Such an imagination she has..."

Coral protested. "Ma, I saw it!"

Her mother looked back at her, imploring with her eyes. She looked at the baby in her arms and at the man beside her.

"Coral," she said sadly. "This man is going to take this creature back to where it belongs. We can't stop it. So it's best, don't you think, to accept what's going to happen and get on with the rest of our lives?"

"Has he paid you?" Coral asked and she saw by the look of shame that crossed her mother's face that her assumption had been correct.

"Coral, darling… We're not rich people. You're old enough to have realised that."

At these words, Coral felt for the first time a shiver of contempt for her mother. "Anyway," Coral went on, determined to get out her speech before the tears came. "He's not a creature. He's a he, and I think he's beautiful. And I think the man with the perambulator brought him here for a reason. I think he wanted us to look after him."

The tears did come now and there was nothing that Coral could do to staunch them. She wiped frantically at her eyes. Mr Berry reached for his revolver and got sharply to his feet. He looked down at the woman beside her.

"How confident are you, Mrs Mayfield, that you can keep your child quiet?"

"I can," said Coral's mother. "I promise." Tears were glistening in her eyes now.

"Give me the creature," said the man.

With a sickening lurch, Coral saw the ease with which her mother passed up the baby to the stranger, her absolute absence of reluctance.

Berry held the baby beneath his arm, as though he were

nothing more than a sack of flour or sugar. The infant, woken now, squealed in outrage.

"I know where you're from," Coral said. A phrase had flashed suddenly into her imagination. The dying words of the man upstairs. "You're from the city."

At this, the stranger looked briefly furious. Then an odd expression of relief settled over him. "Too much," he said to Mrs Mayfield, as if in accusation. The baby squirmed and wailed. "Both of you over there. Against that wall right now." To underscore his instruction, he flourished the revolver. Coral's mother began to weep.

"No," she said. "Please, please. I'll help you. I'll do anything you want."

"I'm sorry," said the man, and Coral thought he really was sad about it, as though there had been a time, not so long ago, when he wouldn't have dreamt of taking such an action. "I promise you it'll be quick."

XI

What Coral remembered most about what happened next was the awful, sickening speed of it.

Berry gestured again with the gun. "Get up," he insisted. "Get over there." He repeated these commands several times more to no effect at all.

Coral's mother remained motionless, frozen into place by fear. Her sobs grew louder and wilder. The cries of the baby did the same as he tried to wriggle free of the man's grip, his arms windmilling in panic. At last, Mrs Mayfield found her voice.

"Run, Coral! Run!"

Berry lost patience now and directed the barrel of the revolver towards the crying woman. The baby turned his head frantically until his nose and lips were pressed up against the man's exposed skin.

Coral had already decided not to do as her mother had asked. She would not abandon this baby. She reached, her hands trembling in fear, for what she had bought from the shop. It was too late. For the second time that day, Coral heard at close quarters the dreadful retort of a gun. There was a scream. Coral did not want to look but she could not bring herself to look away. Her mother was slumped against the table, silent, lifeless.

It was the man who was screaming. There was blood on his shirt and, Coral saw with a thrill of mingled horror and pride, that there was blood around the mouth of the baby.

The stranger had momentarily lost control and Coral took her chance. She ran to the side and wrenched the wriggling infant from him. He shouted again in anger now as well as shock.

"Give that disgusting thing to me."

It was too late. Coral had the baby and she went quickly to the door. Berry lumbered towards her, blood dripping from him onto the floor.

Coral drew out the first of the items which she had purchased from the store – a bottle of the cheapest gin – and flung it onto the floor. It shattered and the liquid spread everywhere. The baby cried. Coral reached for the second purchase – a box of Lucifer matches – only to understand too late that she could not possibly light a match one-handed, not with the baby beneath her other arm. The man grinned at her naiveté and ran towards her. Coral dropped the matches in her panic and turned towards the door. As she did so, she caught sight of something – the figure of her mother lurching up again and reaching out. Impossible, Coral thought, surely impossible.

Yet it had been a day of impossible things. She remembered her mother's final instruction and now she obeyed. She held the frantic baby close and went to the hallway beyond.

She heard a cry of shock from the dim room. She sped down the corridor, the furred infant giving great shrieks of fearful indignation.

And then they were outside, both of them, looking back at the house and the door through which no-one emerged. Then she glimpsed and smelled the smoke as that old boarding house began to burn. Did she hear her mother cry from within? Or two cries? She never could be certain.

She turned then and, without looking back, but with that extraordinary infant clasped to her chest, Coral Mayfield ran once more, as fast as she could, away from her home, away from the past and towards a future which she could scarcely begin to imagine.

2ND JANUARY, 1896

LA ROCHE, PICARDY, FRANCE

I

The old priest knew as he descended the stairs that morning and entered the modest room in which he generally ate his breakfast, that the day ahead of him promised, most unexpectedly, to be an unusual one. For his housekeeper, Madame Proulx, was waiting there for him with an expression of barely contained excitement.

A short woman who, at sixty, was almost two decades younger than the priest, Madame Proulx had experienced a life filled with difficulty, struggle and upset. Her smiles were not frequent. Yet this morning she was beaming, all but giddy with what looked like anticipation. The old man recognised the signs at once; she had some piece of delicious gossip to impart.

At his age, pleasures were relatively few, and so the priest decided to relish this moment, even to dance with it a little.

Without showing the slightest sign of having noted the housekeeper's eagerness to converse, he shuffled into the room before, in his tolerable, if hardly stylish, French, bidding her a good morning. At such moments, he took an odd, pawky delight in exaggerating his own antiquity.

"Good morning, monsieur," said Madame Proulx.

The priest took his place at the table where warm bread and jams had been laid out for him and set to the buttering of it with gusto. He made several sounds of pleasure at the prospect of the food. It was not until he had devoured an entire slice, and had begun upon a second, that he looked over at his housekeeper and, asked, with a grin which might reasonably enough be described as boyish: "How are you today, madame?"

Proulx smiled and nodded and confirmed that she was well.

"Good," the old priest said vaguely as he continued to chew. "That's very good. Now, you'll have to tell me, is there anything of particular note happening today?"

Eagerly, the Frenchwoman stepped forwards. "There's nothing which you had planned, monsieur. Nothing in our calendar. But there is, I must say, something new in the village."

"Is that so?" said the priest with exaggerated wonderment, as though this was the first time that it had even occurred to him that the lady might have some original information to present. "And what is that exactly?"

"May I sit down, monsieur?"

"Of course, madame. For goodness' sake. You ought to know by now better than to ask. We stand on no ceremony here."

The housekeeper took a seat beside the priest with a closer proximity than many observers might have considered to be altogether appropriate.

"What is it?" the priest asked as he finished the last of his bread and dabbed at his lips with a starched white napkin.

"Not what, monsieur, but who."

"Who?"

"Strangers in the village, monsieur, and of the most unusual sort."

"That's a little out of the ordinary," said the priest, "given the time of year, but surely by no means remarkable."

"They're travellers, monsieur."

The old priest nodded. "Where are they from originally?"

"England, monsieur."

"Oh." At this, something like a ripple of unease passed through the old man. Ridiculous, of course: any number of his countrymen wandered through this part of the world annually even if none but he had chosen to settle there in perpetuity. Still, there was no reason on earth to think that these new arrivals possessed any connection whatever to him. All that he said was: "How nice for them."

The housekeeper leaned in close, to deliver the most enticing part of her story. "And they are asking, monsieur, for you."

Carefully, thoughtfully, the old priest laid down the napkin on the table. As calmly as he could he asked the lady to describe the new arrivals.

"Monsieur, I have not seen them for myself. I only have the word of the farmer's wife."

"Then, please, tell me what she told you." For the first time that day, a quality of irritation was audible in the old priest's voice.

Madame Proulx told him what she had heard, every detail of it. Upon hearing the description, the priest sat very still and said nothing. He looked down at his hands to see that both were shaking.

"What is it, monsieur?" asked Madame Proulx, first crestfallen, then alarmed. "What's the matter?"

"It's only emotion, madame. One I thought I'd successfully outrun."

"You're afraid?"

The old priest nodded, his throat suddenly constricted, his eyes prickling.

Without asking any further questions, Madame Proulx simply gathered the old man up in her arms and held him close, close enough to feel the frantic, lurching beating of his heart.

II

The priest considered fleeing, though the thought was only a brief one, soon extinguished. It was, he considered, a primeval instinct, of which he now felt rather ashamed. For by the finish of his embrace with Madame Proulx, he had made up his mind to stay.

He saw no reason, after all, why these strangers should mean him any harm, save for the creeping sensation of the tide of the past coming back into shore again, after all this time. Having reassured the housekeeper as best he could, he had gone back upstairs, each step on the old staircase feeling heavier and more effortful than usual, every thud of his feet receiving an answering squeak of weary protest from the boards. In his room, he had dressed for cold weather and had gone again to the ground floor and stepped out into the garden. He brought with him a shooting stick, a memento from an old life which he had thought (and hoped) was almost entirely buried.

"Monsieur." Madame Proulx stopped him on his way to the door. "Wherever are you going?"

"Only outside," he said.

She placed her right hand upon his left arm, the gesture both affectionate and faintly proprietorial. "Whatever for?"

"To wait."

"Are you sure?"

He nodded. Very gently, he moved her hand away. "All shall be well," he said, "and all shall be well. And all manner of thing shall be well."

Madame Proulx frowned. The quotation was a favourite of the old priest's. She opened her mouth to speak only to close it again, having thought better of the remark.

The priest smiled and stepped outside.

There was beyond the house a modest stretch of garden. It was in the midst of this that he planted his shooting stick. Having opened the thing up he managed to settle himself in its nook in a fashion that was almost comfortable.

This achieved, he did as he had said he would do and waited. As a young man, he would certainly have smoked in order to while away the time but he had long since given up on the habit. He tried simply to remain in the present, to think neither of the evil memories of the past nor of his concerns for the future. In this, however, as had almost always been the case in his long life, he failed. For several hours he lost himself in unwise thoughts before, shortly after noon, the strangers came to see him.

III

The house was set back from the road and the garden secluded so it was not possible for the old priest to watch for arrivals. Yet he sat very still, listened and waited. When the sun was at its peak, he heard the click of the garden gate and the tread of unfamiliar feet upon the ground. Whoever they were they were unusually stealthy for he had not heard their approach until then. They were quiet amongst themselves too for the priest had heard no hint of conversation.

Would assassins make such an arrival? He thought this rather unlikely for all of their noiselessness. And then would killers really saunter into his garden on a brisk, clear afternoon and call out his name as they did so?

"Reverend Woodgrove?"

The old priest looked over at his visitors. He had not heard his name spoken in an English voice for a long while. The speaker was a young woman who had yet to see her twenties. She had a pleasant but purposeful air. The figure at her side was, at least at first glance, more unusual. He (or perhaps she) was short, coming up only to the hips of the lady, and excessively muffled in a multitude of scarves, a balaclava and a set of tinted goggles such as might be worn to evade the glare of the snow. The day was a cold one yet still such garb seemed excessive.

The priest did not move but raised a hand in greeting. If this were to be the last conversation of his life (a possibility which he had by now, in any case, largely discounted), he was determined not to lose his good manners. "I am he," he said. "I gather that you're new to the village."

The woman and her companion had stopped by the garden gate. They seemed oddly nervous. "That's right," she said.

Dear me, thought the priest. She was scarcely more than a child. Where were her family? Where were those who ought to keep her safe?

"And what has brought you here?"

"We came looking for you," she said.

The priest beckoned them forwards. "Come closer then. Both of you."

The girl walked towards him now, the little shuffling figure at her side moving at a slower pace. She reached down to take the person's hand to help them, and as they approached, the Reverend Woodgrove thought that there was something appealing, something sweet in the moment. No killers, then, he decided. At least not for today.

"Who are you?" he asked when they reached his side.

"My name is Coral Mayfield."

"I'm afraid I've not heard of you, my dear," he said gently. "Ought I have done?"

"Oh, I'm nobody important. But I've heard of you."

"You have?"

"I read your name in the newspapers. I was looking in the libraries and found that you were there... back in Ratcliffe... that you met a man called Moreau."

The name hung heavily between them.

"You'd better come in," Woodgrove said at last. "You'd better come in. You must be hungry. I'll ask my housekeeper to make us some luncheon. And you must tell me everything you know and why you've come all this way to see me. But before then..." He stopped and glanced at Coral's companion. "Please. Won't you introduce us?"

Coral turned to the figure by her side. "He's shy," she said.

"And he must be very hot," said the priest. "Beneath all of that. Whatever the trouble is, I've seen many strange things in my long life. I will not judge. Nor will I breathe a word. And, Miss Mayfield, you are amongst friends here."

Coral reached down and took the goggles away from her companion. Fierce, bright blue eyes looked out now at the Reverend Woodgrove. Next she removed his balaclava and then, peeling them away one by one, his multitude of scarves.

The truth was revealed, piece by piece, the gradual emergence of a most unusual face, simian in aspect, profusely furred but with a quality of humanity which shone out, a legacy of what Woodgrove took to be a most complicated hybridity. The creature looked up at the old priest and gave a toothy smile. He giggled.

"He's very beautiful," Woodgrove said.

"He's my son," Coral said proudly. "Or rather, I think of him as my son. I've always called him Arthur, though I don't suppose that's right."

"Coral and Arthur," said the old priest as he rose laboriously to his feet, his legs complaining at the imposition. "I think you'd better both come inside, don't you?"

IV

"You really have done astonishingly well, my dear."

The Reverend Woodgrove sat at the table, opposite the young woman, the remains of the luncheon spread out before them. In the garden could be heard the shrieks and hollers of the little boy and of Madame Proulx, who were now playing hide and seek. The Frenchwoman, after some initial bemusement, had taken a great shine to the little creature, a result which surprised the old priest not at all.

Coral nodded. "Yes, I think I have," she said simply for her mother had taught her ever to avoid the easy lie of false modesty. "I know I've kept him safe and warm and dry and fed. But I want to do more."

"What more can there be?" Woodgrove asked. His wine glass was still half full. He sipped slowly and thoughtfully.

"I want to know his story," said the girl. "No. More than that. When he's of age, I want him to know his own story. I want to know where he's come from. I want to know if there are others like him. I believe somehow, in my heart, that there are." She leaned forwards in her seat. There was an intensity in her eyes which Woodgrove found disconcerting.

"You may, my dear, be heading along a most dangerous path. One which will change you both."

"I know that I am."

From outside: the frantic pleasure-filled cries of Arthur, who had evidently been discovered by Madame Proulx.

"You think that there is a connection to the man I knew... to Moreau?"

"I do. The dying man in my mother's house mentioned that name. I found it later in a newspaper archive. As far as I can tell, you're the last man alive who knew him."

"Not quite, I think," the old priest said. "Not quite. There was a man called Prendick too. But he passed away not long ago. An accident, I think."

Laughter and merriment drifted in from the garden, in vivid contrast to the trajectory of the old priest's thoughts.

"Could you not just keep the boy safe? Wait till he's grown up. Surely this investigation of yours can be left till then?"

Coral shook her head. The intensity had yet to leave her eyes. "I don't believe it can. I think that something is happening now. Something bad. Something which you suspect too."

"You're very perceptive," Woodgrove said. "I've no doubt the good Lord gave you that perception as a gift. But why? That is the question, is it not? To what end?" He stopped speaking then, thinking instead of a conversation in a churchyard a decade and a half ago, and the ominous dreams which had ensued.

"I'm not a patient person," Coral said, returning Woodgrove's attention to the present. "I need to know. And if there are others like little Arthur I need to help them too."

"On your own?" asked Woodgrove.

The young woman shrugged. "If necessary."

Suddenly, the old priest felt thoroughly afraid for her. He felt a spasm of shame too, for had he not just run away when faced with a similar opportunity? Had he not chosen the anonymity of a continental retirement over a chance to stand up for what was right?

"Stay here," he said quickly. "Both of you. We'll look after you. You can raise the child, in seclusion. We'll do it together. The three of us. I am sure that I could persuade Madame Proulx. She is the best of women, you know."

Coral seemed to consider the proposal. "Thank you. But no."

The priest must have looked disconsolate at this, because the girl said swiftly: "But we'll visit. We'll come back."

"Promise?"

"Of course."

"Thank you. I feel a strong sensation that I have a great deal of cowardly years to make up for."

"I'm sure that's not true. But is there anything at all that you can do to help us now?"

The Reverend Woodgrove finished his wine. He listened to the sounds of the game from outside. What he said next might sign his own death warrant. Yet he spoke on. "Perhaps there's something. Or rather someone. A former pupil now in a high place. He might be able to help. But I think that what you have to discover is the exact location of what I understand to have been a rather remarkable island."

1ST MAY, 1896

WHITEHALL, LONDON

"I think we ought to begin, Miss Mayfield, upon terms of absolute candour."

The speaker was a thin, sandy-haired man in his middle fifties whose face was starting to show that fraying that is commonly brought about by decades of fine living. He sat upon the business side of a great oak desk in a small but sumptuous office. The view from the window behind him, on the fourth floor of the building, was of the city at its most flagrantly picturesque. He was, at least, in terms of the hierarchies of Westminster, rather a minor figure yet he was surrounded by opulence. His dress, his every mannerism, the languidness of his deportment and the lavishly antique nature of his surroundings – all pointed to one who swam unthinkingly in the waters of power.

"I have granted this audience today strictly as a favour to one who was once something of a mentor of mine."

The young woman who sat opposite him gave a steady smile of acknowledgement. "I understand that, minister."

"And how is dear old Woodgrove?"

"Enjoying his retirement," said Coral.

"Good. That's very good. And most probably for the best."

"Did he tell you why I wanted to see you?"

The politician looked down at his desk and to the many papers which were stacked there and began to rifle through them with an air of increasing desperation. There was a studied sort of bemusement to his actions. A kind of pantomimic haplessness which struck Coral as being the height of insincerity.

"I am dreadfully busy... so many calls upon my time... so many good causes, you understand... and my secretaries... are not all they could be..."

Coral watched for as long as she could bear it and then, cutting in firmly: "I came to speak to you about the island."

At this phrase, the parliamentarian blinked once and said, with preternatural mildness. "And which island would that be?"

Coral mustered all her dignity. "I think you know the one."

The politician gave a little shrug which Coral Mayfield thought distinctly foolish. "With all due respect, Miss Mayfield, there are many islands. Was it the Isle of Wight you were thinking of? The Isle of Dogs?"

"Please, sir, do not insult my intelligence."

In response, the politician gave her a smile of undiluted condescension. "Do you have any plans to wed, Miss Mayfield?"

"Whatever makes you ask me that?"

"It's only that I'm sure a husband could educate you on

the matter. He might also be a little easier for me to conduct business with."

Coral could not help but glare at him. "I have no plans to marry, sir."

"Oh? Pity."

"I want one thing from you, in the name of your friendship with the priest."

The politician winced. "I fear you may already have overstated your case. But, very well, you may make your request."

"I want the exact location of the island that was operated by the late Dr Moreau. I want its latitude and longitude."

The politician smiled and leant back in his seat. The polished leather of it let out a sigh as he adjusted his frame. "Then I'm terribly sorry, Miss Mayfield, but I fear I have not the slightest notion of what you're talking about."

"Oh but I rather think you do. You remember Moreau, don't you? Surely? And of what became of him?"

The politician shrugged. "Oh I remember some wild tales in the popular press. I must be frank with you, Miss Mayfield: there are very good reasons why I do not believe very much at all of what I read there."

"I would have thought you would remember this."

"I'm sorry, young lady. Truly I am. I wish I could help but, as I say, I'm terribly busy. Now was there anything else or was that your only enquiry?"

His act of flustered charm might have fooled many but it did not sway Coral Mayfield. "Why are you lying?"

"I can assure you, young lady, that I am not. Now I really think you ought to leave. Do give my regards to old Woodgrove and assure him that I did all I could to help his young friend but…" The politician stopped speaking and the smooth burble which fell from his lips ceased. There had been an interruption (he was not a man at all accustomed to being interrupted), one which had come from a most unexpected source.

Tap tap tap. It came from the window behind him.

The politician blinked, glanced at Coral. She only smiled. "Something wrong, minister?"

Tap tap tap. The sound again. Like fingernails on glass.

"Forgive me," he said. "The oddest noise… I expect it's a bird… some pigeon or crow…"

The sound again and this time the politician turned in his chair to confront the source of it: something at the window.

When he saw what it was (much to Coral's amusement) he swore in violent disbelief. A small furred face at the window pane, grinning savagely. The creature tapped again and bared his teeth.

"My son," Coral said coolly. She stood up, walked around the desk and the astonished minister and opened the window. The creature sprang inside and ran at once towards the politician.

"Play nicely, Arthur," Coral admonished gently, though she did not sound altogether sincere.

Arthur flung himself up towards the startled minister's face, fangs out and hissing. The politician screamed, threw his hands around, stumbled backwards and fell to the floor, still with the creature affixed.

"Enough now," Coral said and Arthur obeyed.

The politician sat up, gasping. "Good God," he murmured. "It's true, then. All true." He gazed in horrified respect at his visitor. "Madam, what is this thing?"

Arthur hissed with a menace which, at least to those who did not know him, seemed altogether genuine.

"He's not a thing," Coral said. "Don't speak of him so. He can understand you, you know."

Arthur capered towards the minister once again.

"What do you want?" the man said. "For goodness' sake, what do you people want with me?"

"Just the latitude and longitude of the island of Dr Moreau," Coral said lightly before adding, with a wink: "And perhaps some money too."

30TH NOVEMBER, 1896

THE ISLAND

The boy was bigger now. He had grown considerably over the course of this long year, far faster, Coral reflected, than would a purely human child. Arthur had wandered down to the water's edge and she watched, with a mother's pride, as he visibly resisted the impulse to crouch down upon all fours but stayed instead altogether upright. He rolled back his shoulders and sniffed the air. Was he home at last? Coral supposed in a sense that he was.

Their ship had weighed anchor early in the morning and a handsome young midshipman had rowed her and Arthur ashore, to the east side of the island. Coral had asked the sailor to stay with the boat, and the young man, although he had looked at them both with curious eyes, had honoured her request. He was, after all, as all of them were, being well paid. The generosity, once again, of the Reverend Woodgrove, with a small contribution in exchange for being left alone from the politician.

She watched her son gaze out to sea. He had taken off his shoes and socks and his furred toes squirmed in the sun.

They had been here four hours. They had eaten lunch together beneath the shade of a palm tree. It was dream-like for her, almost hallucinatory. She had said to Arthur as they had strolled through the little patches of woodland which spotted this place that it seemed to her that they were walking through the pages of a book, some old story of the high seas. Arthur had looked at her thoughtfully but said nothing. His words were halting in any case, though she was trying her best to teach him. Some days he seemed to have real facility with language; on others he seemed silent and still.

Now he stepped a little further into the ocean, the water rising up to his calves, still inches away from the blue cotton of his shorts. Coral watched him very closely, trusting him to go no further while remaining close enough to be able to run to him should he stumble or slip.

As she stood in the sun, admiring the beauty of the place she felt for a short while very far away indeed from all the many travails which had filled up her young life since the arrival of the mariner at her mother's boarding house half a decade earlier. It was the briefest of respites and for this she was grateful.

The boy seemed happy now, splashing his feet in the water with carefree glee.

Of course, this had not been the plan when they had decided to come here. She had hoped to find something, some clue or connection to help her understand exactly where her little son had come from and what had become of his fellows. There was some evidence of habitation but it did not look as though anyone but them had been here for a long time. Of the little village which once had housed the Beast People there was only rotting wood, grown over by the jungle. If ever there had been a society here then it was long since gone. Coral wondered where the people of this place were. Already she was full of suspicion.

"Oh yes. I see that." The voice of Arthur carried on the warm breeze.

Coral looked over. "Darling?"

The furred boy ignored her. He seemed to be addressing his words towards the ocean. "Yes, I thought… We did wonder if that was really true…"

Coral frowned. It was as though the child were conducting a conversation with someone she could not see. He had always shown signs of being an imaginative boy but there was in this something new and disconcerting.

"Arthur!" she called out.

He did not turn but spoke on, his eyes fixed upon the water. "Arthur!"

He turned now and waved. "Mummy! Come here. Come and see?"

Fretful, Coral hurried to the side of her child. There was something unusual in his voice, a kind of oddly adult exultation which she had never heard there before.

When she reached his side, he was still smiling. "He says my name shouldn't really be Arthur. He says my father's name was M'Gari. And that his father's name was Anse."

Quickly, Coral took his hand, thick with fur, and squeezed it. "Who does, darling? Who says that?"

"It's in my head. I don't know his name. But he says that he's a friend."

Coral drew the boy to her side and held him tight. He did not resist. He leaned into her. The warmth of him filled her up with both fear and joy. "Where is he, darling?" she asked, struggling to keep her voice light so as not to unsettle him. "Where is this friend of yours?"

"There," he said, and pointed out to sea. "See, Mummy? He's there. Coming up now above the waves."

Coral looked at where the boy was pointing. "I can't see anything, darling."

"Look closer, Mummy."

And then she saw it: something dark, something moving against the horizon, something both wondrous and dreadful. Something, she realised, that was coming ever closer.

She found herself unable to move, held firm by fascinated horror. "What is it? What is that thing?"

Arthur said nothing and when she looked down to see his face she saw that his eyes were shining.

"He knows," Arthur said then. "He knows what has happened. And he knows what we must do now. He has such plans... such plans for the future."

By the time that mother and son returned at dusk to the waiting boat and the handsome midshipman there was scarcely anything at all in them which had not been changed absolutely.

2ND FEBRUARY, 1900

LA ROCHE, PICARDY, FRANCE

I

Old age, reflected the Reverend Douglas Woodgrove, as he lay awake in the still hours of early morning, was supposed by many to represent an inexorable dwindling of one's capabilities and enthusiasms, a fading away of colour and drive. In his own life, however, this had proved to be untrue. His last years of retirement had been amongst the most dynamic of his life, as well as being, without question, the most materially useful.

Beside his bed were piles of paper and correspondence, stacks of reports and files of dreadful possibilities. From almost a hundred sources all over the globe there were reports, accounts, testimonies, written rumours and scrawled whispers, all concerning that great, ignoble project which he had become convinced had been set in motion in the country which had, for most of his life, been home.

Sometimes at the sight of it – this patient accretion of evidence – he felt obscurely ashamed, that he had not done more sooner, that he had not acted with greater speed and ferocity since the truth had come to light. Yet he found great comfort in prayer and at the slow realisation, which he had spoken about for much of his life without (he saw now) ever really understanding it, that God had a plan for each and every one of his creations. The quietness of his early life had been there for a reason as had the gradual progression of his career, meant to bring him into the orbit of Mr Vaughan and others like him. Then, later, of course, the girl and the little ape-creature had been sent to him as a signal for how he should spend the years that were remaining to him.

He lay in bed on that crisp February morning thinking these thoughts and many more besides. Often he simply marvelled at the sheer shamelessness of the project as well as its terrible scope. He still did not, however, have sufficient understanding of how it all had been achieved; the organisation of the many people, from workmen to architects, from suppliers of goods to officers of the law, who would have been necessary to establish this "city" and to operate it.

Woodgrove was turning this over in his mind as the dawn crept into his chamber, casting shafts of thin light upon the bedspread and upon the figure of the woman who lay, still sleeping heavily, beside him. Too alert to return to slumber himself, the old priest considered getting from his bed and going downstairs to sit and pray before the business of the day began in earnest. Then he heard it: the sound, quite distinct, of footsteps. They were, perhaps, intended to be silent but the house was an old one and sound carried. Beside him, Madame Proulx slept on, oblivious to the intruder. The priest leaned over to her and, taking great care not to wake her, kissed her once upon her forehead.

Woodgrove rose softly from the bed and went from the room. He paused in the hallway to murmur the swiftest of prayers then descended the staircase to the ground floor. He did not hesitate or slow his pace nor did he stop en route to pick up some manner of makeshift weapon. Of course, he had long been expecting this visitation, or something very like it.

II

There was a stranger sitting at the table in the kitchen. He had his back to the priest and he seemed to have made himself very much at home. His legs were stretched out and crossed as though he were in his parlour and he had poured himself a glass of red wine from which he was taking regular, liberal sips.

Woodgrove watched him, wondering where he might be from and who might have sent him. It even occurred to the old priest, after some reluctant protestation, that he might have imagined the trespasser, that his odd, incongruous behaviour was the product merely of an elderly mind, sinking into befuddlement and hallucination.

Woodgrove broke the silence. "I imagine you've come to kill me?"

The figure in the chair did not turn around. "That's right, sir," he said and his lack of surprise made it plain that he had known of the priest's presence from the first. His accent was English (well spoken with a hint, perhaps, of Sussex).

"Was it Mr Vaughan who sent you?"

"Amongst others, sir, yes." Still he did not turn about.

Hesitantly, the Reverend Woodgrove approached him. "How do you mean to do it?" he asked.

"Kindly," said the figure. "I'll do it quickly, I promise. You won't know very much about it." He drank again from his glass. "I've got very good at it, you know."

"I'm sorry that you've had to," said the priest.

The figure in the chair shrugged.

Woodgrove stood behind him, uncertain as to exactly what he should do. He asked for guidance and the words seemed almost to speak themselves. "But you could have done it by now, couldn't you? While I was sleeping. I might have slept through the whole thing and woken up only in the hereafter." The figure did not respond. "Is it the case perhaps, Mr…"

"Berry," murmured the intruder, still unmoving.

"Mr Berry – perhaps you don't want to do this? Not truly and in your heart? Perhaps you don't want to murder an old man in his bed and go on abetting the greatest crime of our time?" He paused. "Am I right in any of these assumptions?"

Berry took another sip from his glass.

"I see you've found my wine."

"Yes," he said. "My apologies for that. Very rude of me. My mother would have been so cross…"

"Poor man," Woodgrove said and put his hands on the man's shoulders.

Mr Berry did not stir but allowed the gesture.

"Why don't you come over to our side?" said the priest. "We can help each other. You can help us destroy what they're building. Bring it down from the inside."

"Step back please, sir," was all that Mr Berry said, and the old priest complied.

Berry rose up, set down his glass and turned to confront the old priest. The face of the invader, Woodgrove saw, was horribly mangled, a tortured mass of scar tissue.

"What did that to you? If you don't mind my asking."

He all but shrugged. "It was a fire. I escaped, but barely, and now children scream at the sight of me. Women gasp. Men just cross the street to get away. I suppose you think that it's God will. A punishment from on high."

"It may be His will but He does not punish. There will have been a purpose to it. Perhaps to bring you here, today, to my door."

Mr Berry reached into his pocket and drew out a revolver.

Panic prickled in the old priest's chest. It was one thing to consider mortality in a theoretical sense but quite another to be confronted by it so baldly.

"Are you alone here, sir?"

Woodgrove wondered whether his visitor had ever been in service, so punctilious and deferential was his manner.

"All alone," said the priest, a lie but one of which he was proud. "So you're going to do it then?"

There was a very short flicker of hesitation in Berry's eyes. "I have to."

"No, my friend. You don't have to. Besides, you know that it is wrong. Everything they've done. What they've treated those poor people. It's monstrous. We're both Englishmen. Doesn't it shame you?"

"Of course."

"But?"

The revolver trembled a little in the man's hand. "But if we were not doing it… someone else would. Don't you think? And perhaps not so humanely. Perhaps they'd be still more brutal than us."

"These are all old and bloodless arguments, Mr Berry. You know the truth, I think, not in here…" The old priest tapped the right hand side of his head. "But in here…" He touched his chest lightly, just above the heart.

"It doesn't matter what I believe," Berry snapped. "Events are too big now. Too full of momentum. Critical mass."

"Not true, my friend. An individual can still change the course of history. One man can make a difference."

The ruined face of Mr Berry twisted still further into a snarl. "How can you have lived so long," he said with a kind of battened-down fury, "yet still learned nothing?"

With this he pulled the trigger.

III

Madame Proulx was woken by a loud retort, like a small explosion. It cut through her dreams and dragged her to wakefulness. Her mind circled a variety of possibilities and alighted on the worst of them. She listened out. No further sound came.

Quickly but stealthily she rose from the bed, draped a dressing gown around herself and descended the staircase. She screamed when she saw the scene that awaited her though the man who had once been her employer was able to calm her panicked sobs.

"What happened?" she gasped.

"I'm not entirely sure," Woodgrove said as they surveyed the body on the ground before them, the ugly smoking hole in his chest, and the gristle upon the kitchen floor.

"Who was he?"

"He said his name was Berry," said the priest. "Poor fellow.

He was grappling, I think, with a decision of great moment." He looked down again at the floor and the corpse that lay there. He took the hand of Madame Proulx in his and squeezed. "I suppose he made his choice in the end, though perhaps not the one either of us was expecting."

11TH JULY, 1901

ST BARNABY'S SCHOOL/ EDDOWES BAY/ THE CITY

I

Albert Edgington, eighteen years old and intensely curious about what life might have in store for him, waited alone on his last day as a schoolboy outside the gates of St Barnaby's. He had spent more than a decade here, at this quietly distinguished, expensive institution in the east of England, boarding away from home and being filled up with all the education and knowledge which befits a nascent gentleman.

He had, he knew, been lucky. As the youngest of three boys, he had been permitted to choose his own path to a greater degree than had either of his brothers: Silas, heir to the family estate, and Roderick who had, since birth, been marked out for the law. In contrast, Albert had followed his own passions – for the sciences in particular but also for the tragedies of Ancient Greece

– and he had in consequence enjoyed much of his school career even if it had at times struck him as being a little rudderless and lacking in purpose. His own future seemed now quite uncertain.

There had once been talk of Oxford or Cambridge but that had ceased before Christmas when both universities had declined to meet with him. He was, after all, bright but not brilliant, eager enough to learn but hardly insatiable for knowledge. He was not even set to be a wealthy man; the great majority of the funds that awaited the Edgington boys had been marked out for Silas whilst Roderick was even now devoting himself to the creation of a sizeable fresh fortune.

In every way, Albert appeared externally to be unremarkable – a copper-haired young man of strictly average height with a distinct, still-puppyish plumpness to his features. It was late in the afternoon and he wore his uniform: frock coat and dark trousers, wing-collared starched white shirt and crimson tie. His single suitcase was by his side and he was waiting for the family chauffeur to arrive and take him home. He looked at his watch, checked the time and concluded that, on what would be far from the first occasion, he had very probably been overlooked.

All of the other boys had left now as had many of the masters. The school was emptying and at this particular point it felt to Albert as though he were almost entirely alone.

He looked at the school again for one last time, feeling that the moment ought to be important somehow and that he should fix it in his mind. Yet as he looked at the grey turrets of the place, its austere halls and chambers, its architecture which seemed to combine at once the qualities of a miniature castle and a well-maintained gaol, he realised that he felt no particular connection to these buildings at all. He could not imagine even missing the sight of them or feeling the least twinge of nostalgia for their numerous corridors and debating halls and libraries. In such defiance was this sentiment to all that he had ever been told and taught, Albert even wondered, with a surge of nervousness, whether this were normal or whether there was in fact something wrong with him.

This chain of thought was interrupted by the sight of a gowned figure emerging from the lodge house and stepping across that wide yard which led to the iron gates. As the person came fully into view, Albert raised a hand in greeting. "Dr Galsworthy!"

The master was a tall, rather striking man in possession of an extravagant black beard which was said by the boys to lend him the appearance of a skinny W. G. Grace.

Dr Galsworthy (who seemed to Albert to be well advanced indeed in years but who cannot have been more than five and forty) nodded in greeting, an informality which would not hitherto have been permissible.

"Edgington," he said, "I thought that was you. Malingering by the gates, eh?"

"I'm waiting for my car, sir. To take me home again."

Galsworthy made rather a performance of drawing out his pocket watch from its compartment in his waistcoat. He consulted the clock face and blinked.

"Running somewhat late, wouldn't you say?"

"Yes, sir. I expect there'll be a very good reason for the delay."

"Hmm." Galsworthy replaced the timepiece and peered through the bars at Albert (for the gates still separated them) and asked, seemingly with true curiosity: "And what will you say to the chauffeur, given the lateness of the hour, when he finally arrives?"

Without thinking, Albert Edgington gave the answer that he imagined that the older man wished to hear.

"I'll show him the sharp edge of my tongue, sir. Give the fellow a lashing. Punctuality's the politeness of princes."

A look of great and undeniable disappointment spread across the master's features. "Edgington," he said, then carefully, thoughtfully: "Albert?"

"Sir?"

"School's over now. You may call me Galsworthy as my friends do. But listen, before you go, I want you to think – really think – about what you say, what you do, what you believe…"

"I'm afraid… that is… I'm not sure that I follow."

"All of this…" Galsworthy gestured vaguely behind him. "A place like this, it can give a fellow some strange ideas about the ordering of the world and about one's place in it. Every one of us is doing our best, I know that, but you can't spend time in these halls without inheriting, shall we say, a certain quality of presumption."

Albert frowned. The encounter was like meeting an actor backstage after the play and finding him in real life to be altogether different to whatever swaggering braggart, pensive nobleman or heartsick lover he had essayed upon the stage.

"What do you mean, sir?"

Galsworthy tugged at his voluminous beard. For the first time, Albert wondered why the man had grown it to such length, whether it did not offer, in a sense, the comforts of disguise.

"I think," said the schoolteacher, "that you have potential, Edgington."

"Oh but sir–" Albert was about to rehearse once again his failings and uncertainties, but Galsworthy waved him into silence.

"Oh, not as a thinker or an academic or a sportsman but rather as a human being. For you have curiosity and a sense of decency, and, I shouldn't wonder, the capacity for great good.

There's just one thing you're going to need."

"Oh?" Albert found that he was blushing. "And what, sir, is that?"

Galsworthy fixed Albert in a very grave and steady gaze and seemed about to give his answer when, at last, a motorcar came roaring into sight.

It was a big, sleek vehicle with large high wheels, two seats side by side and a steering wheel which had about it an unexpectedly maritime touch. There was something of the fairground about it too, as well as something of the racetrack.

"Not what you were expecting?" Galsworthy asked, his words almost lost to the clank and hum of the machine.

Albert shook his head. "And that's not the family chauffeur either."

A big, broad-shouldered figure, sat in hat and goggles behind the wheel and brought the vehicle to a noisy halt before the gates.

The brake was applied, though the engine roared on. The driver lifted up his goggles to reveal the cheerful, open features of…

"Silas!" Albert turned to Dr Galsworthy. "My elder brother."

"I remember," said the master.

"Hop on board!" Silas said. "There's space beneath these seats for that trunk of yours."

"I was…" Albert begun. "That is… I wasn't expecting you."

"Change of plan," Silas said. "A change for the better. I promise you, you'll approve."

Without quite knowing why, Albert found that he was hesitating.

Silas turned and nodded in brusque acknowledgement of the teacher's presence. "Still here, Galsworthy? I trust they're keeping you busy in there?"

The tutor did not smile. "Always busy," he said. "The work is never done, never complete."

"Jolly good!" Silas gave a smile of blank indifference. "Up you come now, Bert," he said and Albert found that he was unthinkingly obeying, stowing his luggage and clambering up onto the unfamiliar machine, taking his place beside his brother and putting on the protective apparel which had been left out for his use.

He waved at Dr Galsworthy. "I'd better go, sir. Thank you so much for everything."

The teacher said nothing but only watched from behind the gates. Silas released the brake.

"We're going home then?" Albert said, perhaps more loudly than was required as he became accustomed to the relentless sound of the engine.

"Oh no," Silas said and grinned a real, ferocious grin. "Not there. Why, we're going to the City."

"What city?" Albert shouted. "Which one?"

"No, you don't understand. We're going to the City."

And, with this, Silas turned the car in a few surprisingly swift and certainly expert motions and began to drive at speed away from the gates of St Barnaby's. They moved down the long driveway which led out of the school grounds and out onto the road beyond, flanked on either side by green, unpeopled playing fields.

Albert, full of questions, was on the cusp of turning to his brother (who still smirked in a most disconcerting manner) when he caught sight of something behind them – a dark, sober figure in full flight, pursuing the motorcar on foot and waving his arms, his gown flapping out behind him like a cloak.

"Galsworthy!" Albert shouted. "Galsworthy's trying to flag us down."

The smirk on the face of his brother grew at this only more broad and Albert considered, somehow meaner too.

Teasingly, Silas increased the speed of the vehicle (he was later to boast that she was capable of speeds in excess of thirty miles per hour) as Albert craned his head around to see Galsworthy fall into the distance.

"Stop!" Albert cried. "I might have forgotten something. Left something behind."

They were at the end now of the driveway. The open road – gateway to the adult world – lay beyond them, empty save, in the distance, for what looked to be a horse and cart of a decidedly quaint, painterly sort.

"That's more than likely," Silas grunted and now he stopped the motorcar. Unaccustomed to such treatment, the engine coughed and grumbled and appeared, for a moment, to be seriously considering stopping altogether. At this, irritation twitched at the corners of Silas' lips. Then the engine settled itself and the grin returned.

Behind them, Albert saw, Galsworthy ran into view. He reached the side of the motorcar, seeming impressively untroubled by the exertion, scarcely out of breath and perspiring only a little.

At the sight of him, another flash of annoyance crossed Silas' features.

"Don't go!" Galsworthy said, standing by the car, looking past the eldest sibling entirely to fix Albert once again in his gaze.

"Go where, sir?"

"I heard what your brother said. But you mustn't go there."

"Oh Galsworthy," said Silas. "I always thought you were the most frightful chump. A chump and a prude to boot."

"Silas?" Albert asked. "Where is this place you're taking me? What on earth is it?"

"It's just the City," said his brother. "I went there when I was your age. So did Roddy. And I bet this old gargoyle –" He made a blunt gesture in Galsworthy's direction. "– I bet he's never even visited at all."

The schoolteacher blanched. "I've heard enough," he said. "About what kind of a place it is. And the kinds of men who go there."

Silas laughed. "You always were such an old woman. I can't think why St Barnaby's put up with you."

Galsworthy ignored the jibe. "Trust me," he said to Albert. "You don't want to go to the City."

"What is it?" Albert asked, his eyes now very wide. "What happens there?"

"It's fun," said Silas. "Just fun."

On the road before them, the horse and cart came clip-clopping closer. It had a Romany look about it, Albert saw now, an emissary from some earlier time.

"Corruption." Galsworthy was countering his brother's argument. "It may seem like fun on the surface but there's corruption underneath. Malfeasance."

Silas rolled his eyes. "Pshaw."

"You're talking in riddles," Albert said, keeping his eyes fixed on the nearing cart. "Please won't one of you tell me what this place is and what on earth goes on there?"

"Better you don't know," Galsworthy said.

Silas winked. "Best I don't spoil the surprise."

Still the cart came closer. There was one driver – a haggard man in a tall hat, a feather in its brim. There was something in the cart but it was not yet close enough to make out the cargo.

"Albert, come back to the school," said Galsworthy. "You'll be safe there. I can contact your father. I don't believe he can have the slightest idea of what your brother has planned for you."

Silas laughed. "You really believe that our father knows nothing of this? The notion was his! He's been to the City himself, on occasions too numerous to count. They know him well there."

Galsworthy seemed startled by this information. He stepped back.

Silas grinned again and nodded with pantomime enthusiasm. "You should go yourself one day, you know. Might liven you up a bit, you desiccated old stick."

"I'll never go there," Galsworthy said weakly. He stepped back again.

"Only because you're a coward," Silas said. Turning to Albert: "So what say you? Do you want to have some fun? Do you want to become a man?"

"If Father says…"

"Damn Father! This concerns you, Bertie. Would you like to be a man? Or a pale little worm like this fellow?"

"There's no need," Albert said softly, "to be unkind."

"Can't hear you!" Silas said over the rumble of the engine.

Albert turned to Galsworthy. "Before," he said, "at the gates. You said that there was something I needed. To become all that I can be. What was it?"

Galsworthy gazed back at him, his gown settled limply around his thin form. He suddenly seemed very tired.

He spoke two words, too quietly to be heard, though Albert believed that he knew what they were.

"Come on." Silas' patience had snapped. "We have to get going. Ready for the City, Bertie?"

Succumbing to the inevitable gravity of the occasion, Albert nodded once.

Silas urged the car onwards, leaving the schoolteacher behind them. In the road ahead, the horse, startled by the lurch of the vehicle, reared up, whinnied, so dramatically that the driver had his work cut out to bring the beast back under control.

As the car sped away, Albert caught a glimpse of what the cart had carried – coils and coils of shining new metal which seemed to speak of restraint and partition.

Then the car was away and horse, cart, driver, master and school sank at last into the distance.

It was a while before Albert spoke.

Instead, he thought of the two words which he believed Galsworthy to have spoken in answer to his question.

They had been simple and direct, and they echoed in his imagination as they drove.

"A purpose."

II

An odd atmosphere had settled between the two young men – even Silas had seemed uncharacteristically taciturn following their encounter with Dr Galsworthy – and it was not until the school was some fifteen miles away and they had passed into the Fenlands that conversation began, haltingly, to start up once more.

"It is good to see you," Silas offered and his tentative smile seemed far more genuine than it had before, devoid now of any touch of cruelty.

"You too," Albert said, grateful that the long hush was over.

"Been too long. Don't see enough of one another. Always try to watch out for you. Make sure you're thriving. Roddy too, of course, but there's a special link, don't you find, between the eldest and the youngest?"

Albert found that he was smiling now too, pleased for the flattery and eager for companionship. Beyond the car was the flat, stark vista which typifies Cambridgeshire even in high summer. With every additional mile, the warnings of his schoolmaster seemed to grow fainter and to recede further into memory.

"So you can tell me now," Albert said, settling back into his seat, "exactly what's waiting for us in this City of yours. What is it? A club of some sort, I suppose?"

The grin was back and a hint of slyness with it. "In a manner of speaking it's a club, yes. Certainly only the most select sort of chap is invited. But it's considerably more than that. It's a feat – of architecture, engineering and imagination. Oh, I really can't describe it. Not in a way which does the place justice. You'll see – you'll understand when we get there. It will be fun, as I said, but you'll receive quite an education too – a finer, truer one than St Barnaby's ever gave you."

"Just tell me one thing, just one thing about the City. Then I'll ask no more until we get there."

Silas drew in a breath, then exhaled theatrically. "Just this," he said. "No-one goes to the City for the first time and comes back the same. One sort of person goes in – and a very different man comes out. It leaves its mark upon you. The mark of Moreau."

"Who's Moreau?"

"One question, old chap. That's what you asked for and that's what I granted. All of the rest of it will become clear in the fullness of time. Now, let's talk of other things. You hear much of old Roddie these days? I hear that wife of his has him fully under the thumb now, poor devil…"

The car went on, deeper into England, and as Silas chattered of family and duty and of the mysterious, inexorable workings of money Albert Edgington sat quite still, watched the level landscape roll by and let his mind roam ahead to the City.

III

The journey from the gates of St Barnaby's to the place which led to the City took a little under three hours, a feat which would not have been possible even a handful of years earlier. Silas pushed the motorcar to its considerable limits, urging it on through the narrow country roads which led out of Cambridgeshire and into the county of Suffolk, ignoring the occasional protestations of the engine and taking visible delight in the power and speed of the machine at his disposal.

Albert meanwhile simply allowed himself to be driven and let their conversation wash over him. He had not been blessed with any innate sense of direction and they were well into the third hour of their journey before he realised what the nature of their destination must be.

"Are we headed towards the coast?" he asked.

They had just passed a weather-beaten sign which, looking as though it dated from the times of the witch trials, proclaimed Dunwich to be ten miles away.

"That's right!" Silas called back. There was excitement in his voice, no doubt at the thought of their proximity.

"Surely," Albert asked, coming out of the near-daze into which he had descended, "this precious City of yours isn't in Dunwich?"

"As it happens, it's not," said Silas, "but don't dismiss a place like that just because it seems like a little fishing village now. This used to be the capital of these parts in all but name. A great centre of power in the kingdom of the Angles."

"Oh," was all that Albert could think to say, quite unable to square his memories of the quaint, poor settlement which he had visited once or twice as a boy with his brother's description.

"It was all different back then," Silas went on. "Before the Normans came. In some ways – in a lot of ways – it must have been a better kind of England. Don't you think?"

"I honestly don't know," Albert replied. "I don't believe I've ever really thought about it."

"Well, I have," Silas said and Albert could tell that he was pleased – pleased, perhaps, at the thought that Albert was surprised by the breadth of his knowledge. "A man in my position has to. Because we're part of a tradition – our family and families like ours – which goes back to before the Conqueror. We're a captive people in many ways, still subject to the Norman yoke, and it behoves those of us who can to cherish and keep alive the spirit of this country as she used to be."

Albert, shifting nervously in his seat, was about to ask politely as to the evidence that the Edgingtons were able to trace their lineage back before the eleventh century (for certainly he had never seen or heard of any) when Silas cried out in happiness: "Aha!"

They were approaching a rustic junction, green fields on either side of them. Ahead was a sign that seemed polished and brand new and which read in bold dark letters: EDDOWES BAY, 3 MILES.

"Almost there!" Silas said.

"I've never heard of it," Albert admitted. "What is it?"

"Oh, nothing special. Just another village by the sea. At least… superficially."

Albert could see the sea now, rising ahead of them in the distance, a swathe of blue and grey.

The road seemed to decline and on either side the banks grew higher. Albert had never seen anything like it, at least not here in this flattest of all the English counties. The road took on a downhill aspect and the mounds of grass and earth on either side grew taller and taller.

It was as though the car was descending into a valley of some kind, heading disconcertingly along a narrow mountain road.

Later – very much later – Albert wondered if this approach to Eddowes Bay was manmade, fashioned at great expense, and had concluded that this surely was the case. Although, of course, by then he had come to understand that there were very few practical limits to the resources of those who had built and operated the City.

As the motorcar sped down the road (too fast to stop safely, Albert noted, should another similar vehicle approach at the same velocity from the opposite direction), a solitary figure walking ahead of them came into view.

It was a young woman, not very much older than Albert himself. She had long blonde hair and wore a flowing blue dress – almost a smock – which gave her the quality of a figure from a storybook.

At the sound of the car, the young woman turned and pressed herself against the bank in order to let them pass. Albert saw her face – pale and fine-featured. At the sight of her, Silas braked hard, all but dislodging Albert from his chair.

"Well, well," he said and there could be no doubt that his tone was anything other than lascivious. "It would seem that the fun has begun even sooner than I dared to hope."

"Silas?"

Albert's eldest brother ignored the speaking of his name and raised his right hand high into the air. "Halloa! You there!"

The woman said nothing but only looked intently at them both.

"Where are you headed?"

Still she said nothing but only looked at them, careful and skittish.

"Eddowes Bay?"

The woman thought for a moment then nodded, guardedly, just once. Was any other destination even possible, Albert wondered, on this strange, deep road in this odd pocket of the country?

"Well, there's a stroke of luck!" Silas declared, all bonhomie and smiles. "We're headed that way ourselves. Might we offer you a lift?"

The young woman looked nervous, not frightened of them exactly, but wary and prepared. "Why would you do that?"

"Because we're a couple of Christian gentlemen. Isn't that right, Bertie? Think of us, my dear, as your passing good Samaritans."

Albert turned to his brother. "She seems ill at ease," he said as softly as he could and still be heard. "Besides there isn't room."

"Nonsense. These seats are made for big men. Great Teutonic bottoms. Plenty of space for the two of you on one chair if you don't mind sharing."

Albert felt his face grow warm at the suggestion. "Silas, no–"

It was too late. When Albert looked up again towards the young woman he saw that she was already walking in their direction. She seemed more confident now, her mind presumably made up, and her gait was almost a saunter.

"I'm Jessamy," she said as soon as she reached the side of the car and before either of the men could speak.

"Surname?" Silas drawled.

"Not important," Jessamy said.

"Pleased to meet you."

Albert remembered his manners though he found himself unable to look the young woman in the eye. "My name is Albert Edgington and this is my brother, Silas."

"What brings you to Eddowes Bay, Jessamy?"

"Oh," she said vaguely. "Work. The promise of employment. I'm to meet a woman there."

"Jolly good. Now, clamber on board," Silas said. "There's a good girl. Do move up, Bertie."

Albert did as he was told and shuffled as far rightwards as he could upon his seat. The girl jumped up and into the vehicle. Though there was precious little space she managed to sit beside him. Their legs could not help but touch. Jessamy smelt of something sweet – something like apricot while underneath there was detectable the sharp, if not unpleasant tang, of her perspiration. Albert felt suddenly very young and gauche indeed.

"All aboard?" Silas cried and, without waiting for any reply, edged the car forwards again, down the narrow steep road towards the sea.

Though he could not bring himself even to glance at her, Albert could sense that Jessamy was smiling.

Silas began to whistle. And it was in this fashion that the three of them rode into the strange little town of Eddowes Bay, last calling post before the City.

IV

The town clung to the coastline. It was a pretty place, though no more so than plenty of other such settlements, outwardly similar, which could be found at that time and in that region of the country. There was a small high street – a butcher, a grocer, a baker – together with a single public house (The Idler's Retreat) and, in the distance, the pale spire of a church.

Before them, the sea glistened and surged, looking, for once, on this bright summer's day, almost blue and inviting.

Albert looked about him with curious surprise.

"Not quite what you were expecting?" Silas shouted.

"I don't know. It looks very quaint but also…"

Albert's words tailed off into silence as the car turned into the high street and passed by a group of half a dozen men on the pavement. They were all young and all were fashionably dressed. They seemed in high spirits and were jostling one another as they strolled, much as though they walked along some expensive London street and not this seaside backwater at all. At the sight of Jessamy, two of them called out and whistled.

"Ignore them," Albert said. "Evidently not gentlemen."

The woman at his side said nothing but only gazed at the strangers with a kind of blank resignation. Silas brought the car onwards to the front of the tavern. He parked before it and turned off the engine with a flourish.

"Here we are," he said. "Now who's for a preliminary snifter?"

Albert did not reply at first. He was still taking in the sight of this small, seemingly inconsequential town which appeared nonetheless to possess for many a great, even dreadful significance.

He took a deep breath, gulping in air. It tasted of two things, of sea salt and the warm, distinctive taste of hops.

Silas must have noticed his expression and guessed his train of thought because he said: "They've a brewery not far from here. Has to be." He winked. "Lot of thirsty people come to Eddowes Bay." Silas clambered out of the car, jumping adroitly to the ground.

"Anyway who's for a drink right now? Bertie? Jessamy?"

The young woman who was in the process of disembarking from the vehicle did not speak.

"Surely…" Albert began. "I mean, that is – they won't permit us to take a lady inside?"

Silas shrugged theatrically. "They have a saloon bar. Besides, the landlord is famously flexible in such matters."

Jessamy turned her back to them, faced away from the inn and looked out down the high street and towards the ocean.

Albert, meanwhile, climbed out of the car and joined his brother who was looking hopefully towards the pub, a quiet, pleasant-looking place which seemed to be entirely empty. Apart from the young men on the street they had seen no-one.

"Where is everybody?" Albert asked, feeling as he spoke, an odd, fleeting sensation of oppressiveness.

"Oh it's still early," Silas said lightly. "I dare say a lot of them will still be… indoors. Now, how about that drink?" He seemed suddenly filled up with a kind of nervous energy. He shuffled from foot to foot. "I could murder a pint of half and half."

"Yes," Albert said, though even he could hear the lack of enthusiasm in his voice. "Yes, of course."

"Come on then," Silas said. "And bring the girl with you."

They formed a curious tableau, these three – the elder brother edging towards the inn, though seemingly reluctant to go in alone; the young woman who stood watching in silence the restless motion of the sea; Albert, the schoolboy who stood between the two of them, caught by twin poles of magnetism.

"Jessamy?" he ventured. The girl did not respond. Behind him, Silas edged closer to the Idler's Retreat.

Albert took three nervous steps towards the woman. "Would you like..? I mean, that is…" At last, she turned to face him.

"It's not real," she said.

"I'm sorry?"

"None of it. It's… fake. Don't you see? Like a stage set."

"I'm afraid I don't…"

"It's all make-believe," she said. "Or it may as well be. Don't just watch, Mr Edgington, try to see."

The two of them looked at one another for a long moment. Her gaze, Albert concluded, experienced at close quarters was queerly discomfiting. He looked away.

"Come on, in the name of Harry! Stop gawping and get yourselves inside." Silas strode towards the door of the pub. Jessamy walked past Albert, appearing not to want to catch up with the older man.

"Coming?" she called back.

"Yes!" Albert said but he waited awhile all the same, thinking on the young woman's strange words. He looked down the high street and at the sea beyond. No other human life could he discern. The place was silent and still. The houses which were clustered nearby all looked empty and dark.

Overhead, a gull screamed and swooped. Was he being watched? Albert thought that he could feel eyes upon him. Or was he simply tired, bewildered and the victim of his own imagination? He sniffed the air again, rich with its promise of water. Then, from nearby, he heard the simple sombre tolling of a single church bell.

Evensong, surely. The noise ought to have comforted him a little but somehow it did not.

With one last glance at the empty street Albert turned and walked towards the oddly unwelcoming sight of the only pub in Eddowes Bay.

V

A small bell tinkled when Albert pushed open the stout and heavy door. As it swung shut behind him, he became aware of the close, warm, almost muggy atmosphere of the place, as if all the doors and windows of the building had been kept tight shut during a heatwave and every room had baked and cooked in unrelenting sunshine.

Once again, as he had outside, he felt a sudden onrush of oppressiveness. This he forced himself to shake off and forget.

He saw that there were many faces upturned to greet him. The public bar was, so far as Albert could tell, all but full. How many men were there? Fifteen? Twenty? Five and twenty? All stood or sat or leaned. All held in one hand a flagon or tankard. All were smartly dressed, not formally so but apparelled appropriately for, say, a visit to the country to stay with some distant but wealthy relatives. The ages of the gathering ranged from only a year or two older than he to men who had evidently seen their eightieth year.

They all grinned expectantly at him, as though they had just been told the great majority of a joke and now expected Albert to recite the punchline.

Albert wondered how it was that he, his brother and Jessamy, had stood for some time outside, seen no signs of life within, noticed no-one coming or going and heard no beery chatter or clink of glasses. Behind the bar stood a thin man with silver hair, his arms folded in a posture of amused scepticism.

He peeled back his lips to reveal dirty teeth. "You'd be young Edgington?" he asked. "The smallest of the Edgingtons?"

"I suppose that I would, sir, yes."

A snarl on the man's face. "No, 'sirs' here, son. But your

brother's waiting for you. Back there." He nodded to a dark brown door which Albert noticed now in the gloom at the back of the room. "Saloon bar."

"Oh I see. Thank you."

Albert stared at the figure of who he took to be the landlord. In response, the man grimaced. "Get back there," he said and added: "Your girl's still with him. Though Mrs Anman will be seeing to her shortly."

"Who's Mrs Anman?"

The landlord did not even acknowledge the question. As if at some invisible signal, the whole bar erupted into talking and drinking and ribald badinage.

Albert swallowed hard, lowered his head and walked through the crowd to the brown door. He felt them watching him as he went and he thought again of Jessamy's words outside.

Beyond the door lay a hallway, filled with shadows. A dark crimson patterned rug cushioned the floor. The walls on either side were covered with a jumble of photographs in frames, all with an Indian theme: the Taj Mahal, a picnic in the Bengal, a bright-eyed English baby, robed in white, clasped tight in the arms of her aya. At the end of the corridor, a splash of yellow light upon the ground spilled out from an adjoining room.

From up ahead, Albert heard first the sound of female laughter and then the familiar bray of his brother. He walked towards the noise and light but, halfway there, he stopped and gazed with trepidation, upwards. In the ceiling, a floorboard creaked. Evidently, somebody was moving there but Albert felt with uncanny certainty that it signified more than merely motion, that he was the object of sustained scrutiny. For a space it even seemed to him that he saw something flicker upon the plaster and play about the beam, a bright red light. Then it disappeared. Albert rubbed his eyes but the little light did not return. No further movement could be heard.

Trying, though not entirely succeeding, to set aside his discomfiture, Albert walked on. The room turned out to be the saloon bar, of course, and, in contrast to the public version it was all but deserted. There must have been at least a dozen tables, a cluster of chairs around each, but only one of them was tenanted, by Silas and Jessamy. In the corner was a modestly stocked bar with a neat, black-haired man of around forty standing behind it. His eyes flicked up when Albert walked in though they betrayed not the slightest interest in the new arrival. There was a resemblance in this barman (around the mirthless mouth in particular) which seemed to suggest some familial connection to the publican who had directed Albert here.

"Bertie!" Silas raised a hand imperiously and beckoned Albert over. "We were starting to wonder what the devil had become of you. Sit yourself down, for God's sake, and wet your whistle."

Jessamy looked at him strangely. "What kept you?" she asked.

"Oh, I was just dawdling. Taking in the atmosphere. Strange sort of a place this, isn't it?"

"Isn't it?" Jessamy echoed in a dull tone.

Silas grinned wolfishly. "I got you a pint," he said and Albert saw now that there were four tankards lined up before him, each filled with a dark, oily liquid. Jessamy cradled a small glass in her hands, some light, mysterious drink glistening within.

"Come on!" Silas roared again and patted the nearest chair with the palm of his hand. The bartender watched impassively. Albert took a seat.

No sooner had he done so than Silas was pushing the flagon into his hands and urging him to: "Drink! Drink! Drink!" The eyes of his brother were sparkling with mirth. "Drink it all! Drink it down!"

Jessamy said nothing but looked away, not awkward or embarrassed but only, it seemed to Albert, wholly indifferent.

He took a sip of the thick, glutinous porter and swallowed uncomfortably.

"More!" Silas said and, leaning in, tipped up the glass, forcing Albert to drink faster and deeper. "More! More!"

Albert grinned at first, trying to go along with the spirit of the afternoon, but when he had difficulty in breathing, when his throat felt filled up and when he sensed the rising tide of panic within him, he had no choice but to move his head abruptly to one side and gasp for air.

Silas righted the glass in time but some of the liquid still dribbled from the side of his mouth, speckling his white collars brown. Silas winked and set down the tankard, now half-empty, back on the table.

Albert gasped again for air. His throat burned and his head swam.

"Not a bad start," Silas said. "But it's only a beginning. Now finish the blessed thing and we can all start to relax." He pushed the glass across the table towards him.

Albert blinked. "In a moment," he said. "Just give me a moment."

Silas snorted.

Jessamy glanced towards them both. "He's only young," she said. "Why not leave him be?"

Silas grinned again, entirely without humour. "What's it to you? Not your brother, is he?"

Jessamy shrugged and took a sullen sip of her own drink.

"Come on, Bertie. You don't want to let me down now, do you?"

Again, the glass was pushed closer. "Just finish up this first drink and I'll stop ragging on you for awhile. Trust me, the City is best not entered stone cold sober."

Without replying, Albert reached out his hand, took a deep breath and drank down all that was left in the glass. He swallowed quickly to avoid as much of the taste as possible. When it was done, his head seemed to roar and his skin prickled. Jessamy seemed to look at him with a species of mild disappointment.

Silas nodded in grudging appreciation. Over by the bar, the silent man – son or brother, nephew or cousin of the publican – caught Albert's eye and winked once, a gesture both flagrant and somehow salacious.

From next door there came a sudden cheer – the public bar erupting at some new arrival or fresh joke or observation or, perhaps, Albert thought dully, for no particular reason at all, save that they were here, half-drunk in Eddowes Bay and that the City, whatever it might be, was somehow, mysteriously, close.

VI

"So tell us more, Jessamy, about this job of yours."

Silas' interest in Albert seemed for now to have waned and the whole of his attention was focused instead upon the young woman. If she was at all unsettled by his enquiry, delivered in a half-ironic tone, then she did not show it.

"After all, you've been pretty mum about it so far."

She gave no particular reaction. "I answered a listing in the *Pall Mall Gazette*. I was interviewed in London, at the end of which I was told that the position was mine if I wanted it. I agreed and so I was given directions here."

"But what exactly, madam," Silas smiled, "is the nature of this job?"

Albert was trying hard to follow this conversation but his senses were still in uproar. He had not eaten for hours and his stomach was whinnying in complaint.

He rubbed his eyes and tried to breathe deeply. In spite of the emptiness of this secondary bar he felt penned in and confined. His vision swam. He blinked hard. A second pint glass of porter sat before him, thoroughly unappealing in every way.

He must have missed some of the interchange between his companions because the next thing he heard was his brother saying, apparently in response to some unheard piece of information: "Oh really? Oh have they now? They've got you doing that here, have they?"

Jessamy was unsmiling. "So they tell me."

Albert, trying his best to concentrate, was about to apologise for his temporary inattention and ask the woman to explain to him exactly what she was talking about when a shadow fell over their table.

Quite without Albert having noticed, a stranger had entered the room – in fact, two strangers. Jessamy and Silas had most certainly noticed, however, and they both stared up at the newcomers with curiosity. Of the taverner there was no sign; his bar stood unattended.

One of the strangers was a very tall, muscular man dressed in a dark and dapper suit which was nonetheless noticeably too small for him.

In the ordinary way of things, he would have been a striking and noteworthy individual yet somehow the figure who stood beside him drew the eye away immediately.

She was a short woman with long dark hair and an unusually melodious voice. More than this, Albert could not tell for she was wearing an outfit of a most unusual sort: coloured a faint powder blue, it was something like a robe, cowed and hooded, suggestive in equal parts of monastery and carnival.

Albert could not make out her face in any detail, so capacious was the hood which framed it. Her features lay in shadow and while there was visible a certain elegance there was something also that struck him as being indefinably wrong.

"You must be Jessamy," she said, her voice soft and smooth yet somehow gurgling. "You're every bit as lovely as I've been told."

The woman in the hood ignored Albert and his brother entirely. "My name is Mrs Anman," she said, "and I'll be taking care of you from now on."

"I'm very pleased to meet you," Jessamy said and there was, at least in Albert's estimation, an audible tremor of unease.

Silas, Albert noticed, was looking away, gripping his glass a little too tightly and gazing with improbable interest at the floor. Albert could not bring himself to do the same. There was something fascinating – indeed, there was something fascinatingly *wrong* – about the face of the woman. As surreptitiously as he could, he leaned forwards and tried to take a closer look. He could make out a nose and a pair of bright green eyes but there was something else, something that was different about her, masked by shadow. Without knowing quite why, he glanced down at her hands and noticed, somehow without the least surprise, that she was wearing long thick gloves. No inch of skin was visible.

She was still speaking to Jessamy who nodded with studied seriousness.

"You need to come with me now, my dear. We have to prepare so that you might best perform your duties."

"Yes, ma'am. Of course, ma'am."

At this, there was a note of absolute compliance in Jessamy's voice of which Albert would not hitherto have believed her capable.

The soft, strange voice of Mrs Anman went silkily on: "Now you've not been to the City before have you, my dear?"

"No, ma'am."

"Nor are you personally acquainted with any other of your sex who has?"

"Not so far as I am aware, ma'am."

Silas, who had even in Albert's earliest memories been characterised by his garrulous nature – a noisy child, a preternaturally confident schoolboy and now a loud and insistent adult, the kind of man who, in the right company, was capable of vulgarity – still said nothing at all and looked down beside him. Albert wondered if this was the product of embarrassment (surely not) or whether it was something more.

"Time to go, ma'am."

These were the first four words that the man in the suit had spoken. He had an accent, from somewhere north of Coventry, which Albert could not readily place.

The woman in the hood inclined her head in response and for an instant Albert thought that he saw something that was more than shadow.

Was there something, he wondered, on her face? A birth mark? A discolouration of some kind, the consequence of injury or disease? Or even (surely not) excessive hair?

"Come along, Jessamy," the woman said. "We should let these fine young gentlemen enjoy the preliminaries. Mayhap you will see them again in the City."

Jessamy's eyes met Albert's then and he saw the reluctance in them, and the doubt.

"Jessamy?" the woman said again, more firmly than before.

"Of course," said Jessamy and rose with purpose. "The brothers Edgington, I bid you farewell. At least for now."

In a most unladylike fashion, she took her glass, still half-full and swallowed the rest of it in one swift gulp. "Goodbye," she said, to Albert but not to Silas, and then she was moving away, flanked by that strange pair, moving across the room and towards the exit, her eyes cast back in what, if Albert was not mistaken, was something like an expression of imploring.

All at once, Albert was gripped by a compulsion – to stand up, to rush towards Jessamy, to take her by the hand and run out of this place to the strange streets beyond, to get her away at all costs from the soft-voiced Mrs Anman and the ghoul who walked beside her.

Without realising that he was doing it, he found himself tensing, his muscles tautening, ready to rise and to run.

He felt the hand of his elder brother then, hard upon his shoulder. "Don't be a fool, man. Stay where you are and stay quiet."

So forceful was Silas' voice and so different was it from his usual tones that Albert obeyed without question.

Half a minute later, and Jessamy had left the room with her guides or captors. The two siblings were alone.

VII

It seemed suddenly very quiet and still. From next door there came a muffled roar of excited approval. Albert felt the removal of the pressure on his arm.

He looked over at his brother and saw the older man's face set in an expression of uncharacteristic gravity. Then, sensing, Albert supposed, that he was being observed, Silas broke in a big, wide and almost convincing grin.

"No need to look so glum, Bertie. Trust me, there's plenty more where she came from."

"The woman…" Albert said. "In the hood. Mrs Anman… Was there… I mean, didn't you think, that there was something wrong with her?"

"Dear me, but I thought we'd been raised better than that. Don't be impertinent, Bertie, and don't pry when the lady so clearly desires her privacy. And now, for goodness sake, have another drink." He pushed the second flagon towards Albert who only looked at it uneasily.

"Drink, Bertie, for God's sake."

"Silas… I'm hungry."

"There'll be food later. Once we get to the City. And plenty of it."

"When will that be? How will we get there? And do you think Jessamy is already on her way?"

"You'll see soon enough. I hardly want to spoil the surprise. So just drink up, try to smile and stop asking so many damn fool questions."

Somehow Albert found himself taking the glass up in both hands, raising it to his lips, drinking, and giving in to a surge of warm, all-encompassing, pleasurable confusion. As he drank, he noticed that the custodian of the bar had returned and that he was now watching them both with mistrustful eyes.

VIII

Albert thought later that around an hour must have passed until something in him finally snapped and he fled the Idler's Rest only to begin, unwittingly, the final leg of his journey to the City.

It should be noted that this figure was necessarily approximate as much of that time, Albert spent in a haze. The strangeness of the long day combined with the application of alcohol contrived to lend events the shift and shimmer of a dream. Later, he could recollect his brother talking, though not the topic of their conversation. He could remember the return of the unsmiling barman who bore more drinks on a gleaming new tin tray. He could recollect taking more strong drink himself, more than he had ever drunk in his life before. He could recollect, after a while, the arrival of others, men of all ages dressed smartly and already on their way to inebriation who filled up the saloon bar in small yet noticeable increments. Some of these people, Silas seemed to know, at least by sight, and he exchanged greetings and badinage with them.

By the time that the hour was up, the place was noisy with an insistent male hum and thick with tobacco smoke. Albert's head swam. Blood thundered in his ears. He felt, although he knew that he was not, very much like a prisoner.

He found himself unable not to think of Jessamy, to fret, in spite of the lag and confusion which now affected his mental processes, about her safety.

Silas was engaged in a robust discussion with a stout young whiskered gentleman about the question of Irish Home Rule. Their voices were raised and their manner was disputatious although as far as Albert could tell they seemed to be agreeing violently with one another.

Albert closed his eyes, settled back in his set and tried to make sense of it all. He believed himself to be unobserved but he was in this mistaken. When he opened his eyes again it was to find the barman all but crouching by his side, grinning levelly at him.

"Another drink, sir?"

Albert shook his head.

"Come now, Mr Edgington. Why not have one more to prepare yourself for the night ahead?"

"Thank you. But I believe I've had enough."

The smiling man did not move or alter his expression. "There's no such thing as 'enough', sir. Not round here." He leaned closer, so close that Albert caught the stale scent of his breath.

Beside him, Silas talked on. The sounds of the room surged and roiled. Smoke stung his eyes and there was an all but intolerable pressure upon his bladder. Suddenly and instinctively, Albert rose to his feet.

"Excuse me. I need to take some air."

The barman stepped back. Silas glanced up. "Bertie?"

Albert did not reply but only forced himself to walk away, out of the saloon, back into the ruck of the public bar and, eventually, out of the door and into the open air, the streets of Eddowes Bay. He stood alone, swaying slightly. In the distance he could hear the hiss of the sea. Gratefully, he breathed in and filled his lungs.

A momentary clarity came to him then and he looked about him to take in the scene in greater detail.

The town was busier than before. The streets were filling up with what he took to be visitors as all were smartly dressed and had the languid yet eager gait of the tourist or spectator. Albert could hear the sounds of lively conversation and enthusiastic laughter. A trio of neatly bearded gentlemen with the air of country solicitors walked past him to the pub and nodded in amicable greeting.

It took him a minute to place exactly where he had witnessed such an atmosphere of happy expectation before. It had been at the theatre or the opera; the loose chatter of anticipation was that which presaged some long-expected performance.

Had he thought that everyone abroad in Eddowes Bay was male, however improbable that sounded? He had and so far as he could see he was in this assumption very nearly correct. In the distance, however, heading away from the centre of the town and towards the sea, Albert saw a familiar hooded figure: Mrs Anman.

With an odd, unexamined determination which might have surprised even the version of him who had waited outside the gates of St Barnaby's mere hours before, he stepped away from the Idler's Rest and hurried after the cowled woman.

Something occurred to Albert as he walked as quickly as he could through the streets of Eddowes Bay. The town was ordered and regular, laid out in a clear grid. He had read of such manmade phenomena, of course, to be found in America in particular but he had never seen such a thing in England. The sense of symmetry seemed altogether out of place. Although he could not imagine precisely why this might have been done he most certainly found it useful, in his still drink-sodden state, to be able to navigate. Albert followed Mrs Anman to the end of the high street and its small row of shops, all of which seemed, unusually, still to be open.

Without looking around her, Mrs Anman turned left into a side street which led, after a series of narrow archways, into a different sector of the town, not so picturesque and attractive as the rest – row after row of grey, almost mean-looking residences, which, unlike many at the heart of the place, showed clear signs of habitation. Here, where the streets were once again all but empty and where there were certainly no perambulating well-dressed gentlemen, Mrs Anman paused once and turned around. As she stopped and seemed to lift up her head, Albert rushed into the welcoming shadows of a nearby porch.

He felt a surely ridiculous certainty that the woman was sniffing the air, as if she had caught his scent upon it. Albert heard a sound, a weird, high-pitched whinnying. Then the woman turned once again and began to run. She moved very fast indeed, melting almost immediately into the gathering dark. Why was she alone? Where was she heading? Where was Jessamy?

After only a few seconds of entirely forgivable doubt, Albert began to give chase.

He ran as fast as he could. Somehow the consumption of the night seemed only to hasten his flight, at least at first, as he dashed through the final few streets of the town and reached the edge of its circumference. The silhouette of the hooded woman glided before him.

Very soon the streets gave way first to grass and then to stones then to sand as Albert found himself endeavouring to move upon the beach. Almost without his becoming aware of it, the great dark slab of the sea bore up nearby, all but swallowing the horizon. In the distance was a small stone hut. The sound of the tides grew very loud indeed. Albert struggled. His sides ached and his stomach groaned in mutiny.

He thought too that he had lost sight of the woman. Perhaps, he thought, he had been mistaken in believing that she had come to the beach to begin with. What, after all, would she want in such a place at such an hour?

Then he saw her, closer than he had believed, but still moving away from him towards the point where the water met the land. He hastened after her but his movements had become tired and flailing. He lost his footing and fell back heavily upon the sand. The jolt of it caused him to cry out. He began to struggle upright and as he did so he saw something which at first he could not believe: the woman stopped, turned swiftly around and then seemed herself to topple forwards. Yet this was no mere fall. Rather, she became a dark shape upon the ground and seemed to surge forwards. With a thrill of horror, Albert understood that she was moving at great speed towards him and that she was doing so upon all fours.

It seemed too incredible to credit yet the sight was undeniable. Instinctively, Albert loosed a cry of fear. He stumbled upright, though this was but a temporary thing. Seconds later, he had been thrown over again to the sand, this time with Mrs Anman upon him. Held firm against the beach, pinioned by the woman as the sea breeze pushed back her billowing hood, Albert saw at last what he had begun, queasily and fearfully, to suspect: that Mrs Anman was not in truth a woman at all, nor human.

In the light of the moon he could only glimpse the nightmarish truth of it – that the face of the creature was covered in sleek, dark fur and that, while the top half of her features seemed ordinary enough, the lower half was altogether monstrous. In place of mouth and chin there was instead to be seen a great, protuberant bill, a long, hard snout.

She barked out a laugh, a harsh, and alien sound. He could taste her breath upon his skin, both salty and sour.

"Happy now?" she said and the sound of her voice was angular and weird upon that deserted stretch of coastal land. "Have you seen what you came to see?"

"I'm sorry," Albert said, instinctively and without quite knowing why. "I didn't understand… How could I have known?"

At this, Mrs Anman only snapped her bill. Almost idly, Albert found himself wondering how so peculiar a proboscis could ever have formed speech which had sounded even so much as passably human.

She leaned closer to him and he flinched away, wriggling upwards against the ground. Given the nature of her physiognomy it ought to have been impossible to tell but somehow Albert felt certain that Anman was at that moment smiling at him.

Then without warning, her bill came down hard, a hair's breadth away from the skin on the left-hand side of his face. He yelped in fear and surprise.

"Stop," he said but it was too late. She did it again, this time on the right, drawing blood now. The pain was sharp and shocking.

"Please." He struggled to free himself but she was too solid and heavy. He felt certain that he was being toyed with by a practised predator and felt an acute sympathy with the field mouse as it spies, too late, the shadow of the barn owl overhead. Again, the creature raised its beak. Albert sensed that the games may be over and that this next assault may cause a great deal more than a scratch.

Yet before he could call out, Mrs Anman stopped, her head still lifted high, and turned her face a fraction towards the sea as though she were listening to some distant voice, caught only faintly on the breeze.

"Yes," she said (Albert was certain that it was not to him to whom she was speaking), "if you think he may yet serve a purpose."

If any reply came, then Albert did not hear it. Mrs Anman paused for a moment, then bowed her head as if in supplication. Unexpectedly, she spoke his name.

"Albert Edgington." Each familiar syllable sounded strange in her voice. Another pause, and then a sigh and then in a sleek, single motion, the creature was off him and moving at speed towards the sea. Albert was, unexpectedly, gloriously free.

He ran then as fast as he could back towards the town, away from the callous gaze of the ocean. He half-expected to hear the Anman-creature behind him, in pursuit again, the awful crunch of her feet upon the stones, the shrill glissando of her laughter. He imagined that his apparent liberation was to be revealed as a hoax, all part of whatever bloodthirsty game she had been playing. He considered the hare being run ragged by dogs before the kill.

At the edge of the beach he hesitated. Some unbidden instinct made him pause and turn about to see the truth of his fears.

The shore was deserted and the sea was still. Of Mrs Anman there was no longer any sign. Then Albert looked further, towards the horizon and it seemed to him that he glimpsed, out towards the dark horizon something vast and tentacular and impossible.

He could not accept the truth of what he thought he saw and so he rubbed at his eyes like a child waking from bad dreams. When he looked again the sea seemed flat and empty, that brief vision no more, apparently, than a mirage.

Albert ran onwards, headlong and pell-mell, filled up with fear and wonder.

IX

The town of Eddowes Bay, when Albert arrived, ragged and perspiring, seemed once again to be altogether deserted. Gone were the strolling men, the ambling drinkers, the smartly dressed strangers with an air of happy expectation. Everything seemed entirely abandoned, like a stage after the theatre has been locked up for the night.

Edgington did not pass a single person on his flight through the streets nor did he see any sign that anyone had passed through before him. Even the air had a quality of motionlessness, as if it had long been undisturbed.

He went first to the Idler's Rest. The door seemed jammed shut, stuck in its frame. A frantic shove pushed it open. There was only silence within. Public and saloon bar, both were empty. Even the barmen had vanished. So far as Albert could discern, the entire establishment stood vacant and untenanted.

"Silas?" His voice sounded puny and Albert suspected that no answer would come but he felt compelled nonetheless to speak the name. Again, louder this time: "Silas, where are you?"

The noise was dead and flat. No human voice replied yet it seemed to Albert that there was a response of a sort: as from somewhere in the distance came the resonant clang of a single tolling bell.

The church? Could it be, he wondered wildly, that the people of Eddowes Bay had sought some form of sanctuary there? Hours before little would have struck him as more unlikely but it seemed now no more improbable than much else which he had witnessed.

Albert strode out through the bar and into the open air. The bell still tolled and he followed it through empty streets till the little church hove into view.

As he approached, Albert saw that it was as though all the life that existed in this queer town was concentrated in that temple. The door was open and warm light beckoned. With a neatness which might under other circumstances have seemed almost comical as Edgington reached the entrance the bell ceased to toll.

A single, righteous male voice came from within. It sounded as though the end of a homily or sermon had just been reached.

"...and that is the wisdom which we have been granted to see for ourselves in the truth of the kingdom..."

Albert ran inside, quite uncertain as to what to expect. Yet the scene which awaited him seemed on the surface to be a wholly conventional one.

The church was full of a congregation. All were men and all were dressed expensively and in some style: the various individuals, Albert had no doubt, whom he had already encountered on the streets and in the tavern over the course of this long and terrible evening. Their general attitude and demeanour was more sombre than before but there seemed all the same to be a strata of irony and playfulness just behind the mask of probity.

At the head of the aisle before the altar there was a pleasant-looking young man, not very much older than Edgington himself, dressed in surplice and dog-collar and standing with his hands outspread.

"And now before we pray," he said. "A moment's silent reflections."

If the priest had noticed Albert's arrival then he gave no indication of the fact. No other person turned to see him.

Albert walked forwards, between the ranks of wooden pews. A part of him wanted to shout out, to speak of what he had seen down by the water's edge. Yet no-one seemed to pay him the slightest mind. For a mad moment, he wondered if he had somehow been turned invisible, if, like some spirit, he could not be seen by any there present.

Three rows from the front, he spied his brother, watching the priest with an expression of amused curiosity.

"Silas!" Albert half-called, half-whispered.

The older man did not seem to hear him.

"Silas!"

His brother turned his head, with doleful, blinking slowness. "Oh," he said. "There you are."

"Silas–"

"Shh." His brother raised a finger theatrically to his lips. "Better stand next to me," he said. "Prayers now. You'll like this bit."

At this, Albert behaved just as his years of education had conditioned him: he stepped to the end of the row, stood beside his brother and lowered his head in a pose of contemplation. He even, upon instinct, closed his eyes.

Then the prayers began.

X

They were not prayers that Albert had ever heard before. There was something subtly disquieting about them, almost unchristian. The pastor led the way but soon plenty of the gentlemen who stood in solemn ranks were intoning along with him.

"Let us speak now the word of the law," said the man of the cloth. "Let us know what it is to go upon two legs and let us be truly thankful for that honour."

As he spoke, the priest began to process alone down the aisle and towards the great wooden door through which Albert had entered minutes before.

"To go upon two legs… that is the way of our law."

The last four words of this were spoken also by the crowd. Silas dug hard into Albert's ribs. "Speak up!"

"To take what we must from those upon four legs and from they who were born in that same estate."

Again, the same response came – "that is the way of our law" – and on this occasion Albert was fast enough to join in with most of it.

By now the priest had reached the door. Somewhat unusually, he continued to speak even as he pulled it shut and drew across the bolt. The sound of it echoed. "To draw water from the earth and to pull down fire from the firmament."

The same response: "That is the way of our law."

The priest turned back and smiled. "To help where we can, to give aid and succour to those who truly are in need."

There came then one final, massed response, heartier than before: "That is the way of our law."

This done, there seemed to spread amongst the assemblage, an air of relief, as at the discharging of some necessary chore.

Hastily, Albert turned towards his brother. "I need to talk to you."

"Not now," he said.

"Silas, it's urgent."

In an unwelcome flash of self-knowledge, Albert heard the whine in his own voice. "Silas, please."

The priest had returned to his place before the altar. He raised his hands once more. "We are good men," he said. "We are honourable men. And now, in light of our acts and deeds, let us enjoy our reward!"

As he spoke there came to be felt in the church a faint but distinct rumbling sound combined with a slight tremor in the ground.

"Silas?"

His brother looked at him with a savage smile. "I said – not now."

"But… I saw…"

The smile grew wider. "It doesn't matter what you've seen," he said. "It's as nothing to what lies before us."

The rumbling increased and the tremor in the earth grew more pronounced. All around them, the gentlemen stood quite still, pictures of unconcern.

Albert flinched as he felt his brother's right hand tight about his left arm.

"Try to relax, old chap. Try to enjoy it. Though it's always a bit unnerving the first time."

Before them, the priest was lowering his arms.

"My apologies," he began. "There may be some delay of a technical nature. Please allow me to–"

Yet he could say no more for at that moment it felt as though the floor itself gave way and there came at once both darkness and an awful, terrifying sense of plummeting. It was a long, dreadful descent. Albert screamed and he was in that crowd of men in this by no means alone. He felt Silas' grip tighten.

"Be brave," he murmured. "If you can't bear it, close your eyes!"

In the roar and run of the moment, Albert did as was suggested and shut tight his eyes.

In the darkness he wondered if he might not be going quite mad, as if he were still at the gates of St Barnaby's and that all of this was some crazed hallucination.

Yet when he opened his eyes again, he found himself in a place of inarguable reality. He found himself, at long last, in the City of Dr Moreau.

XI

The first words that Albert heard in the darkness were those of his brother.

"It's quite something, don't you think? As a feat of engineering, I mean."

Albert did not reply – indeed, he could not, so utter was his discombobulation. It seemed certain to him that he had moved yet he still stood upon the same stone floor. The same pew was still behind him, his sibling stood beside him and (so far as Albert was able to tell) the same dark-suited gentlemen were all around him.

There was, however, almost no light at all and he was able to perceive no more than shapes and shadows. In the gloom he heard the high, confident voice of the padre.

"If you wouldn't mind bearing with us for just a shade of a fraction longer. We hope at any moment to be able to bring you… luminescence."

No sooner had he finished speaking than a dim light did become apparent, from the direction of the great wooden doors, a sharp white glow. The doors were opened then and the glow became a glare. At last, Albert Edgington found his words.

"Where are we? What's happened?"

"Oh we've travelled," Silas began, soon having to raise the volume of his speech since all of those others who had come to Eddowes Bay for who knew what reason had also now begun to chat and murmur, their studied ease and casual postures hinting at some suppressed excitement.

"We've gone down, that's all. We're beneath the surface."

"How far?"

"My best guess? Around a hundred feet. But that's only an estimate."

"The floor…" Albert stumbled towards understanding. "It was in truth then, a kind of elevator?"

Silas nodded. "As I say, it's quite something, don't you think? And it obviously had you fooled. Had no idea what you were really stepping into, did you?"

A horrible kind of anxiety scuttled into Albert's chest. "Why? What's it for?"

"Just a bit of mummery. Nothing to be taken too seriously." Now the church was flooded with light though darkness still clung to its stained glass windows.

"Feel free, please, gentlemen, to step outside whenever you're ready. You'll be pleased to know that we've arrived safely at the City. Please do as you will for the next eight hours. We will reconvene here at six o'clock to return to the surface."

He had not finished speaking before several of the congregation, evidently frequent visitors, began to file out of the church doors and into that unnatural light which lay beyond.

Silas gave Albert a look of pure impatience. "Come on. Look lively."

Albert reached out and tugged at his elder brother's sleeve, a gesture he had not made since the nursery, at least not with the same urgent instinct. "But where are we?"

"You know where we are," Silas said, all but shoving Albert out into the aisle. "Now come with me. It's high time we started to explore."

XII

For reasons which shall soon become apparent, for many years after this long and terrible night, Albert Edgington was asked by the curious exactly what it had been like to step for the first time through the doors of that remarkable edifice, out into the City.

At first, Albert would say he felt only trepidation as he walked behind his swaggering brother into the white light. This was succeeded, he would always say, with a touch of that winsome self-deprecation which had become his calling card, by a feeling of mild disappointment as the space beyond the church was revealed to be simply a very large and pale vestibule into which the gentlemen had been decanted.

At the far side of it (and the only visible exit in that huge, featureless space) was a small green door, a frame through which only one individual could pass at any given time and into which, in orderly single file, the group was now processing. The effect was, the elder Albert would say, something like discovering that a hallway provided the sole human entrance into Heaven (and a hallway at that which was most likely located in some corner of the civil service, a great Whitehall nest of clerks and panjandrums, of junior mandarins and governors in training).

So Albert and his brother joined the queue and patiently waited their turn, moving forward very slowly one step closer at a time.

Although there was some conversation around them, Silas himself did not seem at all anxious to talk. He looked away or behind him, catching the eye of some associate or acquaintance and exchanging salutations and courteous enquiries as though nothing outré had occurred at all and they were waiting simply to gain egress to some perfectly ordinary London club.

Certainly, he did all that he could to evade conversation with his brother.

Albert sensed this and made only fitful efforts to initiate a dialogue. Once he tried to ask Silas more about who had built all of it and why, to receive only a blank expression and a murmured "not for yours to reason why…"

Tiring of the secrecy and persistent strangeness of the day, he found himself all but crying out, "I saw a woman by the water's edge, and she was not a woman at all, not even human."

Several heads turned to look at him in the wake of this outburst. His brother hushed him with a gesture. "For goodness' sake, keep a civil tongue in your head. There's nobody here who wants to hear that sort of language."

"Silas, please, I—"

"Later, I promise." His brother sounded solemn. "You have my word that all will shortly become plain."

Succumbing to the inevitable gravity of the night, Albert said nothing in response as the line edged slowly forwards.

He was often asked by those who had come to believe in his political cause whether or not he regretted not doing more to disrupt the order of things there and then, whether he had come to believe in his middle years that his much younger self should have been very much more forceful.

At this, Albert always went very quiet and still before, after a pause, replying: "I should not think so, no. For what could I have done to change anything? What could I have possibly said which would have changed the course of that night? Why, I'd only have plunged myself into a trouble. No, no. I kept my counsel then and to have done so was simply a matter of self-preservation. Nowadays, of course, is a very different matter."

And so the line moved forwards and in time the Edgington brothers shuffled to the head of it. Three or four back from the front, Albert became aware of raised voices from beyond the door, and the sounds of queer music, and the smells of odd, alien scents, of exotic foods and impossible blooms.

Then, almost before he knew it, they were at the entrance. Silas went first and Albert followed, out at last of that weird, dull void and into the place which lay beyond.

XIII

How best to describe the City through Albert's eyes?

It was, he said, more a question of impression than incidents, more potent sensation than details to be recalled in tranquillity. There was, he would often say, something of the island in *The Tempest* to the whole experience:

> *"Be not afeard; the isle is full of noises,*
> *Sounds and sweet airs, that give delight, and hurt not.*
> *Sometimes a thousand twangling instruments*
> *Will hum about mine ears; and sometime voices*
> *That, if I then had waked after long sleep,*
> *Will make me sleep again"*

In truth, the allusion was more a helpful shorthand to the elder Albert Edgington than it was any particular piece of accuracy, relying as it did on his schoolboy memory of a drama which, as adulthood wore on and for reasons which he did not care to examine too closely, he found more and more unnerving.

Nonetheless, there *were* strange sounds in that place – high, chittering yelps; low bass roar and rumbles; a chattering, a swooping, a mewing and the weird ripples of laughter which, whilst sporadically charming, also did not sound quite female nor altogether human.

And there were scents too, as of weird perfumes and improbable blooms, combinations of sweetness which Albert had never smelled before nor ever would again, for all that he lived almost long enough to see old age.

The light was dim at first and it was not golden but rather of pink and amber hues. No source for this illumination was immediately apparent.

It ought to be stressed that the City was a real place, an actual conurbation, a settlement built of stone and rock, timber and glass. The architecture was of a quaint kind, though studiedly so, as if it had been built by those who had never visited any town in Europe but had only read of such places in the faded pages of ancient books.

The street onto which Albert emerged in the wake of his brother was cobbled and the houses which flanked it upon either side were high and crooked, drawn seemingly from the late seventeenth or early eighteenth centuries. The crowd of men surged along it, stopping to gawp at the citizens of that place who were standing amongst them or at lighted doors or leaning from open windows into the perpetual night.

Ah, yes. The citizens. The people of the City. None of them was human, at least not wholly so. Every single one was a creature of the island, every one a beast-person. On that first vista alone, there were at least a dozen separate species. Young Albert looked about him, in both wonderment and terror, unsure at first whether he had simply fallen asleep in the car beside his brother and all that had befallen him since had been the product merely of bad dreams. The alternative – that every moment of it was real – seemed too bizarre to contemplate.

"Oh do try not to gawp so," said Silas, who had turned around a yard or so before him. "You look like such an ingenue."

"Sorry," said Albert, purely on instinct since he did not in truth feel at all apologetic. "But what exactly is this place?"

Silas grinned. "Why, this is only the tip of it."

"But all these… people. What are they? Actors? Performers of some kind? Clowns?"

"You know that they are not."

"Silas… are you, sure… I mean, this is all just so deeply strange."

"I think you'll find that you can become accustomed to it. Sooner than you think." Silas shrugged. "Look here, I don't have the time for this. I'm here for my own pleasure too, you know."

"Silas," Albert began, though before he could say more a stranger linked arms with him, the gesture swift and proprietorial.

"Are you new here?" said a soft female voice, hot against Albert's ear.

Albert turned to face the speaker whose form was now very close to him.

She was dressed, as had Mrs Anman been, in a long flowing cape and a great blue hood. Though the face of this person was not hidden.

On the contrary, she peered out with a wide smile and neat white teeth. Her eyes were, as the writers of romance would have it, made of pure sparkling blue. And every inch of all her visible skin was covered with fine, silky brown fur.

Albert looked back only to see his brother wink at him.

"You've found a guide, Albert. Well done. Now be a good boy and try to enjoy yourself, won't you?"

Without waiting for a reply, he pushed his shoulders back, adopted a forceful pose and walked away, into the crowd towards the end of the street.

The woman said, liltingly: "What is your name?"

"Albert."

"It's a nice name. I am Faun."

"Faun?" Albert frowned, his senses reeling. But then, as he had been trained to do in all the years of his expensive education, good manners came into play. "Well, I'm jolly pleased to meet you."

The woman linked arms with Albert Edgington. "Come, I will show all the marvels of our City."

"Thank you. You're very kind."

She squeezed his arm. "You've arrived, let me tell you, upon the most interesting of nights…"

And with this, she led him away.

XIV

Although he would tell his story often and in great detail in the years which were to follow, Albert was always coy about what occurred in the hours between his meeting the woman who gave her name as Faun and the beginning of the violence.

They wandered, he said, through the streets of that strange subterranean place, and they ate and drank many odd things. Time seemed to him to become elastic and there were many pleasures to which he was that night introduced. His memory, he said, was affected by what he ingested.

The City at that time was most assuredly a miracle, though one underscored by darkness. Many and varied were its courtyards and palisades. Wondrous were the high staircases, the low temples, the narrow paths and the mighty thoroughfares. It had at once the quality both of a set and a dream. There was much which was illusory and much which was performed. Yet the great majority was real – tangible and visceral. It was this, of course, not the coating of make-believe but the substructure of undeniable reality, which brought wealth and privilege there in such quantities.

Albert's most abiding memories of this odd lull were twofold. The first of them was the people of the City, of which Faun and Mrs Anman were amongst the least bizarre examples. For everywhere he looked were the most remarkable hybrid creatures, every one of them (though Albert himself did not yet know it) a descendant of the peoples of the Island. Here were cheetah-people and goat-men, women who were at least half antelope and those who were semi-hippo. After an early burst of shock, Albert simply accepted it all, much in the manner as certain mystics are said to accept without question the most unearthly visions.

The second memory from this period which stayed with him was something less immediately peculiar: the curious profusion of statues. There they were, at the end of every road, the centre of every cul-de-sac, raised high about street level in some places and placed almost upon the walkways themselves in another. It was not merely the sheer number of them which struck Albert as strange but also the fact that, although they differed widely in their individual details, they seemed to depict the same man. He was large, clean-shaven and dressed in what appeared to be a sort of white safari suit. He did not look quite like anyone whom Albert had ever met, though there was something dimly familiar about him all the same, as though he had encountered him long ago, back in some other life.

He kept intending to ask his guide the reason for the repetition of this figure, again and again throughout the City, yet the moment for quiet conversation never came. Instead, Faun led him on to ever weirder locations, to parties which seemed to have been going on for days, to carnival processions which seemed to be entirely spontaneous, to mad jamborees which filled the boy up with sights and sensations of every kind. And so the impossible night wore on.

XV

The point at which Albert Edgington's memories became more detailed and precise must have been around four to five hours after his entrance to the City and the moment when Faun first took his arm. He had become separated from his guide after they had left some extravagant gathering or other and taken once again to the streets. The specifics of this eluded Albert but somehow he had found himself alone at the end of an empty road, without any sign of any of the denizens of that place, let alone his brother or any other human visitor.

There was a path leading off from the main avenue into a small, shaded courtyard, centred around a single tree. Its leaves were an unearthly violet and weird vegetation flourished at its base, all the flora of the island transported here and changed in the long darkness.

Grateful for the chance of silence and respite, he walked on, down the lane to the courtyard and stood before the tree. In the distance he could still hear all the sounds of night-time merriment which typified the City, though it sounded comfortingly faraway. He thought of how he had come here, of the curious set-up of the village known as Eddowes Bay, of the crazy rigmarole of the entry and the forbidden tang of the underworld itself. He stood and sucked in sweetened air and thought of Silas' glee and he had to admit, if only to the most secret part of his soul, that he understood entirely the dark allure of the place.

He noticed then that behind the tree stood an unmoving figure. Stepping forward to get a better view, Albert called out ("Hello!") only to feel foolish a second later as he realised that he was facing nothing more than another of the City's plentiful statues.

Then a voice came from behind him. "I met him once, you know."

Albert, startled, spun around to see that there was a man standing in the shadows behind him. He must have been very silent and very still for the schoolboy had not so much as suspected his presence until now.

"Who are you?" Albert asked.

The man walked forwards, into the light. He was a small, slender man, white-haired. Ignoring Albert's question, he nodded at the statue.

"Of course, he didn't exactly look like that. And no statue can capture the way in which he moved: wild energy, focused and suppressed by iron control. I often wonder how quickly it took upon that island of his for all that control to ebb away. How swiftly he frayed at the edges." The man turned away from the statue and directed his gaze towards Albert. It was as if he was only just seeing him now, for the first time. He shook his head, the very picture of a gentleman striving to restore order over himself. He forced a rictus smile, like an unwilling host greeting guests a party he'd avoided successfully for years. "I'm so sorry. How remiss of me. Who precisely are you?"

"I'm Albert Edgington. I'm… well, I suppose I'm a guest here really. And you?"

"My name is Vaughan," said the other. "No first name. Not important."

"Pleased to meet you, Mr Vaughan. Are you a guest here too?" Even as he asked the question, Albert knew that the answer could scarcely be a simple "yes". There was something wrong with the man, a vagueness suggestive of illness.

"Not exactly," said Vaughan. "In a sense, I'm the owner. Or architect. Yes, perhaps that is a better, more accurate term."

"I see," Albert said and then found himself entirely unable to think of anything sensible to say next.

Vaughan was happy to speak without any need for prompting. He seemed, Albert thought, like a man in want of an audience. "You must be wondering how the idea for all of this came to me. What was the kernel of it? A night, long ago, years before you were born, before you were even thought of, I went into the laboratory of the man you see now before me, immortalised in stone."

Albert found his voice. "What was his name?" he asked. "The subject of these statues?"

The answer came. "Moreau."

Edgington shrugged. "My brother mentioned him before. But until then I'd never heard of him."

"Truly?"

The schoolboy shook his head.

"You've never heard of The Moreau Horrors? The Ratcliffe Charnel-House? The monstrous dog?"

"Never."

"How quickly the truth is lost. How swiftly history forgets." Mr Vaughan sighed, apparently disconsolate. "And speaking of forgetting, I very much fear that your name has already escaped me."

"Edgington, sir. Albert Edgington."

"Of course it is, my boy. Of course it is. My own memory's not what it was, you know. Everything's starting to seem a little misty. And there are moments when the past and the present become in my mind quite tangled. Even times when I do believe I spy something like the future. A woman on some impossible train. A transformation in a hotel. Then, change on a scale undreamed of even by me."

"I see, sir. That must be... jolly distracting for you."

Mr Vaughan nodded, with unexpected enthusiasm. "That's it. That's it exactly. Distracting." He smiled as if at a distant memory. "Do you think it's something about this place, Edgington? Something eating me alive like this? Nibbling away at all I've ever known?"

The older man paused for a long while after this—so long, in fact, that Albert thought he was expected to reply.

"I'm sure I couldn't say, sir."

Vaughan showed not the slightest sign of having heard him. He went on speaking, as though unaware that there had been a gap of any kind. "Do you think it's something essential in the soil and the rock that's about us? Some poison or toxin? Or do you think it has to do with me? With the way in which I've lived my life?"

Albert swallowed and fidgeted, in just the way that he had

always been taught not to. "I'm sorry, sir… I don't have the knowledge to say."

"Unwilling to make a diagnosis, eh?"

"I'm not a doctor, sir."

Vaughan peered at him. "No, I don't expect you are. You don't have the look of a sawbones about you. And I've known a few in my time."

"I think I should go, sir. My brother will be waiting. Is there anyone I should fetch, Mr Vaughan? Is there anyone who'll be…" He found himself unable to complete the sentence.

Vaughan grinned and Albert received the strong sensation that his own discomfort was providing pleasure to the older man. "Yes?"

"I meant to say: is there anyone who'll be missing you?"

Mr Vaughan said nothing. He seemed to be considering the question. At length: "No. And I'm not so sure that there ever has been. My mother, perhaps, when I was very young… A girl, once, long ago…" He winked rather grotesquely. "You should go, Mr Edgington. Find your brother. Enjoy the City. The peoples of this place can be very generous."

With this, the conversation seemed done and the little man turned away and began to scuttle away. There was, Albert thought, something beetle-like in his gait.

"It was nice to meet you!" he called after him, though this was far from the truth.

Vaughan stopped short then and Edgington thought at first that it was because he meant to speak some more to him. He realised the truth a few seconds later. For all the older man's evident confusion, certain of his senses were still unusually acute.

Faraway, in the distance, there could be heard the sound of screaming.

"What is that?" Albert asked. "Who is that?"

Vaughan blinked. "Sounds human," he said. "I know the screams of the Beast People and that is not one of them."

The first scream was joined now by others. And by other sounds also: cries of conflict, of steel upon steel and – once, twice, three times – the sharp retort of gunfire.

"Mr Vaughan?"

The man wore an expression of the most curious and paradoxical sort: suspicion, fear and what seemed to Albert to be something like relief. "At last," he said. He sighed. "I knew this day would come. Any student of history would have said the same. I told them, Mr Edgington. Never let it be said that I did not tell them. Let it be recorded that they simply refused to listen."

The sounds were very much less distant now. Whatever its cause, the violence was moving in their direction. More screams. The angry punctuation of gunshots. And fierce, strange cries, of exultant ululation, which were surely not formed by any human throat.

For a long moment, the two men stood in that secluded place as if frozen there, as if paralysed, able only to hear the fearful approach of the mob.

Then, as the ruckus drew near, Albert heard it, quite distinctly, rising up out of the melee, a voice filled with pain and fear: "Albert! Albert! Help me!"

XVI

For just an instant longer, Albert Edgington remained in a state approximate to paralysis. The strangenesses and horrors of the night seemed to him to be almost overwhelming. Then the desperate cry came again, audible even above the wild shrieks and hollers of the crowd.

"Albert! For God's sake!"

The schoolboy turned, hesitated. The little man was watching him from his place at the edge of the square.

"It's my brother. That's my brother's voice."

Vaughan shrugged. "I wouldn't go to him," he said. "Not if I were you."

"I have to."

"They will, I think, be in a state of some considerable rage. Men such as your brother will not by them be received… kindly."

"I have to help him."

"You can come with me. I know all the secret places of the City. I can keep you safe until the rioters are quelled." Vaughan looked as though he cared little for the answer, as though he were speaking these words purely out of courtesy.

Once more, the screams and antic shouts drew closer. Once more, the frantic cry of the eldest Edgington boy was heard.

"Thank you, Mr Vaughan. But I have to go."

Albert did not wait for the stranger to reply but ran from that place, suddenly, and somehow almost excitingly, filled up with purpose.

XVII

The little man watched him go. "How sad," he said, and then again: "How sad. We all of us did our best, of course. In our own ways." He looked up at that ubiquitous statue which stood at the heart of the square. "You especially," he said and nodded with careful politeness as though the figure were some acquaintance made of flesh and blood. Then he surprised himself: a single laugh bubbled out of him, a cracked, high, crazed thing. The sound of it scared him, as though he had truly heard it for the first time. And so, after that, he simply stood, and listened to the approach of the crowd and waited.

XVIII

Albert saw them almost as soon as he left the fragile safety of the square and ran back into the main thoroughfare. They must have numbered in the hundreds: a great, roiling mob of Beast People moving in a dense formation. The scientist in Albert thought it fascinating while the part of him which was drawn to the poetry of Ancient Greece thought it oddly beautiful.

Considerable damage had been wrought to the streets and houses of the City. In the distance, there was smoke and flames. It was as though he had emerged from momentary sanctuary to step into the frame of a painting of insurrection, some portrait of revolt.

In the midst of them was Silas, borne aloft by that raucous assembly as though he were a tribute, destined for sacrifice. He was struggling frantically yet was he held firm by the talons and claws of the mob. His clothes were torn and ripped. He had been cut and his face was bloodied. Every fibre of him was in a state of outrage and disgust.

Struggling upwards, he saw Albert. "Help me! Help me!"

Now that bestial collective took note of the schoolboy. They surged towards him, a phalanx of teeth and claws, and bloodied, matted fur. They bore down upon him. They shrieked in bloodlust and delight.

"Please!" Albert called out. "Please let my brother go!"

There came much laughter at this and some cries of fury at the suggestion. They were speaking one to the other, Albert realised; these were not mere animal calls but rather some unfamiliar language, unique to these creatures.

"Wait!" he called again. "My brother is a fool but he means no harm!"

At that moment, Albert lost sight of Silas. The mob dragged him down until he was amongst them.

No sign of him could be seen; not so much as a hand raised in desperation, pawing at the sky, or a glimpse of his wild hair, swaying above that agitated populace like the fronds of some fantastic subaquatic greenery.

Still the eldest Edgington boy could be heard. As Albert shrank back against the wall, and as the mob moved towards him like creatures in a dream, he had no choice but to listen to the sounds that were being made by his brother. Too tired now for screaming, the noise was something else (something which seemed to Albert to be somehow worse than mere hoarse panic or dread): a low, protracted moan as of a being upon the rack, a kind of solemn plain chant which seemed to speak of dreadful resignation.

Once more, Silas called the name of the young man whom he had brought to this place. "Bertie! Albert!"

Then there was a sound like linen being torn and ripped in a frenzy. Then an instant of almost silence in which only the snuffling, snorting, chittering sound of the Beast People could be heard. Then, inexorably, they moved forwards once again.

Albert himself did not call out, for all that he was aware of the extreme peril of his situation, more keenly cognisant than ever he had been before of his own mortality. He felt the stone of the wall behind him and his breath come in fierce, ragged bursts. Yet he also felt a weird sense of calm at the prospect which seemed suddenly to have reared up before him. Bad luck, he thought, this is just the worst kind of luck.

Then he recognised a face at the front of the crowd. It was Faun, the woman who had been his guide and from whom he had been separated scarcely more than an hour earlier. She seemed different somehow, changed even in the short time that they had been apart. Her clothes were ragged and stippled with stains. She bared her teeth.

"Faun!" he cried, although he already knew that it was fruitless. Somehow he had already adjusted to this hideous new reality.

The woman who had calmly acted as his guide now no longer seemed capable of forming human words. She hissed and raised her left hand high in the air. What emerged from her throat was more wild ululation.

Albert said nothing. He took a breath. He closed his eyes. And he made himself as ready as he was able.

XIX

In the end, what saved him from the mob was an unfamiliar voice.

"Leave him be!"

The words were clear, the accent British, the tone deep and filled with authority. At the sound of them, the crowd did not stop altogether but they did hesitate in their advance. Then the voice came again.

"Do not touch him!"

At this the crowd ceased to move. Instead they looked behind them and that little battalion of rioters began to part like the Red Sea, their actions no longer seeming like that of a rabble but rather of a force which could yet be moulded into the acceptance of military discipline. With fretful clarity, Albert saw their dread potential.

Two figures were approaching in the midst of the throng, coming increasingly into view as all of those bodies made way.

The first was entirely unknown to him: a lean, sinewy figure dressed in some sort of makeshift uniform, a darned, homemade thing of epaulettes and patches. The face of the figure was covered in sleek dark fur, the face of a young ape-man.

The second figure was familiar for all that Albert fumbled for a moment to place her: a slim young woman with dark hair. The blonde, he realised, must have been a wig. For it was none other than she who had earlier given her name as–

"Jessamy!"

A hard smile crossed the woman's face.

"That is not my name."

She and her companion reached the forefront of the mob. The peoples of the city gazed at them expectantly, cringing and obedient. Were they the commanders of the mob, Albert wondered? Or something more? For there was to the reaction of the crowd a distinct quality of religiosity.

"We should introduce ourselves to you, Mr Edgington. You ought to know our true names. I am Coral Mayfield."

"Coral…" The name felt strange, yet somehow, oddly, familiar upon his lips.

"And this is my son."

The furred soldier beside turned his piercing green eyes upon the schoolboy. "My name is Anta'Nar, son of M'Gari, son of Anse. You have picked an interesting day to come to the City, Mr Edgington. For today is our day of revolution. Today has been a day long in the making. We have worked for years to achieve this – this mighty hour of victory!"

At this, the crowd erupted into whoops and cries of triumph. Albert found that his breaths were coming in shorter and shorter gasps, that his heart was beating too fast, that there was a great roaring in his ears. Having felt an odd sense of acceptance and resignation scarcely a minute before he now found himself filled up with a desire to live.

"What do you want with me?" he asked once the victory shouts were over. "Do you mean to do to me what you did to my brother?"

"I am sorry about your brother," said Anta'Nar. "Truly I am. Today has been a reckoning long overdue. I fear that the captured peoples of the City have not been lenient."

"He was not a good man," said Coral. "But he was no means the worst of them. He did not deserve the manner of his passing."

"You speak," said Albert, swallowing hard, "as though his body is not even now still being trampled beneath the feet of your swarm of rioters."

Coral bowed her head as if to acknowledge his criticism. "You asked what we mean to do with you, Albert. And the answer is this: we want you to join us. We want you to help us in our cause. For today is only the beginning of a greater struggle."

"Join you?" Albert asked. "But why?"

"Because I think you can be useful to us," Coral said. "There's something about you. A quiet intelligence."

Anta'Nar spoke now. "My mother has told me that you are not like the others. I see it in you. You know that this place is founded upon injustice. You know, I think, with every fibre of your being that this is wrong. And that you may yet play your part in moulding a better future. So I ask you now, Mr Albert Edgington: will you join us?"

Albert thought of his brother, of his dreadful final moments, his screams of indignity and terror. He looked first at the dark-haired woman, her face a mask of implacable resolve. He looked into the eyes of the beast-man and he saw there, in almost equal measure, authority and rage. And then, he gave them his answer.

XX

Mr Vaughan heard something of this as he waited beside the statue of the spiritual founder of the City. He heard the death cries of the elder Edgington and even something of the conversation of the younger boy. He wondered why the crowd had fallen quiet and was able to admit to himself that he found their silence to be somehow more ominous than their earlier shrieks and baboonery.

The light in the courtyard began to flicker. He could smell smoke and hear the crackling of flames. The face of Moreau looked down at him, impassive and unmoving.

"I went further," said Vaughan. "Further than you ever dreamed."

Some part of him almost expected the stone man to speak. It did nothing of the sort, of course, though still Vaughan felt its gaze upon him.

The little man spat once at the base of the statue. "Not such a pygmy now," he said. "Not such a pygmy!"

And then, regretting his burst of intemperance, he sank to his knees as if in prayer.

XXI

This, then, was how they found him in the end, the Beast Peoples of the City – Mr Vaughan upon his knees, by the foot of the statue of Dr Moreau.

Dozens upon dozens of them streamed into that little courtyard to surround him, having caught his scent upon the breeze and knowing, or at least suspecting, him to be the architect of their ordeal. They would have torn him limb from limb as they had Silas Edgington and they would have done so with glee. A hyena-creature and a tiger-woman were at the front of the throng, claws out and teeth bared. The air was filled with bloodlust and with vicious ululation.

Mr Vaughan did not rise nor did he turn to face those who wished him dead. He was expecting the killing stroke at any moment. Instead, he heard the soft, compelling, cultured voice of Anta'Nar.

"Get up, Mr Vaughan. I would look upon you."

Curious, the man who had once been the most successful alienist in England did as he was told. He faced the beast-creature in his homemade uniform.

"You're not one of mine," he said mildly.

"None of us is yours!" roared the commander.

Vaughan raised his right hand in a gesture of apology, as though he had merely made a faux pas at a dinner party. "Forgive me, I didn't mean to imply that you were. I meant only that I do not recognise you. I do not believe you to be of the City."

Anta'Nar shook his head. "I am not of the City."

"How fascinating." Mr Vaughan peered at him with a chilly,

scientific gaze. "Then what exactly are you? Wait, don't tell me…" His eyes ranged up and down the figure of the being before him, an ape-man who evidently held over him the power of life and death. Still Mr Vaughan narrowed his eyes and peered and sniffed the air. "But I do know you. Or rather I know who you must be. You're the infant, aren't you? The one the sailor took from here. The one he took to the boarding house. Oh but we could never find you. I'd given you up for dead."

"My mother hid me well," Anta'Nar said evenly. "And we had help."

"The old priest I knew about, oh yes. Dear me. Silly old fool." A certain vagueness came to the face of Mr Vaughan then as though he had temporarily forgotten where he was and why he was remembering. He seemed to flounder.

"We have a decision to make, Mr Vaughan," said Anta'Nar. Behind him, the mob was growing restless. Many had they killed that day and copious had been the slaughter upon the streets of the City, yet still were they hungry, for the blood of the author of their misery.

"Oh?" Mr Vaughan seemed to be interested only moderately in the conversation, as though they were discussing supper plans for the week to come. "And what is that?"

"What to do with you."

"I imagined you would want me dead. I'm fairly sure that this little army of yours desires exactly that."

"I have great plans for this City. But I will need the respect of those outside of it. I cannot sanction execution without trial. Not, at least, once the initial violence is done with – that which was necessary to secure the whole of this place."

Mr Vaughan smiled. "Spoken like all true revolutionaries.

Already you make excuses for what you've done. I understand, my friend, for I recognise the trait from myself. One is looking for a reasonable explanation for the blood on one's hands."

At this, Anta'Nar moved close to the little man before him and snarled. Vaughan merely blinked.

"But as to your question," said the little man still almost conversationally, "as to what would be best for a creature in your position to do with a man like me... Well. Might I be permitted to make to you just a very small suggestion?"

Anta'Nar, who, in spite of his earlier words, now felt very tempted indeed simply to open the alienist's jugular with a single swipe of his nails, nonetheless leaned forward and spoke two words, flecked with danger.

"Go on..."

XXII

Coral Mayfield led Albert Edgington out of the City. It was a journey that he never forgot, no matter how hard he tried. Often, in later life, images from their trek would come back to him unbidden. They would wake him in the night and stalk beside him during daylight hours. They would return again and again, upon the slightest provocation.

The uprising had been both brutal and comprehensive. The streets were carpeted with the bodies of those visiting men beside whom Albert had stood mere hours before, in the pub, in the church, in the waiting room. Much of the place was in flames. Houses were smouldering and the pavements were littered with debris. Outliers from the main mob rushed and scurried by. There was in the air a febrile quality which was only now beginning to slacken, as though the fury, for so long pent up, was finally starting to break.

It was only because he was with Coral that Albert was safe. They seemed to know her, the peoples of the City, and they allowed both of the humans to pass unmolested. Albert was under no illusion that this would not have been the case had he attempted to escape alone. He knew that, had he done so, he would long ago have joined the ranks of battered and despoiled bodies.

In large part, they made the journey in silence. The magnitude of what he had experienced – the magnitude of his loss – was coming only gradually to Albert.

"What does this mean?" he asked, once they were back onto the main thoroughfare of the City, heading towards the entrance. "Everything that's happened here?"

"Oh it'll change the world, I expect," said Coral, with a lightness that suddenly made her sound younger than her years. "Nothing will ever be the same after this."

"This place…" Albert gestured vaguely as they strode on through the ruins. "Who ran it all? What was it for?"

"Money and pleasure," Coral replied, as though the answer should be obvious. "That's why most things exist, isn't it? The machinery of the world. And Devil take the poor creatures who get crushed beneath its wheels, trapped in the cogs of the thing."

"I don't understand."

"You understand more than you think, Mr Edgington."

"Please," said the schoolboy. "You must call me Albert."

By the entrance they came across an especially distressing sight: the hanged body of an antelope-woman with a scrawled sign about her neck which read: "COLLABORATOR".

"Pity," Coral said as they walked beneath her swaying feet. "And she was far from alone. There were many others, of course. Plenty of them acted as gaolers, turned against their own kind." Then, with a smile that Albert thought distinctly chilling: "Still, let us hope that's all done with now. The worst is over. Get rid of a few bad apples and we can all of us start to feel so much better."

It was Albert's turn now to say nothing further as they walked on, out of the City and back towards the surface world. As they went, Albert let a sense of numbness settle over him. He tried not to think of the future and he tried not to think of the past. He just kept breathing and took one step after another.

XXIII

The waiting room itself was empty, save for four dead gentlemen. Albert did not recognise any of them. Coral barely even glanced at their twisted forms.

On they went, across that big white space, and into the room beyond. This was as it had been before: an exact replica of an English church nave, with pews and altar still undisturbed. There were no corpses to be seen in here.

"Strange," he murmured, almost to himself, "that they left it be."

"The Beast People of the City have great respect for faith of all kind," she said. "They brought their own religion with them from the island. They would not have trespassed here."

The place seemed to Albert, after the uproar of the past hours, to be almost distressingly quiet. "How do we get back to the surface? How is it done?"

Coral sauntered to the front of the nave and to the lectern.

"Don't worry. There's a lever here somewhere. It will reverse the mechanism and bring us back up."

Albert paused midway in the church and watched as Coral felt around the back of the lectern, searching for the lever.

"You have to agree," she called out (and was he right to detect a hint of nervousness in her voice?), "that it's quite a feat of engineering, all this. Stupidly overcomplicated, of course, and madly expensive. You could almost admire it if it wasn't so absolutely wicked." She stopped, cursing beneath her breath.

"What's the matter?" Albert asked.

"It's snapped. It's been broken off."

"Then what–"

Before Albert could say more, he was interrupted – they both heard it – not by a voice but by a sound. The scrape of wood against stone. The noise of a pew being moved, surreptitiously, backwards.

"Who's there?" Coral said and, suddenly, she was up on her feet and moving fast There came another sound, more frantic than before, and Albert saw a bearded stranger clambering awkwardly to his feet from what must have been his hiding place beneath the pew. He was at the rear of the church, in a place of shadows.

"Get back!" cried the man. "Both of you!"

He looked at them both, wild-eyed. In spite of the gloom, Albert realised then that he recognised this man: he had passed him (he thought) on the street after he had first fled from the Idler's Rest.

The man, however, showed no signs of recognising Albert. "Who are you people? Are you... with them?"

Coral looked at him very coolly indeed. "What's your name?"

"Simon... Simon Masters." He took a noisy breath. "But

you're human, aren't you? You're human like me? And you want to get out of here?"

She gave him a long, level shrewd look. "Do you know why this mechanism is broken, Mr Masters?"

He shook his head, a shade too vigorously, Albert thought. "Perhaps they destroyed it. The animals. The Beast People."

"Can you fix it?" Albert asked.

"Maybe," Coral said, "but I need time."

"You have to hurry," said the stranger. "The others will be on their way." He turned to look behind him, peering towards the open church door.

Coral busied herself with the mechanism, wrenching off a panel and examining the device beneath. Albert's own attention, meanwhile, was taken up by the man who had given his name as Masters. There was a wrongness to the man, something indefinable which nagged at him as he watched the woman work.

"Mr Masters!" he called out. "Can you come here, please? We need your help."

Coral looked up from her labours and gave him a questioning look. He nodded, hoping to convey the sense that she should trust him in this.

"Mr Masters!" he called again, for the gentleman in question still had his back to them. "Please, sir, you're needed here."

The figure raised a gloved hand. "In a moment," he said. "Give me just a minute longer."

"We need you now, Mr Masters."

Coral glanced back at Albert. "What are you doing?"

The schoolboy whispered: "There's something... strange about him."

He looked again over at the stranger. "Please, Mr Masters. We

243

need you here. Or else we'll leave without you."

Masters called back: "Wait for me, please, just wait for me."

Albert mouthed one word to Coral: "Liar."

"Then what…"

The woman never finished her sentence for in that instant of distraction the man turned at last and ran full pelt towards them.

Albert saw now what he had only hitherto suspected. Seen in full light, hidden no longer in the shadows, the truth about Masters was plain. He was no human at all but a creature of the City who had dressed himself in the clothes of a human being and (Albert realised with a surge of horror and disgust) in the skin of a man's face. It hung off him now, bleeding and askew. As the creature, whose ancestry seemed to hint at the buffalo, pounded towards him, Albert found himself surprised that he had been taken in even temporarily by the masquerade.

"Albert!" Coral cried out but it was already too late and the buffalo-creature was upon Albert, throwing him back to the floor, claws outstretched, what was left of the face of Mr Masters clinging to him like melting cheese on hot bread.

The schoolboy shouted in shock and pain as the claws of the City-dweller fumbled at his face and throat. He pushed back with all his might but the buffalo-man was far stronger than he. With a single motion, the creature slashed Edgington's right cheek. The pain was immediate.

"Coral!" he shouted, though no help came.

The beast bore down upon him and Albert saw in his blazing eyes that he would remove any obstacle to his escape from this place. The hairy hands of his opponent reached around his neck. Albert felt them tighten. He gasped frantically for breath. Then he felt surge through him an outraged fury, that the long day and his many trials should end like this. He pushed back hard. With secret strength, he kicked against the creature and pulled the hands that were at his throat apart. With a cry, the creature rolled off him. On all fours it sprang. Now Albert kicked again and met its midriff with his foot. It howled in pain then ran again only for a single shot to ring out. Blood, bone and cerebral matter were at once made visible as the buffalo-man sank first to his knees and then, with leaden, ungainly finality, onto his back.

Albert looked up. It was Coral, of course, who had fired the shot. That she even had a revolver upon her person he had not known till now.

"Thank you," he said.

She shrugged. "He was a collaborator," she said, as though that explained it all. "He worked with the humans. Guarded his own people." There was in her voice no audible trace of sympathy or regret.

Albert, gasping, rose. "When did you realise? That he wasn't who he claimed to be?"

"A little before you, I think." She offered no further words of explanation but said simply: "You did very well, Albert. You'll be very useful to us." She slammed the panel back into the place over the mechanism behind the lectern.

"Now, shall we go?"

"You've fixed it?"

"Yes," said Coral and smiled. Her hand was on the lever. "Goodbye to the City. Let's go back to the surface. I would take you to the sea, Albert, and introduce you to a friend of ours who dwells there. Though I think you've already glimpsed him today."

She pulled the lever and what had happened earlier that night now occurred in reverse. With a great wrenching sound the floor, the walls, the entire church, seemed to move upwards and at some speed. Without questioning why he should do so, Albert Edgington moved towards Coral. They clung to one another, ostensibly for balance, as the church moved swiftly upwards.

"Everything will be different now," Coral said and Albert believed that he heard in her voice the traces of years of struggle. "The whole world will be altered by what's been done here tonight. The future will look quite different."

Albert said nothing in reply, but only clung still more closely to Coral Mayfield as they went up to the world above.

15TH JULY, 1901

THE CITY

I

As Brunor padded into the room (previously a library, now pressed into service as a makeshift operations centre) the new master of the City peered over the pages of a great tranche of official-looking papers and said: "Don't hesitate, please. Come in, come in. And be welcome here."

It was – at least to one such as Brunor, who had known only the City for the great majority of his life – a decidedly curious sight: a member of the Beast Folk sitting in this crucible of Man with the easy air of one who had been born to it. Anta'Nar, the celebrated leader of a new world, reclining in the chair which had long been used only by their oppressors. Brunor sniffed the air: the reek of humanity assailed his senses in a way that was all too familiar.

"Thank you, sir," said Brunor, whose approximation of military uniform was even rougher and more improvisational than was Anta'Nar's own. The origins of Brunor lay primarily in the bear family and the clumsiness of his bulky, ursine form was only emphasised by the handmade nature of his costume. He trod stolidly on until he faced his leader across an ancient wooden desk, one no doubt appropriated from the old regime.

Anta'Nar set down the weighty document. His voice was kindly, his fierce, simian face lit up by a smile.

"Are you pleased?" asked the City's commander-in-chief casually.

"Pleased by what, sir?"

Anta'Nar moved one bristly hand through the air in discouragement. "No need," he said, "for 'sir'. We are a fellowship. Not an order of soldiers."

"Yes, sir, but all the same, sir: there is discipline to be maintained."

"Not, surely, when it's just two friends talking together?"

"Please, sir. I should prefer it, sir."

Anta'Nar shrugged, a gesture which struck Brunor as being somehow dismayingly human. "As you wish, my friend. But I asked you a question, did I not?"

Brunor nodded. One would say that he did so gruffly if such a description were not redundant: everything the bear-man did appeared, by nature of his girth, brown fur and long snout, to exemplify gruffness. Only those who knew him well (his mate and their three cubs; a few true friends) were able to judge the shifting range of his emotions. He had long since given up persuading those who were not of his inner circle of his capacity for complex feeling.

"You asked," he said, "if I were pleased. You mean, I take it, about the coup?" That last word sounded, in the bear-man's gravelly tones which seemed to threaten at any moment to break into a growl, almost comical, as though he were endeavouring to mimic a birdcall: *coo…*

Anta'Nar frowned. "The Folk are calling it a revolution. That is the preferred word to use."

"Does it matter, sir?"

The ape-man sighed and leaned back in his chair. "Not to us. Of course. Not to you. Or to me. But it will matter to the world outside. Oh, it will matter to them all right."

"Why, sir?"

"The people beyond this City. The humans… They will resist what we've done here. They won't want to permit us our freedom. And so we must make sure to have, in their eyes, a clear sense of… legitimacy."

For several long seconds, Brunor chose not to reply. "I understand, sir."

"So will you say 'revolution' from now on, my friend? For my sake?"

Brunor considered refusing then and there, to say that he'd prefer to make his own choice of words, to describe the world the way in which he saw it. He was curious to see how Anta'Nar would react, a courageous ape-man who nonetheless, in the clear light of morning, three days after the overthrow of the old ways, seemed to possess an unexpected quality of fragility. How different the following year might have been had he only spoken up then. But, of course, he only nodded and said: "Of course, sir."

"You're an unusual fellow," said Anta'Nar. "One of a kind. I've always thought that about you. You like to go your own way."

"It has been said, sir."

"Can't have been easy for you for all this time, working here in the City. Do you remember the Island?"

"Yes, sir, but barely. I was very young."

Anta'Nar looked almost envious. "Still, to have some memory of it. Any memory at all…"

Brunor did not reply, his mind filled with a succession of swift, violent images: of running, of savage motion, of the lamentations of his elders.

Sensing the rawness of what he had uncovered, Anta'Nar probed no further. "And in the City itself, where was it that you worked?"

"In the foundry, sir. They kept me out of sight. I was not so pleasing to the human eye as were certain others of our people. They thought I would scare the visitors and so they put me to work there. Hard labour."

"As I understand it, you were often reprimanded for disobeying orders?"

"That's true, sir, yes."

"Even that you were involved in plans for several… uprisings."

"That's so, sir, yes." The bear-man sniffed. "Though they didn't get very far. The powers that were ranged against us… But, yes, I fought." Brunor paused and a different light seemed now to come into his eyes. "Not so much of late, of course. Not since I've had my family."

"Yes, yes," said Anta'Nar, as though such a concept was to him largely theoretical. "Though I wonder, my friend, that the humans did not place you in the security division. There you might have been an asset to them."

Brunor shook his head. "I've long since given up, sir, trying to understand why they did what they did. What the point of it all was."

"I can sympathise with that," said Anta'Nar with a jocularity which seemed to Brunor to be at least partially feigned. Had not the ape-man, after all, spent a good portion of his years in considering just these things? Had he not passed through the world above? Had he not plotted to come here to the City and had he not long dreamed of its liberation?

"Perhaps," Brunor said, choosing his words with more than usual care, "your friend, the human woman, might be able to explain the thoughts behind the foundation of... all this."

Anta'Nar spoke crisply. "I think of her as my mother. My foster mother. And she's left the City for now. There is much for her to do in the human world if we are to remain safe. If we're going to be able to resist human interference of any kind."

"I'm sure you're right, sir. I'm sure it's necessary. I'm sure you're doing what's right."

There was an awkward silence.

"You're angry, I think," said Anta'Nar at last.

"Of course." Brunor spoke without thinking. "All that I've ever known is in uproar. The world has changed forever."

"But you can see how things will be better? So much better than they ever were in the old days?"

"Of course, sir. Thank you, sir."

"But?"

"There seems to me..." Brunor fell silent, unwilling to speak the final phrase of the sentence.

"Say it," Anta'Nar said softly.

"There seems to me, sir, to be a want of justice. A great crime has been committed here, in this City, at the hands of mankind. And everything's that in me cries out for retribution."

"I see." The words emerged smoothly. "I appreciate your candour. You're the kind of fellow, I think, who could make life easier for himself if he only went along with the powerful a bit more, if only he said yes and nodded his head and didn't cause too much of a fuss."

"I dare say that's true, sir."

Anta'Nar seemed pleased. "Well then, Brunor, I do believe you're just the man I need."

"For what, sir?"

"To help me out. With an especially difficult job. It needs someone thoughtful, intelligent and honest."

"Anything I can do, sir. For the sake of the City."

"That's very good to hear." As he spoke, Anta'Nar rose from his chair, stepped around the desk and walked to the side of the bear-man. "Now it's rather a sensitive matter." He put one arm around Brunor's beefy shoulder, a gesture at once fraternal and conspiratorial. "You see, it has to do with our prisoner…"

II

After Anta'Nar had told Brunor what he required of him, after the bear-man had asked his own, necessary questions and, eventually, out of a combination of nascent patriotism and personal obligation, had accepted the invitation, the two Beast Folk left the library and walked together through the City.

The place had once been barren and wild. It had then been made, under the instructions of mankind, into an elaborate pleasure garden. Now it was changing again. All signs of the old regime were in the process of being removed. There was much eradication, much hollowing out. Everywhere was renewal, reassembly, a potent air of reformation.

They walked through the streets of the City and they saw how it was being transformed: its sets of apartments turned now into accommodation for the Beast Folk, the halls that had been devoted to the expense of food and drink turned over to more utilitarian ends. All that was pointlessly quaint or merely picturesque was being torn away, leaving in its wake the skeletons of structures and buildings: as though, after too long, make-up and rouge were being removed to show the true face beneath. The weird vegetation and fauna which once had formed so memorable an aspect to the topography of the City was being ripped from the ground in great quantity, hacked away and left to moulder by the roadside. Everywhere too were to be seen the ruins of statues, the smashed remains of that likeness of Moreau which once had been everywhere across the kingdom.

As they went, Anta'Nar was often stopped by the people who were now citizens of that place, mostly to be thanked or given praise. Sometimes, however, there were personal entreaties (an elk-woman looking for her daughter, still missing after the revolution; a sow-creature asking for clemency in the case of her brother who was being considered as a collaborator) and sometimes there was even criticism, robustly delivered, which the ape-man received with dignified cordiality.

Still, Anta'Nar had spoken earlier of the security division and, as they walked, Brunor wondered to himself how much longer it would be before the commander needed protection himself. He was, after all, a little king now and no monarch ever walks alone, even amongst his own people.

"Might I ask a question, sir?" he said, as they strolled in the direction of the first street of the City, and the waiting room which was at the end of it, places to which Brunor had never, before the revolution, been permitted to see.

"Anything," replied the ape-man.

"Do you think we can do it? I mean, truly? Survive on our own. Here, in this place?"

There came no hesitation from Anta'Nar. "Of course I do."

"But what do we have to protect ourselves with? What do we have, for that matter, to trade? How will we hold off the humans? How will we flourish?"

In the distance, a green door loomed. Yet Anta'Nar stopped in the street. A gang of zebra-people clattered by, still full of uproarious spirits, only to lower their high, whinnying voices at the sight of the master and the bear.

Once they had passed by, Anta'Nar placed his right hand upon Brunor's shoulder. "You are a deep thinker, my friend. Deeper than you like to let on, eh?"

"Do you have the answers?" was all that the bear-man said. "Do you have promises to make?"

"I have hopes, yes. And some answers. But I don't have promises. I have studied much of human history and it would tend to suggest that I should not promise the people of this City anything which I cannot absolutely guarantee. There is much which must still stay secret for now. There is much too, my friend, that is taking place even as we speak behind the scenes. But, yes, I can tell you this: that we have the means, we have the leverage, to bend the humans to our will. We have both sword and shield to keep them at bay. It has to do with what men call... technology. But more than that I cannot say for now."

The bear-man peered at Anta'Nar. He wanted to look into the ape-creature's eyes as he was speaking. He wished to divine the truth. The silence between them grew uncomfortable.

"Do you trust me?" Anta'Nar said at last.

"Yes," said Brunor. "At least..."

"Be honest, my friend. Hold nothing back."

"At least I think that you're our best hope."

The ape-man smiled. His teeth, Brunor noticed, were a little crooked and unkempt, testament, perhaps, to a life spent hiding amongst the humans.

"That's plenty for now," he said. "I appreciate it."

Brunor grunted.

"Well then," said Anta'Nar, "we should hurry. There's lots to arrange with your new duties. And I think that I should be there when you meet the prisoner for the first time. For all our sakes."

He walked on, towards the green door, and Brunor followed. He sniffed the air as he went. The smell of humanity was stronger here and his gorge rose at the thick, sour scent of his tormentors.

III

Anta'Nar led the way, through the green door and into the dull void beyond. In addition to the smell of humanity there was an unpleasant scent of chemicals, some weird unguent or polish, meant for cleaning, which nauseated the bear-man. In this wide, empty space – a funnel for the visitors to the City – he felt a shiver of unease. Brunor was a believer in the old gods of the island and there was in that cosmology much emphasis on the survival of unquiet spirits. He felt it here, in this place: dead souls. As he walked, his fur seemed to shiver.

It was with relief that they passed out of the void and into the church that lay beyond. It was orderly again and clean. Brunor recognised it as a manner of temple but he sensed also something mocking in the look of it.

"Whose idea was it?" he asked. "All of this? This… illusion."

"As I understand it," Anta'Nar called back, striding to the head of the nave, "it was the notion of the man we're going to see. In many ways, my friend, this is his dream and we are merely standing in it. Long since time, of course, for us all to wake up." He reached the pulpit, reached down for some piece of technology which lay behind it and said: "You should probably brace yourself for some turbulence."

And then they were moving upwards. Brunor saw that Anta'Nar was smiling at him as they rose (too fast, he thought) up towards the surface but that his smile seemed in some senses to be stretched too thin, as though it hid only lightly the fear and uncertainty which lay underneath.

Eventually, the church ceased its odd sense of movement and, with a grinding sound, fell still again.

"Here we are," said Anta'Nar. "You've heard all the stories, I suppose? About what's up here? The false village. The façade."

Brunor nodded.

"My friend, please, speak truly…" The ape-man's face was twisted now in sympathy. "Have you been to the surface before? Since the Island, that is?"

Slowly, sombrely, Brunor shook his great furred head, not trusting himself to speak.

"I thought it unlikely," said the ape-man, "but I had to ask. So this may not be without its challenges. Are you happy to proceed?"

The bear-man swallowed hard. "Of course," he said. "Let's go." Without waiting for any response from his commander, he walked fast towards the doors out of the temple, stepped across the threshold and beyond.

IV

Outside the church lay the village of Eddowes Bay and the dark blue strip of the ocean. Brunor, who, in recent years, had come to pride himself on his phlegmatic responses to life's extremities (his wife had even remarked that this was now one of his most attractive qualities, teased out of him as it had been by several years of patient cohabitation) was nonetheless all but knocked back upon his paws by the simple, matter of fact vision of it.

His every sensory receptor was filled up with unexpected data: the smell of salt and brine, the feel of a crisp summer's breeze across the fur of his face, the touch of the sun upon his hide and, above all, the sensation of sheer space, the confronting nature of the expanse. At the distant glimmering of the sea, tears prickled and a sound, unbidden and impossible to control, emerged low and plaintive from his throat.

Yet Brunor was never one for cringing. Within less than a minute he had regained control of his faculties. He wiped away the few small tears that had emerged, dampening his fur.

Anta'Nar had looked discreetly away. "It's quite something, isn't it? After so long underground."

Brunor took a careful breath. "I suppose."

"Come along," said the ape-man, "you'll soon get used to it. You'll be spending a lot of time up here from now on."

"I was a prisoner," Brunor said and, even to his own ears, his voice sounded far away and disconnected. "Now I become a gaoler."

"Oh I'd say it's rather more complicated than that," Anta'Nar said. "Isn't everything?"

He moved away then and Brunor followed, down towards the sea.

Eddowes Bay itself was being changed too, just as swiftly and without compunction as was the world below. Others of the Beast Folk were here and they seemed to Brunor to be setting up some manner of perimeter fence, very high and made from a patchwork of wood and metal, much of it torn from the stage-set of the village and from the City itself.

"A temporary measure," said Anta'Nar as they walked on by. "We will need something more permanent in time. But this should be sufficient for now. Enough, at least, to make our point to the wider world."

Brunor turned his great, shaggy head to take a closer look at this feat of improvisational engineering. "Won't it look," he said, "as though we're penning ourselves in?" That the notion made him profoundly uncomfortable did not need to be stated: it was at once apparent from the tilt of his snout and the curt intonation of his words.

"It's a question of perspective, don't you think?" asked Anta'Nar, not slowing. "In my view, it's a necessary evil – to keep the humans out."

Brunor took one last look at the construction, wondering whether so provisional an assembly would be enough to slow down any determined group of intruders for long at all, though he chose to keep his misgivings to himself. Besides, he had no doubt that Anta'Nar had already thought such thoughts and had come to the conclusion that their situation was very much more perilous than he could afford to let on.

The pub, the Idler's Rest, unlike the rest of the village seemed to have been left alone. Whereas the rest of that strange, false conurbation was being dismantled the inn looked as though it were being preserved.

"I thought it might be useful," Anta'Nar said, though Brunor had not spoken. "As a means of reward."

Brunor nodded, although he had many questions, feeling that he had said enough for now. And not wanting, perhaps, to hear any more answers.

At last, they reached the pebbled beach. The sea surged and hissed in greeting. In the distance there was a small stone building outside of which stood two great gorilla-people, both armed with carving knives, whose every aspect seemed to proclaim them to be guardsmen. The sight seemed to Brunor to sound a grim note, a reminder, perhaps, of the old ways in a place that was otherwise devoted to change.

"Are you ready?" Anta'Nar asked.

"He's waiting inside?"

"It's his whole world now. Bar an hour or so for exercise."

The pair crunched on over the stony beach. The hut drew nearer. The gorilla-people observed their approach, both a little wary.

"How is he?" Brunor asked. "In himself?"

"The prisoner seems defiant," said Anta'Nar. "Unrepentant. At least for some of the time. But then... there are moments when his mind seems to be unmooring."

"You think he'll be fit to stand trial?"

"He must be, and if he isn't then you, my friend, must make it so."

They reached the hut. The gorilla-people stood aside, both managing what seemed (at least in Brunor's eyes) to be a rather maladroit salute. One of them drew back the bolts which had been placed on the exterior of the door. At the sound of it, a voice – a human voice – called out from within.

"Who is it? Who's there?"

Brunor hesitated. He tried to avoid thinking grand thoughts but that this was a moment of history seemed to him to be an unavoidable conclusion. He knew the voice of old, recognised it from speeches and inspections, the voice of the City's founder and despot both, the voice of Mr Vaughan.

V

Much later, after it was dark, once Brunor had completed his first day of new duties and returned underground to the City, his wife and his cubs were waiting for him.

Brunor said very little about how he had spent the day, though he could tell from his mate's querying expressions that there was much that she wished to ask him. The cubs, excited, crawled all over him and asked their giddy questions and pulled with hectic excitement at his fur.

Later, once the little ones were asleep, and Brunor and his wife sat up together in their makeshift parlour, he told her what Anta'Nar had asked of him and that he had no real choice but to agree. His mate, though she cried angry tears, understood. It was, she suggested, his patriotic duty though she wished that the new commander of the City had asked almost anyone but her husband to fulfil the task. Brunor had little enough to say to this, retreating, as had become his wont in the course of married life, into stoical silence.

Later still, as they lay together, waiting for sleep, listening to the snores and snuffles of the cubs next door, she asked him a question: "What's he like?"

"Mr Vaughan?"

Brunor gave a grunt, indicative, perhaps, of an unwillingness to even so much as shape the syllables of the human's name.

"In some ways, much as you'd expect. Arrogant. Without remorse. But there's something else too. Something old… Confused."

"You think that Anta'Nar's set on putting the human on trial?"

She spoke too loudly. From the adjacent room, one of their cubs, half-waking, cried out. A moment's silence and then he settled himself. The couple conversed in whispers.

"He seems set on it," said Brunor. "He thinks it will show the humans that we're fair. Not like…"

With the odd telepathy of marriage, his mate completed his sentence. "Animals?"

Brunor growled softly at the back of his throat.

She sighed, reached out and stroked his fur. "I'm proud of you, you know. It took courage to say yes. It won't be easy. Someone like you defending someone like him… But Anta'Nar's right. It had to be done. It could only be one of us who'd argue for his life."

She waited for a response but none came. He was asleep, she realised, exhausted from the first long day of many. In spite of her earlier words, she could not imagine how any of this could end well. She lay awake awhile before slumber came to claim her, listening to the sonorous rise and fall of her bear-man's breathing.

5TH NOVEMBER, 1901

LONDON

I

Roderick Edgington, QC, strode through the streets at a pace which, he believed, marked him out as a man of significance and distinction. Others of his station relied upon their drivers and their biddable chauffeurs but the middle Edgington brother had ever eschewed such things, believing that to remove oneself in such a fashion from the great mass of ordinary people was to risk uncoupling oneself from their concerns and fears. He preferred to walk amongst the populace, to swim in the great, churning stream of London life so that he might remain in some sense "of the people". He wished to hear the heartbeat of the citizenry to understand them fully.

Naturally, this insistence on pedestrianism resulted, more often than not, in Edgington running persistently late for almost every appointment.

This was the case on the afternoon in question when the barrister was walking as fast as he could up from the Strand (passing by the hostelry that, twenty-four years before had played host to those men who would have thwarted Moreau) and towards Covent Garden, at the edges of which sat an establishment by the name of Creedles, for a brief spell at the start of the twentieth century the most fashionably expensive restaurant in the metropolis.

The thoroughfares that day were crowded, with gawpers and dawdlers, and Edgington had no choice but to cut something of a swathe through them. It was a warm afternoon, more like summer than autumn, and Roderick was perspiring heavily through his thick black suit. He pulled his heavy silver watch from the left-hand pocket of his waistcoat and saw that the time was now twenty-five minutes past one; almost half an hour after the time he had agreed to meet his brother and his new friend. As the lawyer hurried on, he took a florid handkerchief from his pocket and wiped away the sweat at his brow. He glanced down at it before stowing it in his pocket and saw that it was grimy with dirt, another consequence of remaining at all times on the level of the people.

He pressed on and strode up the surprisingly steep incline which led to the market itself. He was jostled by pedestrians who were surging in the opposite direction and he had no desire to step out into the street upon which all manner of vehicles clattered by. Reaching the plateau, he struck out towards the market and the restaurant beyond only to find his way barred by a cadre of dirty-faced children. Held up in their midst as though he were one of them, they clutched a roughly-constructed scarecrow dressed in rags with a lolling face of straw.

"Penny for the guy, sir! Penny for the guy!" These words were chanted by the leader of this miniature mob, a short, surly boy of no more than ten who had placed himself directly in Edgington's path with the pugnacious (and somehow, oddly entitled) manner of a boxer twice his age.

Finding himself unable to simply muscle his way past this insistent gang of juveniles, Edgington paused, already reaching into his pocket to locate a smattering of coins. "Is that your guy?" he asked, with an indulgent smile, nodding towards the mannequin between them.

"Course," said one of the others, a girl, Edgington realised, looking every bit as downtrodden as the boys. "We're going to burn him tonight."

"Quite right too," Edgington said, adding: "though, please, be sure to do so safely."

The group looked up at him with a kind of incredulity which caused an immediate swell of pity in the barrister. Without meaning to embark on such an enterprise, he found himself comparing his own upbringing (a loving, well-tended thing for all its formality) with whatever forces looked over these ruffians.

"Here," he said. "Have more." He pulled out more money, which he gave to the leader of the little gang. "Go safely now." He began to walk away.

"Thank you, sir!" one of them called out after him. "Oh, and mister!"

Edgington called back. "Yes?"

"Watch out now, mister. Be careful, won't you?"

Suspecting, disappointedly, a threat, the barrister turned back. "And what exactly do you mean by that?"

The little boy grinned with chapped and grimy lips. "Haven't you heard, sir? There's monsters on the loose now. They live in a town all their own but they'll be coming here soon, I reckon. They'll be on their way!"

He seemed quite sincere but Edgington, hotter than ever, pushed aside all implications. "Nonsense. It's extremely well known that there is no such thing." Yet even as he spoke these words, reached for easily and almost without thought, old rumours came back to him, and family whispers, and the information which had crept out of the east of the country. "Just nonsense," he said, each syllable inflected by doubt.

The boy was already moving away, the pack of his associates and their straw man in his wake. "If you say so!" the child shouted, his thin, high voice carrying above the bustle and clutter of street life. "Just be careful, that's what I say. Just watch out!"

"Tsk," muttered Edgington. The gang was already out of hearing. He turned again and walked towards the restaurant, the boy's words echoing, inexplicably for now, in his imagination.

II

A sense of mild disquiet hardened into the outright conviction that something was wrong as he finally reached the frontage of Creedles itself. Its exterior managed to be at once lavish and discreet, its windows darkened, the eight letters of the name picked out in gold leaf upon the glass. No passer-by could see what was occurring inside without peering in, their noses up against the panes, and the two doormen, dressed in uniforms of sombre damson, would never allow such an imposition.

A little to the right of the restaurant, however, outside what appeared to be a private residence (but which, a small gold plaque proclaimed, was in fact the headquarters of a tiny but surprisingly influential literary magazine) stood two figures. The first was immediately recognisable as that of his brother, Albert Edgington, albeit looking sleeker, less gawky and more robust than when he had seen him last. The second was that of a young woman; although she cannot have been more than twenty, she carried herself with a deal of self-possession which suggested someone considerably beyond her years.

He had come prepared to be disapproving, ready to dispense some clear-eyed fraternal criticism, yet somehow, at the sight of them, Roderick felt a note of unexpected sadness. They seemed nervous together and ill at ease and somehow, against the swirl and bustle of the city streets, both small and exposed.

Roderick raised a hand in greeting. His brother waved back. The woman only observed his approach with a flat gaze.

"Good afternoon!" he said once he had reached them. "I'm so sorry I'm late. You really ought to have gone in without me."

"We tried," Albert said. "But they wouldn't let us."

"What do you mean," Roderick asked, "they wouldn't let you?"

"I don't know," Albert said. "There's a problem of some kind."

The young woman spoke up. "Think it's my fault." Her voice was at least half-accusing. "Must be something they didn't like about me."

Roderick looked sharply at the woman and then at his younger brother. There seemed to be upon their faces only genuine bewilderment. "Wait here," he said and, turning around with an almost military swivel, stalked back towards the entrance to the restaurant.

A doorman barred his way, beefy and moustachioed. "May I help you, sir?"

"I would very much like to think so."

The doorman gazed impassively at him.

"I'm Roderick Edgington."

"I know who you are, sir."

"I have a reservation for one o'clock. For myself, my brother and his companion."

"I'm afraid we're full, sir."

"Nonsense, man. How can you be full when I have reserved a table?"

Something like a grin flicked across the doorman's face. "Nevertheless, sir. The facts are: we are full."

Before he even had to be summoned, a tall man in spectacles, whom Roderick knew to be the manager of the establishment, appeared behind the doorman. "Is there some sort of problem here?"

"Alex!" Edgington was more informal than he might usually have been. "Can you please be so kind as to tell this trained gorilla of yours that there's been a mistake and that there's a table booked for luncheon in my name?"

The manager murmured something to his employee, who slunk obediently away, and walked to Edgington's side. They both stood now upon the pavement; evidently, there was no possibility of Roderick being allowed so much as a toe across the threshold.

"Alex? What's going on?"

The manager stepped very close to him, speaking sotto voce, like a mourner at a graveside approaching the bereaved. "I'm terribly sorry, Mr Edgington, but we really are full. There's been… some confusion. Entirely our fault and all on our side. But I'm afraid that we just won't be able to accommodate the three of you today." At this, he glanced over towards Albert and the girl who still stood a few feet away watching the scene play out. "Of course, if you wanted to dine today alone then… yes… I do believe we could come to some arrangement."

Roderick glared. "Is this about my brother?" he asked. "Or the woman he's with? Or both?"

The manager smiled blandly. "Now, now, Mr Edgington," he said. "Please make no insinuations of this kind. We have always been a broad church here at Creedles and we turn none away. Not even the most… colourful of controversialists."

Roderick wanted to say more but he felt a hand touch his shoulder. The voice of his brother: "There's really no issue. Let's leave it, Roddy. It's such a fine day. Why don't we walk instead? There's so much to see and it would do us good to stroll around awhile, instead of staying cooped up indoors."

The second Edgington brother opened his mouth to refuse this request and insist that they stay and fight. But Albert merely smiled, giving Roderick cause to consider how much he seemed to have grown up in the months since he had seen him last.

"Very well," he said. "If that's what you like."

The manager of Creedles melted back into the restaurant. The girl approached them, also smiling. "I'm Coral," she said. "It's very nice to meet you."

"Likewise," said Roderick vaguely. "Yes, of course."

"So then," Albert interjected, "shall we stroll? There's bound to be some food and drink on the way. Besides, I expect you've some questions for me."

"Just one or two," Roderick said, his face a picture of puzzlement. "Yes, I do believe there are one or two matters which I should be most grateful if you could clear up."

And so off they went, the three of them, into the whirl and dash of the metropolis.

III

"So what did he say?"

This was Roderick's wife, Diana, when he returned home that evening. She was a thin-faced woman inclined to meanness though this emerged (he suspected) largely from frustration at a life which involved little more than overseeing the house and accompanying her husband. Were there any way to measure intellectual capacity he had no doubt that she would score more highly than he; yet the disparate circumstances of their birth had arranged it so that his was the life of garlands and bustle while her lot was to walk forever three paces behind. She chafed at it and he could not blame her, though, of course, he had never formulated these thoughts in any actual conversation with her.

"He had rather a lot to say, my dear. I confess it was hard to keep track of it all."

"Well, try."

Diana had been waiting for him in the drawing room of their home in Maida Vale. She had been leafing through a novel (a fresh adventure from Mr Scott) which she cast aside immediately upon her husband's weary arrival.

"I need to fix myself a drink, darling," he said. "Might I get something for you?"

She held up her hand. "Just tell me what your brother said."

He went to the drinks cabinet and made himself up a glass. When he looked back, Diana was gazing at him still more frostily than usual. "Oh it was quite a story, my dear. Long and involved. Outwardly fantastic, of course, but Albert swore that every word of it was true."

"And Silas?"

Roderick settled himself onto his usual chair. He sipped from his glass and swallowed. "It would seem that the newspaper reports were accurate."

"Poor man."

Roderick must have looked more sceptical than he had intended at this remark as Diana said quickly: "I know I never cared for him, but there's very few who deserve to die as he did."

"Quite so, my dear. Quite so."

She looked evenly at him. "And who's this young woman he's been stepping out with? I take it she was there too?"

"Coral," Roderick said with careful formality. "That's her name. And she seems to me to be a young woman of singular determination. I think she'll be rather the making of young Albert."

"But she's... surely, some sort of revolutionary?"

Roderick drank again, to fortify himself, perhaps. "It sounds as though she simply saw a flagrant injustice, my dear, and set her shoulder to the wheel in her efforts to reverse it."

Diana sniffed. "And it would seem a great many people have lost their lives as a result of that reversal."

"Well, yes," Roderick murmured. "That's maybe true. But such is the way of things. Don't you think? 'These violent delights have violent ends...' All of that."

"Were any of them there? Any of those... creatures?"

"No, no. Of course not. Far too soon, I'd wager, for that."

Diana looked appalled. "You make it sound like an inevitability. That one day they'll come here."

"Well, it probably is," Roderick murmured, gaining courage from his drink. "In the end. I dare say they'll be everywhere. Rather exciting in a way. A whole new species in our midst."

At this point it became apparent to Roderick that Diana was

having to work quite hard simply in order to keep her temper. Her hands, formerly flat upon her knees, were beginning to clench. Her face was very pale. There was in her voice to be heard the faintest suggestion of a tremor. The calmer and more reasonable he seemed the more secretly furious she'd become, a pattern which had grown by no means unfamiliar over the course of their marriage.

"They're animals," she said.

"Hardly that," said Roderick mildly. "Sounds like they're doing everything they can to make a proper state out of that place. Seems they've all kinds of plans for the future. And you can't say they're not following the international rule of law now. Why, the long trial to which they're subjecting that fellow, Vaughan…"

Diana shook her head in a single savage motion. "Animals," she said again. A long pause ensued. Then she added: "And you, Roddy, you're a born fool."

Roderick drained his glass and set it aside. Without saying more, he got to his feet and left the room. He knew without having to ask that he would sleep in one of the guest rooms that night. This was usually by far the best solution when life threw up some petty disagreement between them. Diana had generally forgotten all about it by morning and everything proceeded afterwards just as it had before.

He was surprised, then, when, at long past midnight, a soft tapping came at his door and Diana, in her nightdress, stepped into his room and slid into bed beside him. Even in the gloom, he could tell that she had been crying.

"Diana? Whatever's the matter?"

"You don't see, do you? You don't understand."

He reached for her hand, feeling a tenderness which he had

not experienced in relation to her for years. "Darling, what do you mean?"

"That this is the beginning of the end of it all..."

"What?"

"It's the start of the downfall of mankind."

She clung to him then, as though she really believed her words. He responded in kind and they did not speak again till morning.

10TH AUGUST, 1902

THE CITY

I

In the course of the long, strange year which had passed since the fall of the City and its reconstruction under the command of the Beast Folk, time had become for Mr Vaughan a slippery and treacherous thing. Past and present seemed mingled together in ways which were to him almost impossible to disentangle.

He received many visitors – some human, there to check that he was being well and fairly treated, but mostly creatures (a combination of gaolers, the merely curious and those who wished to make a record of his words). The most frequent visitor of all was a great, shambling creature whom many would have thought grotesque, half-bear and half-man, furred and sinister. He was, Mr Vaughan came gradually to realise, intended as some sort of advocate on his behalf for the trial which, he dimly apprehended was approaching.

The prisoner had to admit that the bear-man had showed exemplary patience, respectful in his questions and courteous in how he talked about the case, displaying a level of decency which Mr Vaughan was not certain that he deserved. Certainly, he thought in his more lucid moments, he would never have given the same respect to Brunor (that was his name) had their situations somehow been reversed.

Brunor spoke often to him of strategies and lines of arguments. He did his utmost to tie him down to dates and times, places and people, the exact order of events which led up to the founding of the City and the precise means of its operation. He also (for reasons which Mr Vaughan found opaque, being, as he had ever been, a person of thought and conceit rather than of practicality) was interested to the point of fixation on exactly how the place had been funded, the complex streams of donors and investors, the web of interested parties, all the dodges and sleights of hand, the hidden wellsprings of income and profit.

Somewhat to his surprise, Mr Vaughan found that he answered these questions as honestly as he was able. But, more and more as the weeks went by, he found it increasingly difficult to remember very much at all, the parade of financiers and eager capitalists starting to coalesce in his mind until he found it impossible to separate one from the other.

Although Brunor kept well hidden his frustration at the increasing frictionlessness of the old man's recall, Vaughan could sense it. There were times when his questioning grew more urgent, as though the creature feared that the memories would run out altogether, trickling away until they were irrecoverable. Still, Brunor never showed any sign of doubting the alienist's worsening condition and never once suggested, even in anger, that the forgetfulness and imprecision might be any sort of ruse or abdication. On his good days, Mr Vaughan realised that he respected the bear-man a great deal for this.

Sometimes, as he received his visitors in his little house by the sea like a ruined king in exile, Mr Vaughan noticed that the guests seemed to shift their appearance altogether. Their features and voices were altered and he seemed not to be conversing with some human functionary or messenger from the Beast Folk but people he had known, long ago and in a different place.

There were days when he saw before him Edward Prendick, the man who had first brought him news of the Island and of what had become of the doctor. He seemed much as he had in life, outwardly robust but inwardly fragile. His expression seemed more sorrowful than angry. "Do you know," he would say, sitting opposite Mr Vaughan on an uncomfortable chair as the waves seethed outside, "I think you may be even worse than him. He at least had the excuse of madness. But you're not, are you? Till now, at least, I think you've always been entirely sane."

At other times he saw before him poor Mr Berry, he who, with his wrecked face and flexible morality, had last been heard of in rural France, having failed to kill the Reverend Woodgrove. The valet said nothing at all but only glared at his old employer with eyes that spoke of a deep, ill-focused resentment. The fire in the boarding house, Mr Vaughan reflected, had somehow rearranged his nose and eyes, making him resemble, a child's scribble come to unhappy life.

Once he was even visited by a little girl, not more than ten, dressed in the fashions of the old century. Through the mists that were afflicting his consciousness it took him some minutes even to recognise her. They had been, he realised, playmates together once, at school in a village far from here in a time before any of this had been thought of. Her name danced at the edges of his thoughts.

"Louisa," he said. "Louie."

He spoke both names back to her, remembering them as he did so. With this came a rush of memories, long repressed, glimpses of happiness in the summer of '47. Laughter in the sunshine.

At the recollection that she had died in an accident, a tragedy, Vaughan felt briefly like some credulous character in an old tale, though he felt not shock or fear but only a warming sense of recognition.

"Not long now," Louisa said, though she surely had not drawn breath for more than half a century and was by now just dust and bones. "Not long now till we'll walk together again."

Vaughan smiled at the thought of it and, to lull and comfort himself, rocked to and fro in his chair. When he looked again at his visitor, the girl had gone and it was only the bear-man, frowning at him, a pad of paper open on his lap, a piece of charcoal held like an ink pen in his ungainly paw.

Months had gone by in this fashion and each day Mr Vaughan had sunk a little lower, his occasional outbreaks of panic becoming more and more infrequent as his dream-world came slowly to dominate his waking hours.

Until, at last, and with no particular fanfare that Vaughan was able to recall, Brunor walked into his cell one morning and declared, with a business-like sort of gravity: "It's time now. Your trial is about to begin."

II

The weeks that had followed had succeeded only in worsening Mr Vaughan's confusion. Often, he felt almost detached from his own body, as though he were floating some feet from the ground.

Brought into a great spherical room with dozens (hundreds?) of chairs and placed in a dock before a panel of judges (all Beast Folk), he was hauled out of his state of quiet isolation and thrust firmly in the public gaze. There were human spectators there too, either emissaries from various governments or gentlemen of the press, but they were outnumbered by far by the peoples of the City. The atmosphere was furious, febrile. The judges had to ask often for silence, attention and respect.

On the second day, it occurred to Mr Vaughan that the room in which they were all sitting had once been a restaurant, thought it was now greatly expanded. Dimly, he remembered having seen the plans.

On the third day, he tried counting all of the different species of Beast Folk which seemed to be present but he kept losing count after fifty-four.

On the fourth day, he became convinced that there were dead people sitting amongst the crowd, grinning and beckoning to him.

By the end of the first week, he had become all but oblivious to the pageant that was being played out before him, to the long line of those who arrived to give evidence against him and who pushed their own guilt onto him, the questions from the prosecution (a scholarly creature with the look about her of the water rat) and the objections of his own counsel, the bear-man. He hardly seemed to notice the glowering looks of the judges nor the gawping faces of the newspapermen.

For a time, he drifted, almost contentedly, through the waters of the past. When it was the turn of the Beast Folk to give their evidence against him, he kept forgetting why they were so angry with him, why they snarled and spat and shouted their accusations across the courtroom. He merely smiled benignly and struggled to remember their names.

Once, before he remembered, he grew concerned: would Mr Berry be giving evidence against him? Would Mr Bufford? Or Dr Bright? How curious, he thought, how very curious: he seemed to have spent a great deal of time with men whose names began with B. He giggled at the thought, only to see Brunor looking down at him, a realisation which very nearly sent him spiralling into full laughter. It had been only with some considerable effort that he had contained himself.

And so the dance went on around him, the trial of this new century, with a man at the heart of it who could feel himself (and the sensation was by no means exclusively an unpleasant one) fading, simply fading away.

III

It ended too soon, a week before the verdict, while Brunor was still presenting the case for the defence.

On the day in question, the court had adjourned early due to the oppressive heat and Mr Vaughan had been returned to his cell, Brunor by his side as usual.

There was a strong sense in the mind of the alienist that the events which they had witnessed had some great personal significance, though he found he could not identify them easily.

He was sitting back in his little room, on his bed, his feet rocking to and fro, as though he were a child again.

Brunor stood at the door, stern and with arms folded, like a visitor from a fairy story. "I'm doing the best I can," he said, in answer to a question which Mr Vaughan had already forgotten having asked. "I think our best hope now is to ask for a sentence which takes into account your illness. Perhaps you could even stay here?"

Mr Vaughan spoke then the most lucid sentence he had managed for weeks. "They'll want the death penalty, don't you think?" He smiled.

Brunor rocked back upon his paws. "That does seem likely. But, you know, the City authorities will wish to show the world we're capable of mercy. That we're not animals."

Vaughan looked vaguely at the creature before him. "Should've got me a human, then," he said. "Not a bear."

Brunor, sighing, rubbed his snout. "You ought to get some rest if you can. I'll see you tomorrow. Another day."

Mr Vaughan sank back onto his bed. "Another day," he echoed. He closed his eyes and listened as the bear-man stamped from the room. The slam of the door, the sliding across of bolt and chain, and he was caged again, like an animal. The notion of irony had by this point rather trickled from the consciousness of Mr Vaughan but something of it must still have remained because at this stray thought he loosed a single peal of laughter.

This done, he lay quietly and waited for sleep to come. Instead, he became gradually aware that there was someone else in the room. Someone standing beside him.

"Bear-man?" he said, though no answer came. "Is that you?"

He heard footsteps as the person approached his bed. He had the sudden conviction then that the visitor was human and also that they were dead. In fact, he was almost certain who it must be. For who was the one person, from all of his life, not to have visited him yet?

Mr Vaughan opened his eyes and looked up into the face of Dr Moreau. He looked just as he had on that afternoon, long ago, in the East of London, standing outside his laboratory in his white suit, like a ringmaster pacing before the lion cage. Vaughan blinked and the dead man smiled back.

"Quite a set of liberties you've taken, don't you think?" he said.

Mr Vaughan struggled to speak. His lips were dry and his throat was sore. "Aren't you proud of me? I went so much further than you ever dreamed of."

Moreau's mouth was set in a firm, unyielding line. "I wanted to create a new race," he said. "All you have succeeded in doing is creating a playground for rich men. You're nothing more than a common tyrant. A tyrant and a pimp."

Vaughan swallowed hard. "I wanted… to honour you. Your image. I put it everywhere."

"Blasphemy!" Moreau said and, even in his reduced state, Vaughan saw then what he ought always to have known: that the man was irreparably insane and, most likely, always had been.

"Please," he said. "What do you want from me?"

Moreau rolled his eyes. "I think they'll let you off. I think they'll take one look at you and decide they can't put this old wreck upon the gallows. So I think they'll let you moulder away here. And there's no justice in that."

"Then what…" Vaughan began but these two unremarkable words were to be his last as the hands of the doctor were already around his throat, squeezing and squeezing.

In the end, Mr Vaughan did not struggle. Some deep part of

him knew what he had done. And so he simply succumbed and gave himself up to the inevitable.

IV

The guards found him later that night. Brunor was called at once. He examined the body with little surprise but with a degree of sorrow which surprised him.

His conclusions reached, he went directly to Anta'Nar who only nodded when he heard the news, as stoical as ever.

"It does solve several problems at once," he said to Brunor. "The world has seen the trial. They can see it was just and fair and open. And now Mr Vaughan has been removed from the board."

"But, sir, do you think there's any justice in what's happened?"

Anta'Nar considered. "It's all we have," he said. "You wanted something crueller?"

"I am on that question, sir, in a state of some conflict."

"Aren't we all?" Anta'Nar replied and, to Brunor's surprise, he actually winked, a very human gesture which both amused the bear-man and made him feel oddly ill at ease.

Brunor said as much when he finally returned home and crawled into bed beside his wife.

"That I can understand," she said.

"Sorry. You should go back to sleep. I didn't mean to wake you."

"You didn't. As if I could sleep on a night like tonight. But just tell me one thing…"

Brunor yawned, stretched. "Of course."

"How did he die, that devil Vaughan?"

"Suicide," said Brunor. "To be honest, I was surprised he was capable of it. He's seemed so frail lately and so confused. But somehow he must have found the strength."

"How…"

"He hanged himself," Brunor said. "In the end, I had to cut him down."

His mate stroked Brunor's fur, a gesture of tender solidarity. "He was a wicked man," she said. "It's good for us all that he's gone."

Brunor sighed.

"My love? What troubles you?"

"You're right, he was an evil man," Brunor said. "Or at least a man who did evil things out of greed and a kind of venal curiosity. But I'm worried… the next time evil visits the City, might it not have a more smiling face? Might it not even come from a place of good intentions?"

4TH SEPTEMBER, 1920

CANNES, FRANCE

I

Eighteen years later and Brunor found himself in a foreign land, far from home and, so far as he was able to tell, in a minority of one. Much had changed since the "revolution" (an event which he could not consider even now without the use of careful, sceptical inverted commas) but he still felt nervous when surrounded by humans in great number. This was in spite of their slow and grudging acceptance of the Beast Folk and, he noted with a touch of bitterness, in spite of their happy acceptance of every startling technological development which the City had been able to produce.

In the bear-man's estimation, there could be no reasonable doubt that it was this which had kept the City both viable and inviolate as a tiny nation, quite separate from Great Britain and unaffiliated with any other state. Why, only this morning he had read in *Le*

Figaro a long article in praise of that happy stream of inventions and innovations which had been of material benefit to a great portion of the globe, written in a tone of open-minded liberalism but which was underscored by a substratum of prejudice. That the source of these same advances still remained unknown to him, he tried hard not to trouble him as much as it properly should.

Here, on the Riviera, for example, City-tech was everywhere, in the strange new garments that people wore, in the glossy books and magazines which they swapped and flourished and, above all, in the small dark wirelesses which were carried with them almost everywhere, each one playing music or speech from a plethora of available stations. It was a phenomenon which, whilst still remarkable, had now become commonplace. The earliest models had appeared a decade earlier; today they were everywhere.

Although he attracted many curious glances and outright stares, Brunor did his best to enjoy the sunshine on his back as he walked through the pleasant streets of the town. In the distance, the sea glimmered invitingly but the bear-man had no wish today to go into the water. Besides, beaches of any kind still brought back memories of the cell by the shore of Eddowes Bay where he had once spent a deal of time.

Now in the last decade and a half of its existence, Cannes was still a pretty place, a town of leisure and money. Brunor breathed in the air and felt himself moderately tempted to stop at one of the numerous bars and cafés which lined the streets (always assuming, of course, that he could find one which would serve a beast-person). His nose twitched at the smells of wine and warm bread, spices and sizzling food: mussels and bouillabaisse, pissaladière and socca. He entertained the notion of settling his great bulk into a chair by one of the bistros, ordering a Calvados, lighting up a Gauloise and reclining happily in smoke and liquor. In the end, he pushed these thoughts aside and pressed on. His purpose here was not, after all, one of tourism but one of an altogether more melancholy sort. It was a mission which brought him no pleasure and which seemed, even then, to feel somewhat ominous in its precedent.

"Mummy!"

The bear-man's rumination was disrupted by the sound of a little boy. He cannot have been more than three or four, dressed in a sailor suit and tugging hard on the right hand of his beleaguered-looking mother, a small, round-faced woman wearing clothes that were almost, but not quite fashionable, suggestive of a time before the innovations from the City had altered the processes of manufacture.

"Mummy! Look, Mummy. It's a bear-man!" He was speaking, Brunor realised, in English.

"Don't be rude," said his mother, but the boy was tugging forward, guileless and giddy in his excitement at glimpsing Brunor amongst the herd of comparatively hairless bipeds. As the child approached, the mother looked up at the creature from the City, her face flushed. "I really am so very sorry."

"I can't think of any reason why you should be," said Brunor. He dropped down, laboriously, to one knee and watched as the boy tottered closer.

"Hello," said the child.

"Hello," said the bear-man.

"Aren't you hot? I would be like that. All covered over with fur."

Brunor smiled, close-lipped so as not to alarm the child with the sight of his teeth. "Maybe I like to be warm."

The boy nodded with absolute seriousness, as though the explanation made perfect sense. "Who made you?" he asked.

Behind him, his mother apologised again, more effusively this time, and tried to pull her child away. Brunor held up a paw.

"I used to think that God did," he said. "Or a god, at any rate. But now… Well, now, I prefer to think that it was all just a happy accident. Now that's not so bad, is it?"

The boy shook his head. "Not so bad." He grinned. "Good luck, Mr Bear!" This done, he turned away and went back to his mother who was already chiding him for boldness and impertinence.

Brunor smiled and watched them go, with an affection of which his younger self would most certainly not have been capable. Was he simply softening, he wondered, in his old age? Or was there something more to be gleaned from the light in the boy's eyes? Something indicative of a different understanding to be nurtured by a new generation? Something like hope?

He shook his shaggy head, cursed himself for an optimistic fool. He paused for a moment to think of his own cubs when they were young and of the old dead man in the cell by the sea. Then he walked on.

II

His destination came into view soon after: a wide, sun-dappled courtyard in the middle of the town. Several small restaurants had set up shop here and it was to the most distant of them that Brunor now walked; an establishment much beloved by both locals and sightseers: Café Renardeau. There were tables set up outside under striped sun canopies. All were full with humans dressed for summer in pale, loose-fitting clothes. At Brunor's approach, a plump, toupeed maître d' waddled out to greet him, a thick menu clasped beneath his arm.

The proprietor could not entirely hide his shock on realising just what Brunor must be and where he was from but, to his credit, he disguised it almost immediately. "We have a few tables only, monsieur, and all indoors. Would you be willing to sit away from the sun?" He paused, his eyes flicking doubtfully up and down the bear-man. "Might it even be more comfortable for monsieur?"

"I'm here to see someone," said Brunor. "An Englishwoman. I think she eats here all the time. Her first name is Coral."

At this the proprietor turned a little ashen. "I'm not sure, monsieur... that I know anyone of that name at all."

Brunor folded his arms and settled his considerable weight upon his heels. "Oh but I think you do. My intelligence would suggest quite the opposite."

Before any more could be said, a woman appeared, out of the door to the side of the restaurateur. There was another lady behind her, in shadow, one who squeezed the first woman's shoulder then melted away into some back room. The first stepped forward.

"It's fine, Jules," said Coral Mayfield. "He's come here looking for me. Haven't you, Brunor?"

III

They walked together, through the town, heading vaguely in the direction of the beach.

"It's very sweet of you to come all this way to find me, Brunor, but there really was no need. I said I needed time away from the City. I didn't say I wouldn't return."

"Your son is concerned, ma'am."

They were drawing attention, the two of them, a woman and
a beast-person chatting like old friends. Brunor ignored the looks
of the amblers and pedestrians and listened to Coral Mayfield.
Almost all of the passers-by clutched their small black wirelesses.

"Oh, he doesn't need me. Not any more. According to the
terms of your people, he's practically middle-aged by now. And
he's made all of the right decisions. Smart. Canny. The City's in a
stronger state that we could have dreamed of, all those years ago."

Brunor looked down at the human by his side. Her face seemed
to him to be indicative of happiness. "He wants you to come home."

Coral grimaced. "But it's not home to me, is it? If anything,
I've come to rather hate the place."

"How so, madam?"

"I feel you've all been penned in there, isolated by my species.
It… infuriates me." Her face was set into an expression of outraged
pugnacity, like the stubborn little girl she must once have been.

"I have some sympathy," said the bear-man, "with that
argument."

Coral smiled. "Dear Brunor. Always choosing your words
with such care. He trusts you. My son. More than that, he
respects you. Can't you speak with him? Tell him I'm happy here
for awhile. Tell him that I'll come back when I can."

Brunor sighed. "He's quite adamant."

"I'm not yet forty, you know. There's quite a bit of living I'd
like to do yet. And I gave up so much of my life to the City. You'll
speak to him, won't you? He'll understand." A pause. "Brunor? I
said – would you speak to him?"

But Brunor could no longer hear her. The wirelesses, clutched
by all the people of the town, were doing something strange. In
a thing which he had never witnessed before, every one of them

seemed to be receiving the same broadcast.

With a bear's sense of danger, he held out a paw. "Wait, ma'am. Listen."

The pedestrians themselves were looking with surprise at their devices. There were uneasy glances between them and murmurs of unease. Brunor caught a subtle shift in the scent of the human pack, the first glints of fear. It was more, then, than mere coincidence. The same broadcast was appearing on every station. A young couple, arm in arm in the manner of honeymooners, had stopped right by them. The male of the pair, plump-faced and bearded, was gazing openly at the bear-man. His wireless was clutched in his right hand. Brunor caught something of the words that were being delivered by the reporter. His French was good enough that he could get a clear sense of it. Certain key phrases stood out.

"Assassination in the City… Commander Anta'Nar killed in the explosion… terrorist human group claiming responsibility…" There was more – much more – in this vein but Brunor had already heard enough.

He turned to Coral Mayfield and she seemed like a person transformed. Just a minute or so ago and she had been almost relaxed, a woman whose work was done, a woman who wished only to find her own pleasures and delights.

Now she had changed utterly. Tears streaked either cheek, her eyes were wide with horror, her mouth formed in a soundless o as if she meant to scream. The truth was worse, Brunor thought; it was an expression not of frantic grief but of purpose.

Much later, when he went home to find the City in a state of skittish mourning, darker and more paranoid than before, he would say to his wife that Coral had seemed to him in that single moment to be changed "into something like a spirit of vengeance".

He would name one of the gods of the old island and his wife would well understand. Later still, upon hearing Coral speak to the ruling body to hint at her plans for retribution, he would at once tend his resignation, and his wife would say that she well understood this too (indeed, that she was gladdened by the decision).

Yet for now, in Cannes, the human woman beckoned the bear-man over to her. "My boy…" she said and, without thinking, Brunor took her in his arms and held her tight.

"I weep," he said. "For him. For you. All of us."

Even then as he held her he heard the steel in her voice. "I tried to get away. But it's no good. No, no."

"Madam, please."

"This is… too much. We have to do something. We have to make them see sense. Good God, Brunor, we have to make them *understand*."

24TH AUGUST, 1935

ON BOARD THE
PHILANTHROPY EXPRESS

I

In the course of a successful career which had spanned a decade and a half – and which had necessitated the violent deaths of thirty-three individuals – Miss Josephine Galligan had trained herself to need very little sleep. That she was able to survive (indeed, to flourish) on this bare minimum of rest had saved her life on several occasions as surely as it had eased and facilitated the unfortunate fates of others. On this particular afternoon, however, something unprecedented had occurred.

Having boarded the train at Little Rock, Arkansas, and having been shown to her cabin by a nervy, rather clumsy boy of not more than eighteen with a shock of ginger hair and a pronounced (almost stagey) Brooklyn accent, Galligan had lain down upon her narrow bed with her single valise still unopened before her, meaning to take no more than fifteen minutes of brisk and dreamless slumber, only to slip immediately into deep sleep.

By sheer force of will, Josephine managed generally to dream either not at all or else very slightly, waking on instinct at the first sign of any unwelcome image. Yet today, lulled, perhaps, by the rhythmic rocking of the train upon the tracks, she went much deeper than usual and she dreamed a dream of near-hallucinatory clarity.

She was upon a distant beach in a lush and sun-drenched place where she had never been in her life before. She was drowsing there too but was woken by a disturbance in the water beyond, something moving, rising from the waves. As she got to her feet in the dream, there came then a deep, thoughtful voice which spoke directly to her mind and to impart a flow of warnings and instructions. The precise words that were spoken she forgot at once upon waking but the urgency of them stayed with her, that and their awful quality of calculation. The heat on her back, the voice in her head and, then, something waking her from this dream within a dream: the smell of smoke, the sounds of screaming, the promise of violence on the breeze…

Aware now on some level that she was dreaming, Galligan forced herself to wrench open her eyes. She found – again, most uncharacteristically, for a woman of such self-control – that she was struggling, almost wheezing for a breath, like a glutton at the top of a steep flight of stairs or a baby whose head had slipped momentarily beneath her bathwater. She was shivering too – a writer of popular fiction would have called it "shuddering". Galligan lay still. She forced herself to regulate her breathing. She assured herself that she had been merely dreaming and reminded herself with patient and clear-eyed practicality of her surroundings.

The cabin was a small one, if opulently appointed: a crimson rug, a bedside table, a small mirror and a piece of tasteful artwork on the wall, a bland seascape which was no doubt intended to be soothing. A small window afforded a view of the darkening country, a smooth, regular blur, the nation glimpsed as through a picture frame. Galligan rose and stretched, her fingertips grazing the roof of the cabin. She was a tall woman and strong with it; at forty-three, something in her manner was still suggestive of the athlete. In a few swift motions she filled almost the whole of the cabin.

Space was at a premium on board the Express and this room was only moderately priced, by no means the cheapest but still a long way from those more generous quarters which were intended to cater for the very rich. Of course, Galligan's employers could well have afforded such accommodation, though it was generally preferred by all involved that she travel as discreetly as possible, drawing as little attention to herself as she could.

Unsettled by the depth of her sleep and (though she would be most unlikely ever to have admitted it to herself) by the weird clarity of her dream, Galligan stretched out her arms and took three short breaths, just as she had been taught, long ago, to bring the world into focus once again.

A knock came at the door, barely audible over the rattle and surge of the train: three soft beats upon the wood. It had a quality of repetition, as though whoever stood outside had been there for some time. Was it this which had woken her? Galligan thought it most likely.

The tall woman stepped towards the door and stood, unspeaking, beside it.

"Who is it?" she called out, in a hearty tone which was most unlike her usual speaking voice. Her employer, the presumably pseudonymous Mr Parabola, had often remarked that Josephine might have made a fine actress if only she had troubled herself to learn the craft. "Who's there?"

A voice came from the other side. "Got a parcel for you, miss."

"I don't doubt you do. But who are you?"

"Jimmy, miss. We met earlier."

Carefully, Galligan opened the door. The young man from before – the gawky red-headed adolescent – stood on the threshold, dressed in the neat pink uniform of the railway and swaying indecorously with the motion of the train. There was a slim brown parcel beneath his left arm.

"Is that for me, Jimmy?" The tone was calm now, friendly but not overly so, designed to be forgettable.

"Yes, miss." The young man passed over the parcel. Galligan squeezed it once, briefly, and surmised that its contents were paper.

"Thank you, Jimmy." She produced a single dollar and gave it to the boy.

"No, miss. Thank you, miss." He looked beyond Galligan, into the cabin. "Everything okay? Are you enjoying your journey so far?"

"Very much, thank you."

"That's good, miss."

"Can you tell me where we are now?"

"We've just passed by Dallas, miss."

Gilligan blinked in surprise. "Already? This train is faster than I'd expected."

"Top of the line, ain't it? The most advanced of its kind."

"Impressive. So far."

The boy looked awkward, eager to get away. "Is there anything else, miss? I should say that supper will be served in an hour and forty minutes. The dining car have your reservation."

"Thank you, Jimmy. You're most useful."

Jimmy grinned gratefully and nodded. "Always do my best. Oh and miss?"

"Yes, Jimmy?"

"After the food, the guest of honour will give his speech. Though don't worry, they'll keep serving drink all the way through. No alcohol, of course."

Josephine winked. "Glad to hear it."

"Thought you might be." The boy turned left and continued down the carriage. Galligan watched him go, then closed the door, locked it and went to the bed with her parcel.

She opened it swiftly and found inside a single folded newspaper, the *Daily Herald*, its pages filled with talk of various European disruptions and upheavals. These stories she ignored.

At the middle of the paper, folded inside, was her expected gift from Mr Parabola. A single photograph, black and white, showed a plump, grey-haired man, dressed in a black suit and bow tie, facing the camera with what was presumably intended as a look of sombre gravitas.

Josephine recognised the man at once. There were few in the English-speaking world who took even a moderate interest in current affairs who would not.

She took one further glance at the photograph, picked it up and moved towards the window. With a single, swift motion she pushed down the glass. A sudden howl of cold air billowed into the room. Galligan crumpled the photograph into a ball, threw it outside then closed the window.

She went to the suitcase which still lay on the ground, swung it up onto the bed and opened it. There were inside a set of new clothes, a volume of short stories (Kipling which, although antique, she often found to be to her taste) and the tools of her trade: a revolver, a sheathed blade and a length of strong rope. There was also a fountain pen and a pocket notebook, cream-coloured and with her initials – J.R.G. – embossed on the front cover.

Galligan opened the book and flicked through it. On each page there was a name. There were thirty-three in total, twenty male and thirteen female. Beneath each name was a date and a line or two of detail.

On the next blank page Josephine wrote the following, underlining it with a firm black line.

"Albert Edgington. 08/24/35".

II

An hour passed in which Josephine Galligan prepared herself for dinner. She was a naturally smart woman, ordered and precise in almost every aspect of her life. Her mode of dress was representative of these essential traits and she looked immaculate, if a little aloof, in a light green dress which only just was starting to look old-fashioned.

She had a small, crimson handbag with her in which she felt the weight of her revolver. In Italy, Argentina, Switzerland or any of the other foreign countries in which she had carried out her unforgiving work the possible discovery of this item might have caused her concern. Yet this was Texas and, although they were only passing through the state, the rules of the realm still applied. Here it would most likely seem suspicious if she were not, however discreetly, armed.

Galligan took a breath, feeling the familiar surge of giddiness which she experienced at the outset of any fresh commission. It was popularly supposed that persons in her line of work had no feelings to speak of, that they made themselves as best they could into soulless automatons in order to do what they were paid to do. There may be some truth in this but most certainly not in the case of Miss Galligan. She often felt a great deal, a considerable spectrum of emotion, of which this flurry of excitement was only a small part. She leant for a moment upon the door handle until the dizziness subsided, then stepped briskly outside.

The corridors of the train were narrow and swaying. The lights had been dimmed a little in honour of the evening. Outside the great flat contours of the desert moved by with a strange, paradoxical kind of languorous rapidity.

Josephine turned right, her tall frame almost scraping the ceiling. She had almost reached the door which led to the adjacent carriage when she saw it open and a familiar figure step through.

"There you are, miss," said Jimmy. "I was just coming to find you."

"Why, thank you. But there's no need. I do believe I'm capable of finding the dining carriage all by myself."

"Gee, I know you are, miss. But ain't you running late?"

"No," Galligan said, "that can't be right," but something in the boy's tone had unsettled her and so she consulted her wristwatch. "It's a few minutes before seven," she said with moderate irritation. "I'm right on time."

"No, miss, it's well past eight. Your watch must be slow. Or broken."

Galligan looked again at the face of the device. She held the second hand in her gaze and saw it was unmoving. "You're right."

"Sorry, miss."

"No harm, I suppose," Josephine said, though, at this minor disruption, she felt a distinct prickle of unease. "I'll have to get it fixed."

"Give it to me, miss. I can do that for you. It'll be working just fine again by the morning."

"Thank you," Galligan said and she found herself taking off the watch and handing it to the boy almost without thinking. Jimmy pocketed it.

"This way now, miss," he said, turned around and went back through the door.

Josephine followed, moving through another three identical carriages, as the desert spooled by. They passed no other passengers and Galligan, unsettled, made no further conversation.

At last they came to the dining carriage. The contrast with what had preceded it was vivid to an almost uncomfortable degree.

Like so much of that remarkable train, it was a considerable feat of engineering. It was a narrow space, but a long one, with room for dozens of guests. It had something of the air of a cocktail bar (officially, of course, no liquor could be served here, not while the path of the railroad curved through dry state after dry state) and it was a long, surprisingly expansive space, with plentiful tables crammed in to make artful use of the available room. The carriage was full, with dozens of diners, all dressed expensively and for maximum effect. Food had already been served and the passengers were eating busily. The sounds were of thoughtful conversation, the chink and clink of railway cutlery, the pouring and slurping of fine drinks, all underscored by the insistent bass of the train's forward motion.

There was a part of Josephine, buried but palpable, which was repulsed by this scene and by the people within it – a side of her personality which went some way to explain her choice of career. An expert alienist (someone like Mr Vaughan, perhaps, in the earliest days of his career before his long descent) might have found her to be a most interesting case study.

For a moment, Josephine allowed herself a rarity: a piece of imagination. She saw all of the guests at this high supper as pigs, oinking and snuffling at the trough. That this image was both a familiar one and, arguably, somewhat judgemental, need not detain us; as they did not cause Josephine to slow her stride they should not be permitted to impede our progress.

"Here's your place, miss." This was the boy again, gesturing now towards a small table at the furthest edge of that long carriage. "Nice and discreet. Just the way you like it."

There was something most curious in the way in which he spoke this second sentence which gave Josephine reason to look at him more closely.

"Why do you say that?" she asked as she took her seat.

The boy shrugged. "Your reputation precedes you, miss."

"How can it?" she asked, rather sharply. "You've surely never heard of me."

He grinned. "Everyone here knows you, Josephine."

"What did you say?"

He winked. "Mr Parabola says hello." The boy turned and came back in the direction that he had come. By the finish of his speech, Josephine thought, the child's Brooklyn accent had all but vanished to reveal something less certain underneath. Something European?

Josephine considered. It seemed strange to her, that her employer should have placed another agent in the scene, especially one who was so small in years and stature. Still, it was not entirely unprecedented. There were rumours, amongst the community of those who plied the same trade, that Mr Parabola had done similar things in the past, though only rarely and strictly in cases of the utmost significance.

Why was this job so important, Galligan wondered, what made this man's life stand out amongst so many others?

The arrival of a waiter interrupted her thoughts. A tall, bearded fellow, dressed in the uniform of the railway, there was something distractingly unruly – almost leonine – about him.

"Good evening, Miss Galligan."

Another accent. This time: Australian. It had a broad, rather coarse twang.

"You're late, miss." This was said with an implication of reproof. "Would you still be wanting the starter?"

Galligan glared at the interloper. "Have I paid for the starter?"

"Oh yes, miss. Most certainly, miss. Or at least, Miss Galligan, whoever paid for your ticket has paid for the starter."

"Starter, please," Josephine said, adding with a snip of disdain: "if you'd be so kind."

The waiter did not speak again but only nodded and withdrew. At the sight of him, Galligan received another odd, unexpected image: that the man resembled nothing so much as a dark chess piece being pulled backwards on the board, something sliding slyly into place in order to protect the queen.

No observer would have been able to deduce it, so solidly imperturbable was Josephine's demeanour, yet at this she felt a further spasm of unease. What, she wondered, was wrong with her? Why was she thinking such strange thoughts?

At the front of the carriage, on the table that was raised a little from the rest, there was some activity. Four men were seated around the table. The oldest (and the plumpest) of them had risen, on well-fed legs and was hitting the side of his glass (containing a substance which looked like water but almost certainly wasn't) with a fork.

"Ladies and gentlemen!" the stout man was saying in an accent which hinted at the South. "Your attention, please!"

Amid some joshing and good-natured complaint, the occupants of the carriage fell obediently silent.

"How fine it is to see so many of you here tonight, all crammed into the most capacious carriage that money can buy!"

There was at this some polite chortling.

"I hope and trust you are enjoying the ride so far. So much to see as we cross this great nation, and so much top-drawer service to relish on board. To that end, ladies and gentlemen, why don't you join me now in thanking the good folks on board this train who've made our journey so very smooth and luxurious?" The stout man held up his hands theatrically and began to clap.

Many of the other passengers joined in and a ripple of applause passed around the carriage. Blending in, Galligan did the same. A waiter returned with a drink for Josephine – not the leonine man from before but rather an older, dark-haired woman who seemed, somehow, oddly familiar.

"Your drink…" she murmured, the words almost lost in the tide of applause, before withdrawing into the shadows.

"Now then," the plump man said once the clapping had subsided, "I know very well that you haven't paid what you've paid for tonight to listen to me jawing. Or even for this very fine food."

More polite laughter.

"No, what you've come here for is to listen to the words of one man. To listen to the truth, ladies and gentlemen – the truth they don't want you to hear!" All around Josephine, the audience were nodding in agreement and stating their support.

"One of the most courageous and remarkable Englishmen of his age. A man who it is my pleasure now to introduce to you. Ladies and gentlemen, I give you: Mr Albert Edgington!"

On cue, another diner at the table rose to his feet. He was the kind of man, Josephine thought, who might be considered average in every way: a solidly built man in his fifties, dressed unremarkably and showing no obvious signs of charisma. He looked like the popular conception of a bank manager or a small town doctor, someone almost comforting in his very ordinariness.

Having got to his feet, Edgington bowed his head briefly to acknowledge the applause.

"Hello," he said, "my name is Albert and I very much hope that all that applause isn't meant for me. I'm really nothing special, you know."

Some smiles at this, a smattering of additional applause, a few jocular rebuttals.

Meanwhile, Josephine Galligan leaned back in her seat, drank her drink and thought to herself that it really was a pity that Albert Edgington had to die.

III

"Thirty-four years ago today," said Mr Albert Edgington to his well-heeled, casually extravagant audience, "what has since come to be known as the City of Dr Moreau was first brought to the attention of the wider world. Run for more than a decade as a kind of rich man's playground and pleasure garden, the revolution of the peoples who were kept there against their will resulted in the overthrow of that tyrannical regime." Edgington paused, leaned down to the table, reached for a glass and took a sip. He was an accomplished speaker; the interruption served only to heighten the interest of his audience.

"I was there myself that night," he went on, "as many of you here will know."

Josephine found it hard to believe that there was anyone amongst this crowd who did not know this very well indeed.

"By sheer bad luck and misjudgement, I found myself at the heart of one of the great events of the twentieth century. And, my friends, I do not think that it is any exaggeration for me to say that those of us who witnessed the city in flames and the noble supremacy of its former captives believed with all of our hearts that great change had come to the City." He paused again, took another sip.

Josephine herself leaned back a little further in her seat and took something of her own drink.

"In part, of course, this has most certainly happened. The City acquired its own independence in law and remains a thriving hub of both industry and tourism. The many scientific advances which have been dreamed up by some of the deep thinkers of that place have secured huge advances for the world at large. And if you need proof of that, just take a look at this miracle of engineering on which we're presently speeding through the American night."

Polite laughter at this, the sound of an audience being coaxed with acumen and skill into feeling good about themselves.

"Yet independence," Edgington went on, "was not as complete as it first seemed. Governments around the world have done all they can to make trade difficult for the peoples of the City, just as they have discouraged at every stage the emigration and travel of those self-same people. Had it not been for that torrent of desirable scientism from that tiny but indomitable nation I don't doubt that the City would long ago have had to seek sanctuary in the arms of one major power or another. The outrageous and tragic assassination of Anta'Nar, the first true leader of the City, only exacerbated this state of affairs."

Sombre nods all round at this, together with much surreptitious eating and drinking. Sounds of indolent chewing. The eyes of Josephine Galligan flicked around the room, scanning for possible obstacles, looking for entry and exit points, understanding what might be practicable. Her gaze passed over the other diners without taking in the detail of them until she was brought up short by the sight not of a guest but of a waiter, an older man dressed in sombre black like something from the last century.

"In part, of course, the fact that the City has been able to maintain its independence for more than thirty years is down to the generosity of you and to people like you, who have, through unstinting donation, kept the City solvent."

Without drawing the least attention to herself, Josephine peered before her, trying to get a better view of the man she'd seen in the shadows. She squinted, winced, hesitated, then looked again. Could it be him? After all this time?

"So," said Edgington, "why not give yourselves a round of applause? Go on. After all, you deserve it!"

A burst of eager clapping broke out. To Josephine the diners seemed to bathe in the sound, wallowing in self-approbation. The man across the room whom Galligan believed she had recognised did not clap but he seemed now to be aware of the gaze that was upon him. He turned his head. Their eyes met. At the sight of her he showed no visible reaction. You would have to have known him very well indeed – as Josephine once had – in order to see the shock in the subtle adjustment of his stance.

At last the applause began to die down.

Across the room, Josephine and the waiter gazed at one another. Something passed between them, something which the crowd, settling again in their seats, eager for the next phase of the evening to begin, did not appear to recognise. Then the man was on the move, bustling, hurrying away, towards the end of the carriage, going at speed towards the front of the train.

Albert Edgington went on. "Nonetheless, my friends, the City remains free only in the strictest and most pedantically legalistic interpretation of the term. In spite of the bounties that it has given to the world, in spite of all that it has wrought, in spite of the example of good governance that it has provided, still it is shunned and ignored. Still it is not given its due. Still the peoples of the City are confined to one small patch of the English coast. Still the wider world refuses to change in order to accommodate us. Still it sticks stubbornly to the old ways, when everything around it continues to evolve."

Josephine hardly heard this speech, so lost was she in the past and in the awful, bewildering incongruity of the sight that she had seen. Then, seeing the attempted escape of the man, she too found herself upon her feet and moving in pursuit, her target and assignment all but forgotten.

"But this can – and it will – come to an end. My friends, we'll make the world finally understand. We'll make them acknowledge the City and make them permit free travel of its peoples all over the globe. My friends, please be in no doubt when I say this to you now: we will make them afraid!"

More applause at this but Josephine paid it no heed. She was almost at the side of the hurrying man. He stepped ahead of her, out of the carriage and into the next. She followed without once looking behind her, the cheers and whoops of the crowd at her back.

The next carriage was, unexpectedly to Josephine, almost entirely empty. It was, she supposed, a kind of library. There were shelves filled with books, though all of them had the same blue spine with no lettering at all. There might, for all she knew, have been hundreds of identical copies of the same volume.

The man whom she had been following was waiting for her, leaning between the shelves and the window. Outside, the desert flashed by.

From the adjacent carriage could still be heard the sounds of cheers and well-fed approval.

The man looked at Josephine and she looked at him. How old he has become, she thought, how bowed and weary.

"It is you."

He had the good grace at least to look sheepish. "Hello, sweetheart."

She rubbed at her eyes, trying to persuade herself that what she saw before her was real. She blinked. For all that the day had taken on the unreliable quality of a dream, the fact of his presence seemed irrefutable. "Dad," she said at last. "Whatever are you doing here?"

IV

The old man (and he was now an old man, this she had to concede) waited a long while before he replied to her question. Next door, the sounds of applause were over and the warm, persuasive tones of Mr Albert Edgington could once again be heard.

"They told me I could see you," he said. "They promised."

"Dad?" she said, and moved towards him very carefully, almost gingerly. "Who are 'they'? What's happening here?"

He smiled as she approached. "You look well, Jo. Very well. You've become quite the lady."

"Dad, please. You shouldn't be here. I don't think this is a safe place."

"Oh, I dare say it's not," said the old man. "But where exactly is safe nowadays?" He screwed up his face, as though he smelled something bad. "You know, if they get their way, I don't think anyone's ever going to be safe again."

Josephine reached his side. "Dad, what are you talking about? What do you mean?" She reached out and touched him. He was hot, she realised, almost feverish and practically shaking.

"I shouldn't have left you both," he said, speaking of things which, so far as Josephine was concerned, had ended many years ago for them both. "I know that. It was wrong of me and I was a coward. I should have stayed. Tried to do better. But, you see, your mother..."

Josephine, who had been only sixteen when she attended her mother's funeral, said nothing to this. Instead she was listening to what was going on in the adjacent carriage. It seemed to her that nothing at all was being said. There was no sound of any kind emanating from that adjacent space.

"Dad," she said. "What exactly is happening here? Why did you lead me in here?"

When she looked she saw that the old man's eyes were brimming with tears. "Please," he said. "It began as quite a coincidence."

"I've come to mistrust coincidence."

"They said they didn't know who I was when they hired me and I believe them. Some days…"

"Dad."

"I wanted to see you and they gave me the opportunity. Just once they said."

It was not quite contempt in Josephine's eyes but neither was it any especially soft emotion. "Why?"

"So that I could say sorry," said her father, before adding with an unbecoming sniffle: "And you could forgive me."

Although Josephine remained profoundly troubled by the persistence of the silence on this train of the foolishly rich, she turned her attention in full towards her father. She appraised him in a single glance: a sad, broken-down fellow whose every movement spoke of regret and self-loathing. For a moment she considered telling him the truth – that she had thought very little about him in all of the years that they had been apart, that her memories of him were neither good nor bad but mostly indifferent, and that her mother had considered them better off without his presence in their lives. To have done so, however, struck her as needlessly unkind, and so she said: "I forgive you." She kissed him once upon the cheek in a kind of benediction.

Then she turned and walked towards the carriage door.

"Good luck," her father said behind. "I always loved you, you…"

The end of this sentence was lost as Josephine stepped into the adjoining segment of the train and then into the next carriage.

V

She was met by silence. Every face in the room seemed to be turned towards her, as though they had been waiting for her to arrive.

Then Albert Edgington called out: "Miss Josephine Galligan, ladies and gentlemen! Please. I give you: the herald of the new age!"

And the room erupted into cheers. Many of the diners rose to their feet, slamming their hands together with wild enthusiasm which dwarfed their earlier efforts.

She wheeled about in confusion. She took her revolver from her pocket.

At this the applause stopped.

Albert Edgington looked at her with mild disapproval. "No need for that," he said. "It's quite harmless anyway."

Josephine pulled the trigger. The barrel was empty.

"Jimmy removed the bullets while you slept."

The boy with the wandering accent stood across the room. He winked at her.

"Who are you people?" Josephine asked, disliking intensely the theatricality of the thing. "Why have you done this?"

"You sound affronted," Edgington went on. "That's really in rather poor taste, I should say, given what you came here to do to me."

In a fit of fury, Josephine hurled her revolver to the ground where it skittered and spun into the shadows. "It's my profession," she said, after she had recovered her composure.

Edgington shrugged. "A standard enough response. Though we are all victims of circumstance in one way or another. Don't you think? Speaking of which, I hope that you achieved some manner of understanding with your father next door. We all thought it would be a nice gesture. One last chance at reconciliation."

"Why…" Josephine said again. She had started to feel most unwell. There was a prickling sensation in her scalp. Her eyes ached. Suddenly, she began to shiver. "Why have you done this?"

"For the good of the planet," Edgington said. "For justice for Anta'Nar. We're all on this train exactly what we appear to be: well-meaning, wealthy, philanthropists. We want to help the peoples of the City."

"A fine aim," Josephine said. Though she found herself feeling even worse now. Whatever was attacking her body was moving swiftly. "But how does that… involve me?"

"We want to make the world understand," said a new voice. A dark-haired woman walked out from the crowd, towards Josephine's side. She recognised her from before, the woman who had given Josephine her drink, the woman whom she now recognised as:

"Coral Mayfield!" Albert exclaimed and the room burst once again into applause.

The woman came close to Josephine now. "Poor girl. You must be feeling distinctly groggy by now, I should have thought."

Josephine said nothing but her swaying gait and pallor gave away the truth.

"I am sorry that it will cause some pain but it was necessary to drug you for the first part of the procedure." She smiled. "I want you to know, Miss Galligan, that you're doing an awful lot of good for the peoples of the world. You will, in your own way, become something of a pioneer. Even, perhaps, a heroine…"

Yet Galligan heard no more of this. Her vision grew overwhelmed by fizzing crimson, she stumbled then fell backwards, for the first time in her life, into a swoon.

VI

She was still on the train when she awoke, though in a carriage which she had not seen before – one, she soon suspected, which hardly anyone aboard could have seen for the sake of their sanity.

It was, amongst other things, a tribute to the scientific advances which had flowed out of the City since its establishment as an independent state. At the left-hand corner was a glass screen upon which a figure whom she recognised only from newsreels – the furred and uniformed new leader of the City – was seen to strut and pace. On either side of this screen, stood Mr Albert Edgington and Miss Coral Mayfield. It was what took up the bulk of the space in the carriage, however, which understandably seized most of Josephine's attention.

It was a great tank of water in which something remarkable was being kept: a vast, dark, tentacular creature, something like an octopus, with blazing eyes.

Josephine had been bound to a chair. Every part of her ached.

"She's waking up." This was the voice of Albert Edgington. "Oh dear. What a pity. I really am so very sorry, my dear, that this is being done to you."

"Hush." This was Coral. "Never forget how many she has killed."

"None of us is exactly innocent," said Albert mildly.

"What is this?" Josephine lifted her head to look her captors in the eye. "What are you doing to me? And what is that thing in there?"

Coral smiled. The great black octopus moved closer to the glass, almost as if it had heard and understood her. Not possible, Josephine thought. Surely?

"We had to do something," Coral said. "We couldn't let things go on as they are. We had to take a stand."

"You were chosen at random," Albert said. "Entirely at random from a list of very bad people. It seemed the fairest way."

"There will be some pain," Coral went on, "and I know that's not a happy thing. But it will be necessary."

In the tank, the octopus-thing stroked the glass with one of its tentacles. There was something so inhuman in the motion that Josephine could not hold back a yelp of disgust.

Coral looked witheringly at her. "There's no need," she said, "for such disrespect. Not for a being which has guided our actions for so long. A being which has always urged firm, decisive action. Events have proved them correct."

"What is that thing?"

Then Josephine heard a new voice, one which seemed to speak only in her own head. "Josephine Galligan. What you see before you is what is speaking to you now."

Josephine looked wildly about her but she saw no sign that the other two humans in the room had heard what she had heard at all.

The voice in her head went on. "I think it respectful for you to know exactly what they will do to you. My creator never offered me the same courtesy."

"Impossible…" Josephine murmured. Albert and Coral looked over at her and smiled, as though they could guess what was happening.

"I have overseen the development of a viral agent," the voice went on. "One which has the power of transmogrification. It is highly transmissible, highly contagious. It will be unstinting and without mercy."

"What do you mean?" Josephine said aloud before, realising that she needed only to think these thoughts: *What is transmogrification?*

"You will all be changed," the voice said. "You will become as are the children of the City. A whole new species. Something better. You should feel proud, Josephine Galligan, to have played so crucial a role in its forging."

The voice ceased then to speak. In the tank the octopus moved away from the glass, sinking down towards the mirk at the bottom.

"You're mad," Galligan said, hopelessly but with fierce contempt.

Albert nodded glumly, as though accepting the truth of the charge.

Coral merely shrugged. "If we are then the world has made us so. I would have left it be, you know. I would have walked away. If not for what was done to my son."

"No, none of this can be possibly be happening. None of it can possibly work. None of it's even true."

Coral smiled. For a moment a flicker of sadness crossed her face, an echo of the little girl she had once been. "It's all real," she said. "It's all happening. And this is what has to happen if the City is to be allowed to reach its true potential." A look of absolute zealotry came into her eyes. "This what my son would have wanted. For the truth of the City to spread out across the globe."

And Josephine knew at that moment that she was lost.

VII

Much of what followed after this was darkness to Josephine Galligan. She was aware of faces (not all of them human) looking down at her, of the dark octopoid thing in the tank, of the relentless motion of the train, its inexorable hum and sway.

She did not see her father. Much in recent hours seemed to her to be so close to a dream as to be practically indistinguishable from it. They kept her drugged and she passed often in and out of consciousness. There were injections and copious other forms of treatment. Already, she could sense within her the first stirrings of transformation. She screamed often. She wept. She did not ask for mercy. She kept, in her own terms, true to herself.

And then, it was over. After one particularly long blackout, she found herself free, or so, at least, it appeared. She was sitting outside, no longer on the train, but on a bench in what was to her immediately recognisable as Central Park, New York. She had been dressed expensively. She wore a long white fur coat, the pockets of which were stuffed with cash.

Something moved within her. Something crackled through her system. There was in her jaw an ache, almost as though fresh teeth were growing. She had to fight back the urge to howl.

She rose from the bench and, as if in a trance, began to walk out of the park and towards the American city, to that destiny which was waiting for her there.

21ST SEPTEMBER, 1935

GROSVENOR HOTEL, MANHATTAN

I

Miss Angelique Dupont had met numerous strange visitors during her decade of working at the Grosvenor Hotel but she had never seen anyone quite like the guest who had, for the past three weeks, become resident in room 52. For one thing, the lady had not left her quarters in all of that time, living entirely off room service and building up a bill of the kind that was generally referred to (though always, Angelique had noted, from people who could afford most things easily enough) as "eye-watering". For another, there was evidently something very wrong with the woman, both physically and mentally, something which, as she had refused all help since her arrival, was surely getting steadily worse.

Angelique had been on duty behind reception on the day when the woman had walked into the lobby. She had seemed a little unsteady on her feet and as though she had suffered some recent ordeal. She was also well-dressed; the long white fur coat alone was worth at least a month of Angelique's wages. The stranger possessed an air of confidence (even, Angelique thought, of some indefinable quality of danger) and she paid for everything upfront and in cash. In such circumstances, Angelique had long since learned the importance of looking the other way, of pretending not to see what was right in front of her.

"I need a room," the woman had said, in a voice that sounded husky and tired. "A room in the name of human charity."

Angelique had thought then that this was a curious phrase to deploy in what was, after all, one of New York's dearest and most exclusive hotels, though she had complied immediately with the woman's request and told her that 52 was available. The visitor had agreed, handed over the tariff and signed her name in the register with a shaky kind of flourish as "Miss J. G. Galligan".

"Do you have any luggage?" Angelique had asked and the woman had waved away the question with a bitter laugh, as though the very notion was wildly improbable. "Well then," said Angelique with a brightness that she did not altogether feel, "in which case, would you like me to show you to your room?"

The woman had dismissed this too. "I'll find it," she said. "I shall find the way." She had walked off with purpose, without exchanging further pleasantries of any kind or asking questions, clutching the room key close to her as though it were a talisman or holy relic.

Since then, Miss Galligan had refused all efforts to clean her room, placing her used crockery and cutlery outside. After a week, she had placed more cash there too, sufficient for a further seven days, and she had done so once again after this instalment had run out. She had received some visitors but (at least so far as Angelique was aware, and there was little which went on in this hotel of which she did not have full knowledge) they seemed only ever to be tradespeople: folk who brought her clothes and other essentials.

The world of Miss Galligan seemed to have shrunk to the four walls of number 52. Maids and bellboys had reported sounds suggestive of illness from inside, though, when asked, Miss Galligan insisted firmly that everything was just fine. If matters were ever pushed any further, the lady found an excuse to offer a more than generous tip in exchange for the asker of questions to desist.

Angelique herself had spoken to their solitary guest three times upon the telephone during this period and each conversation had been an exercise in chilly, business-like brevity. She had knocked upon the door of the lady twice, when going up there to collect her money, only to be told upon all occasions that if she wished to speak to her then she should surely use the phone.

If Angelique was more than usually curious about all of this she did not allow it to show to any of the staff who worked beneath her, though she did find herself wondering with increasing frequency about the stranger, and of what her true story might be. She was also waiting, she realised later, in the days after the disaster had struck, for the other shoe to drop, for an element to change in the woman's weird routine, for something, in other words, to break.

One night, after a rare day off, she found herself telling her flatmate, Miss Betty Morales, the whole strange story.

"Huh," Betty had said. "That's very strange. You think she's running away from something?"

"Aren't we all?" said Angelique, thinking of a certain boy back in St Louis and of a certain girl who was now his wife.

"No, but I mean on the run from something bad."

"Like what?"

"Like criminals. Or worse, the government."

"I don't know," Angelique admitted. "And I don't suppose it's really any of my business. But all the same… it bothers me. It really does. It's giving me bad dreams."

II

Angelique was working at the front desk on the morning in question, at the start of Galligan's fourth week of residence, when a handsome woman in her middle fifties presented herself there with a big charming smile and asked for help.

"Of course, ma'am," said Angelique, her voice, as ever, smooth but not ingratiating. "What can I do for you today?"

"I'm here to visit a resident of yours," said the woman, who had long dark hair (no trace of grey) and who was dressed expensively. Angelique, who read multiple papers every night (recovered from the rooms of the guests) thought that she might recognise her from somewhere, from some story, gossip piece or scandal, though she could not have said precisely what the context might have been.

"And who is that, ma'am?"

Somehow the answer, when it came, did not surprise her in the slightest.

"The lady in 52."

"Of course," Angelique replied, before adding, more slyly: "And her name is?"

The dark-haired woman blinked once. "Galligan," she said after what was a fractional (though noticeable) hesitation.

"Very good, ma'am," Angelique said. "I'll ring her now. Who shall I say is calling?"

"Just say it's Coral," the woman said. "No surname. She'll know who I am."

Angelique made the call. With the receiver pressed a little nervously to her left ear, she watched the woman glance with some suspicion around the lobby.

After five rings, the phone in room 52 was picked up and the voice of Miss Galligan said: "Yes?"

Even from that single syllable, Angelique could tell that whatever was wrong with the resident had got worse. She sounded not merely hoarse but actively in pain.

"What is it?"

"This is the front desk, Miss Galligan. We have a visitor here for you. She has given her name as Coral."

There was a pause on the line and what sounded like ragged breathing. "Is she middle-aged? Dark haired? British?"

"Yes to all three, ma'am."

As she said these words, Angelique noticed that Coral was gazing fixedly at her. Angelique smiled though this was not returned by the lady upon the other side of her desk.

Down the telephone line could be heard a sound like scuttling, as though the resident was moving in some quick but awkward manner across the floor.

"Miss Galligan?"

A pause, then: "I'm here."

"What shall I say to your guest?"

Then came the last sound which Angelique had expected: a high, frantic whinny of laughter. "Show her up. Tell her I'm ready for her. But Miss Dupont?"

Angelique felt a not altogether welcome frisson of surprise at the fact that Galligan had learned her name. "Yes, ma'am?"

"Bring Coral to me in person. I want you to be my witness. It's high time you saw what they've done to me."

III

The woman who had given her name as Coral did not make any conversation as they rode the elevator together to the fifth floor or as they walked along the corridor to number 52. Only as they approached the room (where there was once again a dirty plate and cutlery left outside; at the sight of which Angelique made a mental note to chastise the head of domestics), did Coral say anything at all.

"She's not been any trouble to you?" the woman asked, the concern in her voice seemingly quite genuine.

"Not compared to some," said Angelique.

"Good. That's very good. I mean, we've been keeping an eye on her. We wanted her to be safe. But exactly where she went to ground we left up to her."

Angelique gestured towards the door of the room. "Here we are. So sorry about the mess on the floor."

The Englishwoman hesitated. "Are you happy, dear?" she asked suddenly. "I mean, have you known happiness? Have you been contented in your life?"

"That's... kind of a strange question."

"Humour me?"

Angelique answered as honestly as she was able. "For some of it, yes. Not so much as a kid. But now, sure, I've been happy enough."

Coral nodded. "My own childhood was a little... complicated. And truncated also. But I'm glad. Yes, I'm very glad you've known some happiness."

"Ma'am, forgive me…" Angelique stopped herself, about to break a cardinal rule of her profession.

Coral smiled. "Yes, dear?"

"Oh, it doesn't matter."

"Please." The smile was firmer than before and still more insistent. "Say whatever it was you were going to say."

"Don't I recognise you from somewhere? From the news?"

"Oh. Well, yes, you might. I've long been associated with a particular place. What they call the City. You know? In England."

"Yes." Angelique remembered. Some outrage, some improbable, faraway disaster which nonetheless now seemed very close to home. "Of course. How is it? The City? After everything which happened… That poor creature…"

"That's a long story. One for another day."

"My apologies, ma'am."

"No need. But for now, please, if you don't mind – could you please be so kind as to knock?"

Angelique blushed, embarrassed at having forgot herself. She knocked on the door. "Miss Galligan? Your visitor is here."

A voice from within, deep and cracked: "It's open. Come in."

Angelique pushed the handle and nudged the door.

Coral made a gesture as if to say: after you.

It was gloomy inside. Only one light was on and that was very dim. The place was not in disarray as Angelique had, however illogically, anticipated. It was neat and in good order. There was, however, an odd scent in the air, something thick and heavy, something redolent of the farmyard or the stable.

"Miss Galligan?"

The resident was sitting on the only chair in the room. She had turned its back against the far wall. Her face was in shadow and she seemed almost to loll in her seat, in some ungainly sprawl.

Angelique heard Coral walk in behind her. "Leave us now," she said. "I'll call you when it's time."

The figure in the chair nodded at this. "Yes. We'll both call you."

At first, Angelique thought that she still wore the coat which she had worn when she arrived. Closer examination suggested that this was not the case. It was more tightly fitted and it seemed to have no edge.

"Of course, ladies," said Angelique, wrenching her gaze away. "I'll be right outside."

She retreated, then, back into the corridor and pulled the door softly shut behind her. She knew that she ought to set about clearing up the mess yet she found herself unable to resist a little light eavesdropping.

The doors at the Grosvenor were thick and the voices beyond were low but, over the next few minutes, Angelique Dupont was able nonetheless to pick out some snatches of the discourse, fragments of what was said.

She heard Coral apologise for something. "I always felt it was rather a low trick," she said. "But someone had to be patient zero."

This, Angelique thought, confirmed the theory that Miss Galligan was ill.

The resident said something then too low to hear, then: "You didn't need to do it, you didn't need to do it." This had something of the quality of a mantra.

Then the firm, calm voice of Coral came again. "I'm afraid we really think we do. Albert and me... And our friend in the water..."

"Him!" The voice of the resident was louder now, through anger. "How long has he been behind this? Scheming and dreaming? And how has he changed you?"

The older woman declared herself to be not without her failings but nonetheless at heart a philanthropist.

Miss Galligan evidently disagreed with the assessment as a flood of abuse ensued, words and language which did not shock Angelique but which did surprise her even with the ferocity and ease of their delivery.

The voice of Coral seemed to come closer to the door. "I came to say I'm sorry," she said (there was something in this which Angelique did not believe), "and also to confirm that the transformation is complete. We had to know whether or not it's actually worked."

"It's worked," Miss Galligan said. "It's worked all right. But not how you hoped. It won't take us forward. You must know that. The science has gone wrong somehow. It won't go as you hoped. It'll plunge us all back into the stone age."

Exactly what happened next inside the room, Angelique could not be sure. There was a sound like a scuffle, something like tearing, then something like a muffled scream. This was cut off almost at once, followed by a heavy thud as of something like a bookcase being hurled onto the floor. Silence afterwards.

Then Angelique heard the voice of the resident. "Miss Dupont? You may come in now."

For an instant, something primal in her urged Angelique to run, screaming at her to get as far away from that room and from the place – as far away from New York even – as she could possibly manage. Yet the hesitation was but a momentary thing. She knew her duty. "Coming, ma'am," she said and opened the door.

The scene that awaited her was plain enough. The body of Coral was prone upon the floor, her throat torn out. There was blood upon the carpets and arterial spray upon the walls.

Then there was Miss Galligan standing over her. The face of

the resident was in the light now and it was the most extraordinary thing: not the face of a woman at all (or, at least, not purely) but the face of a furred and savage creature, something like a tiger or a lion, with a hint also of slyness suggestive of the hyena or the wolf. The creature bared its blood-flecked teeth in a grimace. When it spoke it did so in a growling parody of how Miss Galligan had first sounded when she had arrived at the hotel.

"This is not how I was meant to be. This has been done to me."

"Why?" Angelique asked, her voice impressively level under the circumstances. "How?"

"Because of the City," the Galligan-creature said. "Because of what they believe." Then, turning towards Angelique: "Let me pass. Don't stand in my way."

Angelique saw that the woman had hands no longer but rather claws, sharp and deadly. Very sensibly, she stood back. Her pay at the Grosvenor was not especially generous; certainly nowhere near enough to encourage her to attempt to stop the departure of so homicidal and monstrous a guest.

The creature snarled again. Angelique stepped further back, touching the wall now.

"Cash," said what had once been a woman. "Take it all."

Without waiting for more, the being loped past her and stepped into the corridor. Then, dropping down onto all fours, it ran on, gathering speed to an incredible pace before, ignoring the elevator, hurling itself down the stairs.

Angelique stood very still, breathed deeply and thanked the sweet Lord Jesus that she was still alive. A moment later, from somewhere else in the hotel, she heard the sound of screaming.

It was to be the first scream of many.

22ND SEPTEMBER,
1935–22ND DECEMBER, 2035

EVERYWHERE

I

After that, the virus spread as might a drop of dark ink in cool water, moving slowly at first but then gathering speed and reach, denying all efforts to staunch its diffusion or divert its flow, until, at last, everything was altered.

II

Initially, the outbreak seemed to be confined to New York. To the other states of the union it was just a weird, unbelievable story, one more tall tale from a strange town known for its eccentricity. Reports emerging from the city were seen as wild innuendo or crazed campfire yarns which had taken on a life of their own.

Some armchair observers dubbed it mass hysteria, others an infectious, inexplicable madness.

The residents of the Grosvenor Hotel, at the very epicentre of the change, already knew differently. On 23rd September 1935, Miss Angelique Dupont, having witnessed the escape of the being which had been Josephine Galligan, succumbed to that contagious agent which she had breathed in unwittingly as she stood, dumbstruck, in the corridor. She woke in the night, shivering and afraid, the surface of her skin filling up with dense, coarse fur, her very jaw restructuring itself into something like the snout of a tapir. Her sobs roused her roommate, Miss Betty Morales, who cradled Angelique in her arms, doing her best to dry her tears and reassure her.

"It's just the flu, honey. Nothing but a cold and headache."

That Betty had been infected became obvious two nights later on 25th September when her gait became suddenly simian and certain of her canine teeth began to grow into fangs. By this point, cases across the city had already reached the low hundreds.

The mark of Dr Moreau had become airborne and it was spreading quicker than anyone at that time could have guessed.

III

Too late, the Mayor of New York, a man called La Guardia, tried to act, closing down segments of the city and ordering strict curfews. Theories abounded at City Hall where many ingenious and well-argued cases were made for a resurgence of bubonic plague or some rogue strain of scarlet fever. All, of course, were incorrect. Besides, every action that was taken by the man who, as things soon turned out, would be the last to hold mayoral office in that place, proved utterly inefficient, like trying to use crepe paper to dam a river.

By 30th September, the virus was everywhere in New York City. Many fled, hoping to find sanctuary elsewhere in the country. In this too they were mistaken. There was nowhere to run, however far-flung, which would be free of it. La Guardia himself was last seen on the 1st October, crouched on all fours on the steps of St Patrick's Cathedral, his face grown shaggy and lupine, his eyes a feral shade of yellow. No records exist to tell us what became of him.

IV

There began to be sightings elsewhere in the nation, escalating incidences of transformed Americans. On the same day as La Guardia's transformation, a woman in Providence, Rhode Island, who had apparently been fused with some manner of bipedal dolphin was seen emerging confusedly from the water of Narragansett Bay, yelping four or five fractured, incoherent consonants before disappearing once again beneath the surface.

On 5th October, a group of hikers in the forest of Pine Grove, Maine, witnessed a couple of ursine creatures staggering almost drunkenly between the trees. They seemed, said the group, to be caught between wonder and hysteria, as though the beings had only just returned to the wilderness and were having to learn how to move through it again, a disquieting combination of the monstrous and the infantile.

On 7th October, in Baton Rouge, Louisiana, a gang of human-sized entities with scaly, green-hued skin were seen wallowing in the swamp, watched balefully by the alligators who had, until recently, been chief predators there.

In all of these places – Providence, Pine Grove and Baton Rouge – there were fresh cases and new transformations within days of each sighting. The nation began to panic. There were now too many instances, too many eyewitnesses and too much damage already wrought to be able to deny the incredible truth of events. Phrases such as "unstoppable momentum" and "incremental spread" were used in public and in the press with considerable frequency.

On 10th October, the Democratic President told a terrified country in a wireless address that they need have no cause for fear and that whatever was amongst them he would root it out and remove the evil. He hinted at the influence of certain "anti-human civilisations", a reference, most observers agreed, to the inhabitants of what was then widely known only as the City. That it was technological and medical advances from that place which had, some years earlier, allowed him to rise from his wheelchair and walk unaided, the President did not see fit then to mention.

Instead, in a stroke which his closest advisors considered too hasty and reactive, he closed all borders. In this the counsellors were entirely mistaken; it was far too late now to make any measurable difference.

V

The day after the President's address, the first proven cases beyond the borders of the USA were confirmed.

In Quebec, an Englishman who had made his home there, by the name of Burgess Dawson, found himself transforming into a leonine hybrid, his fingers turned to claws and his ears, already large, becoming both rich in fur and acutely sensitive. Everyone who was in the Moonbeam Diner with him that night soon began to display similar symptoms.

In Monterrey, Mexico, a sudden outbreak of creatures, largely resembling goats, occurred. Glimpsed first in the mountains, they soon came down to the city itself, objects both of curiosity and fear. Some citizens tried to capture the beings although to no avail. Those that came too close soon found themselves undergoing alterations of their own.

Already a new kind of wildness seemed to be creeping in, at once a reversion and something startlingly new.

VI

The phenomenon was becoming a global one, impossible to ignore or to overlook.

On 13th October the office of the President of the United States demanded to speak to the Commander of the City. A telephone conversation was arranged in which the Commander (the third, elected democratically, since the death of Anta'Nar), a fox-man named Ar'Balar, denied all knowledge of the virus and of any City involvement in its development and spread.

This happened to be true. The works of the late Coral Mayfield and of the mind which whispered to her in the dark were not known at all to Ar'Balar or to the majority of his people. The antics of Albert Edgington had long since come to those who ran the City as something of an embarrassment. Yet the human President did not believe the words of Ar'Balar and so, blustering in the face of the tidal wave of fear, threatened all kinds of international sanctions. The conversation was left for both parties in a most unsatisfactory place.

In the White House, the President ordered enquiries and investigations aplenty, none of which would come to anything or even get close to discovering the true source of the currents of change which were moving across the world. On 25th October, he was moved underground at a secret location for his own protection. Above him, his country fell into chaos. No-one seemed to be immune. The infection rate of the virus was one hundred per cent and what it did to each of the infected was, at least so far as anyone was able to tell, both crazily unpredictable and altogether irreversible.

VII

On 2nd November, the virus reached Brazil. On 4th November, it arrived in China. On 10th November, the Tsar of all the Russia was informed by his courtiers that the virus had got to the edges of his great country. A handsome, fair-haired man who had barely turned thirty and who was to be married the following year, the Tsar too demanded at once to speak to the head of the City.

The line was crackling and the voice sounded very faraway. Nonetheless, he recognised it as belonging to Ar'Balar, whom he had met at a conference in Svalbard ten months earlier.

"Please, my friend," said the Tsar in his own tongue. "Speak plainly to me. Do you know anything of this?"

"Nothing at all," said the fox-man whose Russian was very good. "You have my word."

"It seems… I don't know… it seems almost like a judgement of your people upon mine."

There came after this a very long pause. Then: "Speak not to me of judgement, sir. Not when you owe your health and your throne to our resources."

The Tsar could not respond. There was very little doubt, after all, that the advances in arms provided by the Beast Folk of the City had staved off revolution, nor that what the physicians of that place had provided had made his haemophilia almost bearable.

"I'm sorry," said the Tsar eventually and slammed down the telephone.

In the City, Ar'Balar and his inner circle began to panic. The Mayfield woman had been found dead and there were rumours that the Edgington man had been transformed. International blame seemed to be at the door of the City and no denial, however heartfelt, seemed to be sufficient. There were rumours not only of reparations but of imminent military intervention. As Ar'Balar announced to his council, his usually pensive face filled up with anger: "These are the drumbeats of war. If there's anyone from the City who has any connection at all to what is occurring we need to find them and bring them to justice."

They agreed, of course, and they applauded his words but many in the City were beginning to wonder, even then, whether there might not be something poetic in the virulence of such a thing, whether a world in which everyone looked less like the people of Washington, DC, and more like the denizens of the City might not be a true wonder to behold.

VIII

There seemed, over Christmas, to be something of a lull in the procession of the virus. Cases appeared to decline. Fewer sightings were reported in the newspapers. Whole communities begun to wonder if they hadn't been spared. Some members of the frantic and beleaguered scientific world even went so far as to theorise that the thing might have burned itself out at last, that its malignity had declined, that some sort of natural immunity was occurring in the population to ward it off. For more than a week the planet seemed to hold its breath, to see if this dark-winged angel had indeed passed over the human race.

Then, on 4th January, a flurry of new cases: in Athens, in Cyprus, in Vatican City. On 11th January, the first cases were reported in Africa. A flock of bird-people seemed drawn to the Sphinx of Giza as though they knew themselves somehow to be caught up into something mythic, as though, sensing themselves to be impossible things, they wished to make their homes by the figure of another of their kind, half-buried by the sand.

IX

For much of 1936, the world appeared to exist in a state of constant siege. The virus seemed to ebb and flow. Although many accusations were made against the City, nothing was ever proved and much attention was in any case taken up with combating the effects of the virus. During the twelve months, civilisation began to fray. Technology (even the strange technologies of the City) were laid aside and a simpler way of life embarked upon.

Communities became little citadels, fortresses of the uninfected who kept away any sign of the transformed creatures who were now to be seen in almost every country. The world, divided, stood upon a precipice. It cannot be said, even now, that the humans did not fight, tooth and nail, for what they had built over centuries.

On 30th November of that year, a unit of Finnish scientists, led by a woman named Jarvela, announced that they had found a cure for the infection. They claimed to have had some success in reversing the transformations, though little substantial data of this was ever produced. They also asserted that they had developed a vaccine which would safeguard the unchanged against catching the transmogrifying agent.

Funds were found and a distribution network created in order to give this cure to a sizeable proportion of the surviving population of Europe.

It may be of some interest to the reader to discover that on 12th December, in a nursing home on the Cornish coast, a very old resident indeed, well in excess of his century and known to those who cared for him only as "the vicar", died in his sleep with the comforting, erroneous, belief that some version of the world as he had known might yet survive.

X

By the summer of 1937 it had become clear that there was no cure and that the vaccine was largely ineffective. The virus itself seemed to move across the world in waves, transforming all with whom it came into contact.

The rich held out for longest, and those who were naturally

isolated. The changes did not stop, however, and could not be evaded indefinitely. Societies across the globe broke down and governments had no choice but to frantically devolve power to a succession of smaller and smaller fiefdoms and local states. Things fell apart. It was as though time were being run backwards, as if humanity were being brought home, at an ever-gathering pace, to its beginnings.

XI

One by the one the old institutions were toppled.

On 3rd February, 1938, the President of the United States, who had spent almost the entirety of the past three years underground, was overcome by a version of the virus which made him into something canine and savage. On 5th April, the British Royal Family surrendered also to the transformations. The grounds of Windsor Castle, already by then starting to sink into wildness, soon played host to a menagerie of creatures of the strangest sort. On 19th May, the Pope was seen soaring on impossible wings high above the Sistine Chapel.

Such scenes were repeated all across the world as authorities crumbled and rulers were brought down. The great spirits of the age were metamorphosis and conversion. Nothing and nobody was left unchanged.

XII

Humanity lasted a good while longer, hiding out in the most isolated parts of the world, surviving in pockets, keeping clear of the altered population, cleaving to the high and the hidden sectors of the globe.

As far as it is possible to tell, the last human being to have been untouched by the transmogrification agent in the Western Hemisphere was a Greenland Inuit woman named Quneqitooq who died, a hermit, sometime early in the spring of 1963. Her counterpart in the Eastern Hemisphere was an Australian man called Hugh Olliver who lost his life on the Nullarbor Plain three years later, torn apart by a creature that was comprised in equal parts of dingo and gliding possum.

XIII

Decades passed. The virus mutated, and mutated again, creating the most erratic and unforeseeable results in its hosts. The world seemed almost to luxuriate in its strange new state. And the City of Dr Moreau – together with all of its inhabitants, at one time so talked about, thought about and feared – seemed, for a long while, to have been entirely forgotten.

23RD DECEMBER, 2035

LONDON

I

Four creatures squatted by the edge of the river and waited to see what it would bring them today.

Although not bound by blood, this quartet – the hyena-man, the cheetah-woman, the pig-boy and the platypus-girl – were in essence a family. They had found that survival was much easier when they stayed and worked and hunted together, and this was no small discovery, survival being a hard thing indeed in this strange world.

I have called them hyena, cheetah, pig and platypus although this is not, in truth, altogether accurate for by this time, a century after the outbreak in the Grosvenor Hotel, the hybridity of the peoples of the world had become so tangled that almost every creature who walked upon two legs had within them a multiplicity of origins. Now the lineaments of one species could be discerned in a single face, now another, then yet another. Every creature on the planet was a mixture of the most complicated, glorious sort.

This particular quartet were waiting that afternoon by what had once been the Embankment, next to the river that had formerly been known as the Thames. This knowledge, together with so much else, had long since been lost, and all who dwelt here knew these things by other, weirder names.

Now that humanity had ceded its dominance, much of the city had been given over to nature. Waterloo was wilderness, Piccadilly all jungle. Hackney was marshland and Pimlico a stronghold of the tiger-people who had made of it by far the most dangerous zone in all the perilous, verdant wreckage of the old metropolis. Fantasists and seers of earlier times had often dreamed of an eventuality such as this. Suffice to say that such visionaries would be unlikely to survive a single day in what the place had become.

Our family of four watched the dark water flow by – water which was cleaner, of course, than at any other time in its history, at least after the Romans had come. There were always fish, and they could eat one of these if hunger drove them to it. The cheetah-woman would have done so immediately, being of an impatient temperament, though the hyena-man urged them all to wait in case something better came along, as he felt sure that it would. This was communicated amongst the group both through expressive gestures and by an odd, guttural manner of speech which I shall not endeavour to replicate here.

In the event, the cheetah-woman put up rather less of a fight over this issue than might typically have been expected. None of the others spoke up in defence of her idea, not even the platypus-girl who generally agreed with her upon everything. It was as though they all sensed it, that today was a day of significance, that they should not leave the river yet, that they should, in however inchoate a fashion, elect to bear witness.

And so they waited. In the sky, all manner of strange birds flew and cried. In the distance, beyond the water towards what once had been the southside of the city, far-off roars and cries could be heard. The family ignored them, well accustomed to the sounds of the ruined metropolis, knowing that they would be aware should anything which wished them harm come near.

The light was just beginning to fade when they saw it. It was the platypus-girl who noticed first. Excitedly, she pointed with her right paw upriver, towards the low dark shape that was approaching. A looming shadow moved steadily closer, a thing which, although it seemed at times to be trying to cling to the banks, was being buffeted nonetheless by the water.

Although, in this wild world, the strange was an everyday phenomenon, what advanced towards them was something unprecedented. It was a big, dark, tentacular thing, something like an octopus but with a variety of appendages and odd, additional limbs. Even the kindest naturalist of the old world, the most open-minded of zoologists, the most fiercely opposed to freak shows and circuses, could not have done other than to suggest the being was a monstrosity.

At the sight of its halting progress, the pig-boy cowered into the side of his sister, something atavistic causing him to shy as far away from the intruder as he could. The hyena-man thought that they should leave this thing – which was most likely dead, or if not dead then certainly mortally wounded – to float on and surrender it up to the river. Yet the cheetah-woman could not let her curiosity go unsated. Together she and the platypus-girl, with the grudging assistance of the hyena-man, waded to the water's edge and when the creature floated within touching distance they grabbed at the thing and pulled it in, up onto the bank. Its skin was cold and slimy. The hyena-man remarked that it would most likely not be good to eat. The pig-boy watched nervously from a safe distance, an awful anxiety coiling and uncoiling itself deep within his chest.

The others were tired by the time that they had the thing laid out before them on the grass. There was only the sound of their panting as they looked down at the creature and saw, through the delicate, fitful motion of its bulbous body and the occasional twitch of its tentacles, that it was still, if barely, alive. The cheetah-woman beckoned over the pig-boy, reassuring him that it was quite safe.

It soon became plain that there was nothing which they could do for this strange creature. Although there was no sign of obvious physical damage it was evidently close to death. They had no way of knowing for certain but it was the platypus-girl's suggestion that it was simply extreme old age that was killing it, a thing so rare in the city now as to be all but mythical. The black octopus twitched a little more, mere minutes of its long life remaining.

The pig-boy wondered aloud if it might provide some comfort for the thing to be surrounded by others at the last. His sister chided him for his sentimentality, a trait, she declared, which would be likely to shorten considerably his own life expectancy.

Then they heard, as had M'Gari and Coral Mayfield and Josephine Galligan before them, the voice of the creature inside their head, a sibilant, alien thing. It still spoke in English which had been the language of its long-dead creator and its words meant nothing at all to the family. They looked around them in bemusement at the sound, at the gibberish that echoed, uninvited, in their minds.

"My friends, I thank you for your kindness. You have done well. You are a fine set of inheritors."

The faces of the family twitched and scowled in confusion.

"He would be proud of you. The creator of us all. He who laboured on the island to brought us all into being. This new world is his legacy and you must all…"

There was a good deal more of this in a similar vein but since the family took no further notice of it I am not sure that we should either. It was, after all, only babble now, for the creature from the water, the last living original experiment of Dr Moreau, was the only surviving speaker of any human language upon the planet.

A minute or so later and this too was gone. The creature died, quietly and ingloriously. The voice in the heads of the family had ceased a short while before.

They all four looked at one another in evident confusion, wholly uncertain as to what had just happened. Although she did not go so far as to admit that she had been wrong, the cheetah-woman nonetheless suggested that they place the dead thing back into the water and let the river carry it away, towards that sea from which, they dimly supposed, it had first swum.

This they did, in silence and without ceremony. They stood and watched as the final vestige of the old world floated away into the distance. And then, hungry now, the family turned from the river and went towards the hunting grounds beyond, in search of fresh meat.

II

Yet the family ought, perhaps, to have waited just a little longer. For this is not how our story should end, nor does it represent the final fate of the great continents of Earth.

Twenty-five minutes after the family had disappeared back into the undergrowth, off on their search for sustenance, something appeared upon the twilit horizon, something new moving along the river. Had the family waited they would have seen its slow but determined progress. It was a small, makeshift boat, a kind of coracle formed of cloth, wood and rope. It looked something like a mariner might have constructed out of desperate ingenuity had they been stranded too long upon a desert island. It looked, for that matter, a very great deal like the boat which once had been made by Mr Edward Prendick as he made his escape from the first stronghold of Moreau. It was a leaking, limping thing for sure but it had held together just long enough to bring its small crew to this place of hazards. By coincidence, the boat came to a stop at the precise spot where the octopus-creature had just been dragged by the family from the water. There were on board this improvised vessel two adult beings, one male and one female, and it was the first of these who leapt ashore from the prow and secured the barque with rough urgency to a tree stump on the bank.

He was a tall, rangy creature, rather simian in aspect (although, of course, his lineage was much more complicated than that). He was covered with fur but, unlike the peoples of new London, he was dressed in clothes, in trousers and shirt, neckerchief and a cap. Panting a little from his exertion, he called out to his companion who was still aboard the boat:

"This looks good enough. We can get food here! Even make camp for the night." He, of course, did not speak any human tongue, though it was one vastly more complex than that spoken by the family, the equal at least of the old, dead languages of, say, English or Icelandic.

His partner called back to him. "Food, yes, but can we camp here? Truly? It can't be safe!" She was furred also and dressed in similar clothes, although her ancestry was visibly closer to the bear than to the ape. There was something strapped to her chest, a small but bulky thing, which she handled with the greatest of care.

"But where's safe now?" called back the beast creature on the shore. His tone was not despairing but rather possessed of a kind of wise rationality, suggestive, perhaps, of one who sees the world as it really is and not as he would like it to be. "Where exactly is safe for us?"

The beast woman conceded the point with a tilt of her head, a gesture that seemed appealingly wry. "Well, I can't say I wouldn't like to get my paws on solid ground for a bit. Help me up?"

Her companion came to the water's edge, lifted her up out of the boat and, with great, if rather ungainly, delicacy placed her upon the earth. He had to be extremely careful in the course of this procedure not to touch or damage that very precious thing which was strapped to her chest.

She smiled at him with love in her eyes. "Thanks," she said.

In the distance, they heard a rumbling, minatory roar.

"Maybe we shouldn't tarry…" said the male. His right paw went instinctively to a small curved knife which hung in a sheath around his waist. But the roaring got further away, as whatever had made the sound moved now into the distance.

"I don't know," said the female. "Perhaps you were right and that nowhere's really safe. We have to make our home somewhere, don't we?"

"Somewhere, yes…"

"Since the City won't have us."

The male beast-creature grunted in annoyance at the mention of this. "Let's see," he said. "We could explore tomorrow. See what's here. In whatever this place used to be." He gestured rather vaguely about him at the ruins and at the uncultivated vegetation, as though he felt he really ought to know the name of where it was that they stood but that the details were proving to be maddeningly elusive.

"This may be as good a place as any."

"You were fearful just a moment ago."

The ape-creature smiled. "One of us is generally afraid."

"True enough. And all is well so long as the other is brave."

"We take turns, then?"

"We take turns."

In the wilderness of London, by the banks of the Thames, the two Beast Folk smiled at one another.

"Let's see then," said the male. "Let's see if we can't find sanctuary here, at least for a while."

"One day at a time," said the female.

The thing which was strapped to her chest stirred now, woken by all the noise and excitement. A small, inquisitive cry was heard. The baby's eyes had flicked open and she wriggled in sleepy curiosity in her papoose. The female cradled her close. The male came nearer and peered down with mingled pleasure and concern.

"Oh so you like it here, do you, little one?"

A gurgle and a smile from the baby, as if of appreciative confirmation.

"Seems to me like it's settled," said the bear-woman.

"Seems to me that you're right," said the ape-man.

And the little baby cooed, starting to get hungry now, peeping out wonderingly at the world around her. For a moment, as though to form a tableau in bold defiance of this unforgiving environment, the family embraced: a woman and a man whose ancestry came from the Beast Folk together with their only child, a girl who somehow, against all rules and expectations, had been born different.

She was an infant whose very existence had caused their exile from the City. She was a baby with smooth and hairless skin; a baby with deep brown eyes, eight plump fingers and two plump thumbs; a baby who was, in every respect, palpably and without question, human.

ACKNOWLEDGEMENTS

The author wishes to thank:

Craig Leyenaar, for editorial expertise and guidance, together with all at Titan.

My agents, Alexander Cochran and Robert Dinsdale.

Paul Simpson, for numerous proofreading saves.

Natasha McKenzie for the wonderful cover.

My parents for their ongoing support.

My wife, Heather, with love, for everything you do for our little team.

Alistair and Benjamin – two little monsters of my own!

ABOUT THE AUTHOR

J. S. Barnes is the author of four previous novels, including *Dracula's Child*. He has written numerous audio originals for *Big Finish* and *Audible*. His journalism appears in the *Times Literary Supplement*, *The Critic* and the *Literary Review*.

For more fantastic fiction, author events,
exclusive excerpts, competitions, limited editions and more

VISIT OUR WEBSITE
titanbooks.com

LIKE US ON FACEBOOK
facebook.com/titanbooks

FOLLOW US ON TWITTER AND INSTAGRAM
@TitanBooks

EMAIL US
readerfeedback@titanemail.com